A WAKE OF CROWS

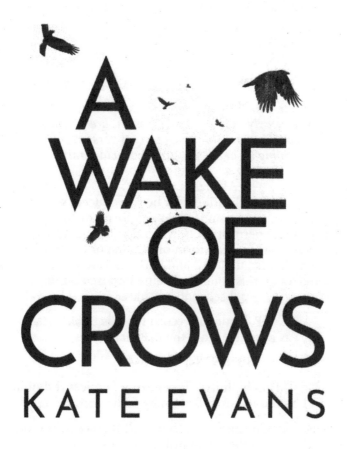

A WAKE OF CROWS

KATE EVANS

CONSTABLE

CONSTABLE

First published in Great Britain in 2021 by Constable

1 3 5 7 9 10 8 6 4 2

A CIP catalogue record for this book
is available from the British Library.

ISBN: 978-1-47213-475-2

Typeset in Calson by Initial Typesetting Services, Edinburgh
Printed and bound in Great Britain by Clays Ltd, Elcograf S.p.A

Papers used by Constable are from well-managed forests and
other responsible sources

Constable
An imprint of
Little, Brown Book Group
Carmelite House
50 Victoria Embankment
London EC4Y 0DZ

An Hachette UK Company
www.hachette.co.uk

www.littlebrown.co.uk

To Claudia Hempel for the love and friendship going back forty-three years, which not even The Wall could thwart

Prologue

Then

Run. Turn around. Run away. Stop this craziness. She could turn back. Back to her parents. They need never know. She looks up and sees the slick of his dark hair settling on his wide shoulders. He is walking quickly but nonchalantly. *How does he manage it?* She keeps tripping and slithering. *I don't want to look a fool.* She must be grown up in front of him, a lot more than her seventeen years and ten months. Otherwise, otherwise, well the otherwise is so unthinkable, she squashes the attempt of her mind to bring it to her attention.

It is dusk and getting darker. They avoid the circles of yellow light thrown down by the street lamps. It is cold. It has been raining all day – the droplets like a beaded curtain she is continuously trying to push through. She slips again. She halts. She is panting as if she has just run the last couple of kilometres. There is a stitch beginning to ache in her side. As she tries to slow her breathing, she hears a vehicle, a van perhaps. It is going fast. The tyres squeal, taking a corner at speed. *Are they coming for us? They must be coming for us.*

She heaves herself forward. He is some metres in front of her now. She wants to shout out to him to slow down. But he had said not to communicate. If they are not seen communicating, they can deny all knowledge of each other. They are out for a stroll. Separately. Why through an industrial estate in the rain would be a question they'd have to face. Separately. And come up with an answer. Separately.

She quickens her pace and follows him around the corner. She can see his car hidden in the shadows. There is a young man and a young woman, jeans and denim jackets intertwined as they lean against the side of the vehicle. They are the passengers. They look up as he approaches, but do not unwrap themselves from each other. They nod and swap muffled greetings.

All is quiet in front of her. Inside, her lungs and heart are pumping like parts of a steam engine, overcompensating for her exertion. She stops again to collect herself. She wants to walk up to them as cool as they are. The change in their faces and body language – from nonchalant to stricken and rigid – comes before she hears the footsteps and voice behind her.

She turns. He is as startled to see her as she is to see him. *What is he doing here? In that uniform?* Her brain cannot compute. Luckily, or perhaps unluckily, surprise appears to have befuddled his brain too. All he can do for a moment is repeat her name. He backs away as well, as if attempting to withdraw from the situation.

She shoves her right hand into her pocket – it hits metal. Her fingers grip the smooth curve of it. She pulls it out. Merely to frighten him off, make him run away. Leave. Her hand shakes, the other comes to steady it. His mouth falls open. He doesn't move. He is frozen. In that moment it is as if her hearing has regained its acuity and then some. She hears the flap of a piece of paper as it is caught against the base of the street lamp. She hears a scratching of tiny claws on tarmac. Then she hears the van. The rest of his squad come to find him. Suddenly there is a detonation of sound in front of her. The retort cracks at her wrist and batters up through her elbow to her shoulder. She drops the gun. It has become a roasting iron.

There is a scream and shouting behind her. Her arm is grabbed and she is flung round. 'Let's get the fuck outta here,' he says, his moustache a limp dark worm against the chalk of his face.

Chapter 1

Now, 2013

When the call comes through, Donna has been in Scarborough for twenty-four hours and on duty for five. DS Harrie Shilling has been introducing her to the different floors of the police station and some of the staff who work there. Now, the DS cuts the phone connection and looks Donna up and down, her gaze resting on Donna's shoes, a pair of robust brogues. They obviously pass muster. Harrie gives a curt nod. 'We've a male found dead in Raincliffe. You're coming with me.'

As they leave the building, Shilling says, 'You might want to keep some decent boots to hand, the countryside around here can get a little rugged.' She doesn't add, 'not like the soft Southern streets you're used to'. However, it hangs in the air.

Harrie drives to the back of the town and up a steep hill. Turning off at the top she keeps to a gravelly path. Donna notices how focused her DS has become. She is petite compared to Donna, with blonde hair pulled back tight, emphasising her sharp cheekbones which have reddened under the blusher as Shilling stares ahead of her.

Donna imagines she is making a mental list of what needs to happen. It is what Donna would be doing, only with the current vagaries of her memory she would need a pen and paper too. She lets her gaze move past Harrie through the driver's-side window. There is a fine view of toy-sized housing splaying out from the two bays, with the ruined castle keep sentinel on the cliff in between. The sea is navy this afternoon; there is a firm horizon between it and the paler sky. Many have come to Scarborough for views such as this, for the light, for the waters, for the sea. Donna has not. On the whole, she would prefer to be landlocked.

Switching her gaze to out of her own window, she takes in a field of sheep and what she presumes are television masts held by slender metal wires which glimmer in the low-wattage September sun. Then Harrie explains this is GCHQ, Government Communications Headquarters, the government listening station. Donna is surprised. *Who'd have thought it, here?* She gives it a second glance. It still looks like a gathering of TV antennae.

The track runs out, they park and begin to walk. Soon they are in among the trees – a mix of pine, birch, beech and oak. The path becomes steep. It is claggy from the recent rain. The leaves occasionally float from the branches around them, a confetti of yellow, burgundy and brown. Donna can sense the heatwave brewing. She pauses. She sucks in air. Her mouth is dry. She unzips her coat and pulls at the scarf around her neck as if it might be throttling her. Then she plunges on. Her DS is waiting for her at the outer cordon looking as if she has merely strolled to the corner shop. Donna can feel the dampness in her armpits and around the collar of her shirt. She hopes her face has not gone too beetroot. She suspects Harrie will be checking whether her new (temporary) DC has really passed her fitness test.

The inner cordon is being managed by a tall broad officer, made more bulky by the usual plethora of implements and devices hanging off his regulation fluorescent jacket. Donna remembers how wearing one made her feel corseted as well as safe, though she never expected to feel this pang of nostalgia for it. Shilling introduces her to PC Trevor Trench as: 'DC Donna Morris, she's with us for a while, from Kenilworth, during her probationary period.'

For a while. It seems no one is very clear how long she will be here, least of all Donna.

'Trev,' says the PC, grasping Donna's hand in his warm bear-paw, 'pleased to meet you.' He is probably around the same age as her, a smidge the wrong side of fifty. He is the first officer Donna has met who hasn't made her feel ancient. Even Shilling can't be more than her mid-thirties.

'Trevor's a Scarborian through and through,' says the DS. 'A fount of local knowledge.'

Trev grins, presumably at the label. When Shilling asks him to bring them up to speed, he does so with slow deliberation. The body had been found by a lassie who had been riding through the woods on her horse, a usual route for her. The lassie turns out to be a woman in her forties. She had noticed a tent just off the path for a couple of weeks, but hadn't reported anything, believing the woods a better place for the homeless than the town's streets. 'As long as they don't make a mess,' she had added, and Trev now faithfully conveys. Donna notices Shilling balling her hands into her knee-length puffer-coat pockets and letting her weight move from foot to foot. However, she doesn't hurry Trev and Trev carries on unhurried. The body is male, Caucasian, aged anywhere from his thirties to his sixties. The CSI are on the way. The area has been secured. He closes his notebook.

'We'll take a swift gander any road,' says Shilling, her tone also betraying the local accent, though lighter than Trench's. She leads the way along the designated route to the body.

It looks like Elizabeth. For a moment. It is something in the mismatch of ill-fitting clothes and the outstretched emaciated arm. Though she has been informed the victim is male. And she knows where Elizabeth is. Even so, Donna hesitates.

'You have seen a dead body before, haven't you?' asks Harrie.

Donna nods. 'Of course. But you don't ever really get used to it, do you?'

Shilling gives an encouraging smile. 'The boss says when you do is when you should think of doing summit else.'

The boss, the one Donna is waiting to meet, he's beginning to sound all right.

They approach the body. Donna is aware of sounds beyond her own internal workings. They ease her fluster. She can't hear any traffic noise. There is the croaky caw of a crow. Donna glances up. Jet mourning beads decorate the tree branches. Then one ruffles its feathers. They are in a clearing. To one side is a huge spreading beech, its smooth bark folded and twisted from ancient pollarding. Beechnuts plop through foliage to the ground. Those already on the ground crunch under her feet. It's as if the dead man's fingers are reaching to pick one up. Fern, bracken and brambles form a tangled barrier to where the ground falls away down a steep incline. They also create a green and brown shroud for their victim.

'What do you think?' asks Harrie.

Donna takes her time; she wants to show she knows what she is talking about, because she knows she does. 'Looks like he's been sleeping rough for some time. There's signs of drug misuse.' She indicates the familiar tracks on his arm. She leans slightly forward, swats at a fly which has risen to greet her; the smell is rank. 'Decomposition, or maybe a fox has made a meal of him. Could mean he's been here a few days.' She glances at the collapsed heap of tarpaulin and metal poles at the other side of the clearing. 'That would have hardly kept him dry and warm. He's very wasted. Could be he starved, died of hypothermia or an overdose.'

Shilling nods. 'In which case our only job will be to find out who he is and the next of kin.'

'Sad,' says Donna, then wishes she hasn't. Is it revealing too much emotion? She's still testing out her new colleagues. She is gratified to have her DS agree with her and add that unfortunately this kind of death is becoming all too usual.

Behind them a pheasant suddenly hurtles itself into the sky with a great flapping of wings and screeching. It has been disturbed by the arrival of the crime scene manager and his team.

'At least he'll get a decent tent now,' says Harrie flatly.

It had been what Donna had been thinking. Her DS turns away and into duty-mode before Donna can be certain this moment of connection has clocked with her.

Chapter 2

Now

Her new house is bland. She is glad of it. Of course, it is not entirely hers. She is renting it. It is all she can afford. Jim won't finance this 'mad escapade' of hers. They have a house, he says, a four-bedroom detached 1930s house with a wrap-around garden, which they have both lavished time and money on. It is a revelation to Donna that, on the whole, at this moment, she prefers this bland brick box attached to a line of bland brick boxes in a cul-de-sac, each with their own narrow drive and patch of lawn front and back. It is on the outskirts of town, away from the sea. This too Donna finds comforting.

She boils the kettle for her fruit tea. She had always been a two-cups-of-coffee-in-the-morning-to-get-her-going type of person, but she finds she now treasures rest over everything and fruit tea means better sleep. She is show-ered. Her cropped brown hair is already dry. She is dressed. Layers – she has found layers work best. A light sleeveless T-shirt under the cotton shirt and cardi. The offices appear to be hermetically sealed, she has to be prepared for heat. Especially as Harrie has said the CID turned incident room can get a little snug. She's also wearing a skirt. Trousers are more problematic these days. But she has bought some sturdy boots, much like the ones she wore as a PC, and the skirt could manage the roughest terrain. She's relatively confident she's kitted for whatever happens.

She sips her brew and eats her porridge topped with raspberries. She realises she is looking forward to the day, relishing the challenges which are to come. She'd always been a relish-er, ever since she – to the consternation of Jim – had become a special constable, when Elizabeth and Christopher had settled into school. More recently she's noticed having more off days, when fatigue drags her down. But not today, she is determined. She runs through what she expects will happen. They have to get an ID for the man and the pathologist's report should tell them whether a crime has been committed. *It's a crime whatever,* she thinks. *A crime a human being ends up like that.* Jim wouldn't agree with her. Some people bring it on themselves, he would argue. He had argued, even when speaking about Elizabeth. She is glad not to have to spend another breakfast countering him – or not, and feeling impotent for not doing so.

She considers leaving her crockery in the sink for wash-ing later. There is no one but herself to please. She cannot do it. She might be back late – she wouldn't want to have it there waiting for her. Then she goes to the bathroom for one more check. Satisfied she has everything she heads out the door.

As she does, she encounters her neighbour, Rose Short. She'd already been round with home-baked biscuits and a beaming welcome. She lives up, or maybe down, to her sur-name, is stout and has a long grey plait snaking against her

10

back. She is dressed for the allotment in baggy dungarees and wellies. There is something of the hippy about Rose. In their first and only conversation she'd told Donna she is a member of the Green Party and had been at Greenham. She had tried not to look disappointed when Donna had said she wasn't political. 'Not possible,' Rose had said. 'Everything we do is political.' Donna hadn't felt strong enough to defy Rose and had quickly nodded. However, for good measure, she had added it was because of her job with the police force. 'We're not allowed to show political allegiance.' Interestingly, Rose had seemed mildly intrigued that Donna was a police officer, a detective constable, no less. She probably had her down as a bank clerk. Most people do. Rose had also been curious about the faint accent she detected in Donna's diction. 'German?' Rose had responded when told. 'I would never have guessed.' 'I've lived here longer than I ever did there,' Donna had offered as an explanation, pleased how her German inflection mainly goes under the radar when she is speaking English.

Rose now says, 'There'll be more raspberries and some apples and potatoes. I'll leave them in a bag on your back fence.' The raspberries this morning had been delicious. Donna begins to be effusive in her thanks. Rose waves them away. 'Maybe, if you've time, you can help me turn the soil.' Donna nods, not entirely sure what she is agreeing to.

She is one of the first to arrive, so she helps set up the room. The desks are positioned around the side. She assists in bringing every available chair to the space in the centre, pointing them towards an interactive board at one end. Then she boils the kettle and sets the coffee machine going. The other officers exchange bits of news about their days off or nights out or sometimes about wives, girlfriends, boyfriends, husbands. Few of them look old enough to have a driving licence to Donna. Then she chides herself, *I'm not that old.* She gets included in the chat and asked a few questions. She keeps her answers light and guards the real reason for her move north. 'Your husband must be very tolerant to let you come,' says one female PC. *Let me come? Do young women still ask for permission from their partners?*

'Oh yes he is,' replies Donna. 'He recognises how important this is for me.'

Jim is possibly the least tolerant person Donna knows. He had actually forbidden her move to Scarborough. Very rarely does Donna defy her husband. Since joining the police she has got better at it, and this time she really had to hold her ground. She found silence and just getting on with it are the best defences. She has discovered there are imperatives more vital than pleasing Jim.

She sits at the back as the meeting gets underway. DS Shilling is leading it and the DI is standing with her. Theo Akande. The only black officer in Scarborough and one of very few on the North Yorkshire force. His skin is dark mahogany, his hair twisted into cornrows, his eyes conker-brown. He's wearing a dark suit, his shirt is maroon, as are the frames on his glasses. He listens attentively to Harrie and there appears to be a warm rapport between them, she glancing over for his encouraging nod. If the gossip hadn't already told her about his sexuality as well, Donna might have suspected something going on between them.

Harrie is summarising what they know so far. It is not a lot. Professor Hari Jayasundera, the pathologist, has not reported; apparently a rough sleeper found dead in a wood is not a priority. Similarly, the forensics are not being fast-tracked. Shilling lets her disapproval seep into her voice. *It would have been different when forensics were in-house and not parcelled off to hastily created private companies,* Donna thinks her DS might have added. *It's not the staff's fault, there's just more money or more prestige in working other cases.*

'The CSI took away several bags from the tent, but so far no ID,' says Harrie, 'which means it's where we start. We've got a pretty decent mugshot. Trev, get a team together to go and talk to other rough sleepers around town. There's a group currently congregating down by the old South Bay Pool huts. Go easy, we want information, not to frighten them off. Plus get up to St Jude's Community Kitchen and see if our man is known there.

'Donna, can you begin a Miss Pers search online, please? Also we need to try and pin down a ToD. We all know what our Prof Jayasundera will say, "summit between the last time he was seen alive and when the body was found".' She emphasises the Yorkshire accent and there's a ripple of amusement. 'So Donna, can you get a formal statement from our horse rider, Lynne Ritchie, concentrating on what she saw and when? Thank you. We still need to do a finger-tip of the whole area. I'll work with Brian on that.'

DC Brian Chesters is sitting to the side of Donna. He is tall and sprightly with large ears. His dark hair is gelled into spikes – when Harrie mentions his name these appear to lift a little, like a peacock's tail. The youngsters get to go out into the field. Donna doesn't know whether she should feel slighted. She's been given tasks of her own; this shows trust.

'Anything else?' Shilling looks first at her DI and then out into the room. The officers are already shifting around ready to move.

Donna finds her voice. She begins tentatively, 'Um, I was just thinking, is it significant that he was found so close to the GCHQ complex?'

'It's a fair point,' says Theo.

Donna glows, perhaps a little too much.

Shilling nods. 'He didn't look like a GCHQ employee, but looks can be deceiving. As part of your search, see if you can speak to someone up there, get the photo over to them. Someone might have seen him, even if he wasn't one of theirs. OK people, let's go.'

The small room erupts into noise and movement. Donna feels like a small boat in a harbour of rough water. Then she realises DI Akande is in front of her and addressing her. He's apologising for not being around to greet her yesterday, asking would she care to come and see him now.

The DI's office is up some stairs and down a corridor. It has a square window framing the roofs of houses in the street at the back of the station. There are the usual functional chairs and a desk with a computer on it. There is a filing cabinet in the corner. It is all very ordered. The walls are painted a minty colour and there is a bold abstract on the one the occupant of the desk would mostly see. DI Akande indicates Donna should sit in the chair he has placed by the desk, then he busies himself with the kettle to produce a camomile tea for both of them. Once he has these he sits. He leans forwards, elbows on the desk and smiles. 'How are you settling in? Must have been a bit disquieting to have a case like this on your first day?'

Donna smiles. It is difficult not to. 'I'm fine, sir. DS Shilling has been very welcoming and supportive. They all have. It'll be good to be doing work which could lead us to knowing who that poor man is and hopefully finding his loved ones.'

'Call me Theo, unless we're interviewing or the formality of the situation demands otherwise. I think Kenilworth is about half the size of Scarborough, and Scarborough has higher indices for all the issues associated with deprivation.'

'I did get rotations to Leamington Spa.' Donna does not want him thinking she has not got the required grit.

'Scarborough was a spa town too, you know, over a hundred years ago. It has one of those chequered histories. Its booming years were up to the 1970s when package holidays came into their own. But they say there might be something of a renaissance now with creatives moving in. I grew up in Birmingham and worked in Manchester, so coming here took some getting used to. Partly it's the small-town mentality. But it's also the sea. When half your patch is the sea, it changes your outlook.'

He sounds enthused. It's only then Donna notices his slight Brummy accent. Or at least she assumes that's what it is – she's never been good with accents. She doesn't think she can match his eagerness. 'Yes.'

He sips his drink. 'I love the walking and the cycling around here. There's some who swim in the sea, all the year round.'

'Are there?' She shivers inside.

It must have shown as he laughs briefly. 'Yes, I imagine it's cold. Prefer warmer water myself. The Balearics or the Canaries.'

Donna nods. Jim had never taken to foreign travel. She had enjoyed their one trip to Florence and Rome, despite the hours on the coach.

There's a slight pause before the DI goes on, as if he is choosing his words carefully. 'Obviously, I am aware why you chose Scarborough for part of your probationary time as a DC. Your daughter.'

She moves her head forwards and backwards a bit too manically, says quietly, 'Elizabeth.'

'Elizabeth,' he repeats gently. 'As far as we can see there is no conflict of interest currently, but we would expect you to be hypervigilant in case one should arise. As I said, this is a small town.'

'She's not in the town.' Donna struggles to get her voice above a whisper. 'But, yes, I see there could be a problem if people she associates with . . . Well, if there is, I will come straight to you.'

Another pause. 'It must be very tough for you. It must have been very tough for you for a long time.'

Donna feels tearful and then stupid for feeling tearful. She tries to force her tone to be more assured. 'It's not what you expect, what I expected would happen. But there, it did. And I want, I want . . .' What does she want? For it all to be different. For things which have occurred not to have occurred. To have a happy, functioning family again. Again? Was it ever? 'I want to be here to support her.'

'Yes, I understand.'

Do you? She feels the roar entering her throat never to escape: *Do you really understand? You handsome, successful, sorted man. You can't possibly understand.* Donna feels shabby. She remembers the man in the wood. Suddenly she feels more akin to him.

Theo drains his cup. 'Well, if there is anything you want to discuss, my door is always open.' He stands.

Donna can't finish her cooling tea, she would choke. She wonders whether she should take the mug with her to wash. She stands with it still in her hand.

'Just leave the mug there,' says Theo, kindly. 'I'll deal with it.'

She nods. It rattles as she puts it down.

'Perhaps take a walk to the sea,' says Theo. 'Ask someone to go with you. I always find it very reviving.'

'Thanks,' she says softly as she leaves.

Chapter 3

Then, thirty-six years ago

It is Erika Neuhausen's fifteenth birthday. It is early in the spring, but they have come to the summerhouse on Grosser Müggelsee to celebrate. The house belongs to the Party. It is far older than the Party. It was built in the late nineteenth century, with generous bay windows and wood panelling on the ground floor. On the upper two floors capacious bedrooms have been converted into dorms with bunkbeds. Even so, there is something of its former elegance which remains – elegance and decadence. Decadence the Party has always raged against. A contradiction Erika has only just begun to consider.

Former occupants would no doubt be horrified at the decline of the place. The wood around windows and in the porch is in dire need of repair and paint. The sticks of furniture are mismatched and sagging. The kitchen and bathroom have had anything which isn't nailed down pinched. The water pipes knock and rumble every time the toilet is flushed or a tap is turned on. The cooker and oven is still the old 1930s version which wheezes every time it is lit and smells slightly of gas. No one is allowed to smoke around it. However, the lawn runs into a sandy beach which borders the wide expanse of green-blue water. The still lake reflects the pale sky and the dark pines which crowd the opposite bank. Despite the slight chill in the air, some of Erika's birthday guests have already changed into their bathing costumes. They crash into the water fracturing the mirror.

They may be guests at her birthday party, but they are not her friends. They are her parents' Party colleagues and their children. One now calls to her to come and join them for a swim. Erika lays off chewing at her thumbnail cuticle and stands. She sweeps her long brown hair up into a ponytail held by a band. She has her swimsuit on under her trousers and shirt which she now sheds. Her mother insisted she brought a dress for later, however she doesn't think she will wear it. She steps into the lake. There is the thrilling moment when the cold stings at her feet. Every autonomic reaction is pushing her to jump back. She holds still. '*Komm schon*,' '*Treten Sie uns bei*,' the swimmers shout. Erika moves in deeper, the water stretching its fingers up past her ankles, past her knees to her thighs. Again she stops. She is hyperventilating. From her school biology lessons she knows her flight response is going into overdrive. She steadies herself. Slows her breathing. Then quickly, as if to catch herself off guard, she lets herself fall, landing on her back, the lake a frosty cushion. She is rolling, first to her front and then onto her back. Her arms and legs are moving strongly in unison, pulling her forwards. The icy water slithers across the bare skin of her shoulders and under her suit at the slight cleavage being formed by her budding breasts. She is laughing.

There are ball games both in the water and out. Later in the afternoon there is a picnic in what would have been the sitting room. Erika has been persuaded to put on her dress, a white lacy affair she's had for several years which has recently become tight and short. There is the usual array of sandwiches and bits of battered fruit. The cake, however, is a confection with chocolate and cream. Erika is shocked. All the guests will be aware some of the ingredients must have come from West Berlin. Though if no one points it out then nothing needs to be done. Both her parents make a little speech about how proud they are of their only child. Erika would once have basked in this. Today she squirms. She gets her first taste of a rather sour wine. Everyone else seems to be enjoying it. She makes an effort to drain her glass and then another.

Her head feels groggy and tender, as if a headache is threatening. Everything and everybody is getting too noisy. She wanders outside and then down a path, which leads into some trees as it follows the shore. She wishes her best friend Sofie were with her, but her mother had said no. She had said there would be enough of her friends at the party. Only she doesn't understand these same children who, under their parents' watchful eyes, encourage Erika and invite her into their games, but at school make fun of her, especially her accent. Two years since her family's move from Dresden to Berlin, Erika isn't able to hide her accent. The accent of a bumpkin; worse, a dolt. Sofie never laughs at Erika. Sofie knows what it is to be an outsider.

Deep in thought, Erika doesn't hear him coming up behind her. He is merely unexpectedly there. Ralph Lerner.

Erika doesn't really like him. He is too full of himself. He is very blond. He is bigger and older than the other boys. But he is the son of the head of the Party Committee her parents belong to. Erika knows to be polite. As they walk, he says all the right things about how he's enjoying the day. Erika would like to turn round, go back to the others, however she is feeling marched along. Suddenly Ralph halts. He grabs her by the shoulders and pushes her against a tree. The bark scratches at her spine. His soft full lips ram onto hers, his tongue pokes out and is trying to pry open her mouth. Tongue kissing. She's heard about it. She tries to turn her head. He whispers something and she realises what he is saying. 'What about that cake, Erika, where did your mum get those ingredients? You do as I say and I won't make a report.'

Still she twists away from him. 'No, no, I don't want to.' She doesn't even know what she is saying no to. She doesn't like his fleshy lips and tongue. She shoves at him. Then she remembers something Sofie had said once about boys and their sensitive parts. They had giggled then. Now Erika brings her knee up into his crotch. It is harder than she expects as she makes contact. It is enough for him to yelp and leave go. Erika twists away. She loses her footing, lands with a jolt onto her backside. She is sliding down the slope. She tries to grasp hold of roots, grass, the very earth itself – nothing holds and she falls inexorably into the lake.

It is no longer a cushion. It is a freezing multi-limbed creature dragging her down. It grasps at her. It holds her under. She hadn't had the wherewithal to take a deep breath as she fell. She has no oxygen in her lungs. They are

21

beginning to burn. She wants to open her mouth, to take in air, but she knows, if she does, only murky slimy water will gush into her stomach, into her lungs and she will drown. *I don't want to die. Help me. Help me.* All this is inside her head. There is no one to help her, only Ralph, and why should he?

Chapter 4

Now

Donna had known from the beginning the parameters were too wide. They had no age, no ToD, no idea where he had come from. They had no idea how long he had been missing – whether, indeed, anyone considered him missing. Even so, she has given it her best shot and has come up with nothing. She's tried the police's own database for missing persons as well as a national charity's, and then uploaded the photo and a query to both. Then she contacted GCHQ and found someone to email the image to. She is waiting to hear back. Finally, she has set up a meeting with Lynne Ritchie for when she is back from her job in Pickering.

This won't be until 6 p.m. Donna has an hour and a half before she has to think about leaving. Lunch was a sandwich eaten at the desk. She decides to follow DI Akande's, *Theo's*, suggestion that she get out for a walk. She has no intention of going to the sea, only to find a café still serving. But in this town it's difficult to avoid the sea. All streets appear to take her there. She ends up on North Bay. Dusk shadows collect on the shore as the sun struggles to maintain its height over the hills to the west. Donna is glad of her coat and scarf, and that she had thought to bring a woollen hat, which she now puts on.

She rests her arms on the rusty railings. The beach is below her, a matt brown slowly being eaten away by the incoming tide. Steely water stretches out to grey clouds amassing on the horizon. The headland between the two bays rises up on her right. On its crest is the tumbled-down castle tower. Its one casement is blank, an eye blinking. A gull swoops down onto the pavement beside her and tilts its head. It has a yellow eye. It has a yellow beak. Its pink feet are as large as side plates. It makes a chittering sound as if engaging Donna in conversation. Then it loses interest and lifts itself effortlessly into the sky. Donna feels lumpen in comparison. She looks down. The sea has nibbled closer and one wave hits the wall below, spitting up an icy gob which catches her on the cheek. Donna steps back. She feels stiff and awkward. She thinks she might slip, then fall through the railings and be consumed by the waves. She knows it is ridiculous, impossible. Yet she quickly turns away.

The café across the road is still open. Donna orders a bowl of soup and sits. The warmth of the place begins to make her feel dizzy. She takes off her outer layers, down to her T-shirt. Still the heat radiates from her. She gulps down some water. The waitress brings over the soup. At first Donna takes tentative sips. Slowly her stomach and throat stop resisting and the furnace which has been lit in her cheeks begins to subside. But there is another feeling to attend to. She has come on again, only two weeks since the last time. The blood is sticky between her legs and there is a slight ache below her guts. She sighs and goes to find the bathroom to clean herself up. At least these days she knows to be constantly prepared. The toilet light gives a yellow tinge to her skin, it emphasises the bruise-like discolouration under her eyes. She feels flabby and exhausted. She remembers vaguely a time when she was relatively contented with her body, occasions when she even felt sassy. She feels a different woman now. A woman she doesn't know. She returns to her seat and finishes her soup.

To get to her appointment with Lynne Ritchie, Donna has to drive the twisting road which skirts the bottom of Raincliffe Woods. Donna has brought to Scarborough her little 'runaround' as Jim puts it. It's nippy at the corners, but it is really a town car – it wouldn't cope with bad weather or some of the muddy tracks Donna notices breaking off at intervals. The evening turns the wood into a different place. It seems more densely packed. One half-naked tree stretches its branch into the roadway with accusing fingers. It taps with a loud snap at the roof of Donna's car. For a moment she is uncertain what the noise is. When she realises, she has to unclench her hands on the steering wheel, unhunch her shoulders and pull her foot back from the accelerator. She thinks about 'our boy' living out there for at least a week: the cold, the wet, the darkness. Had he chosen the life? Or had he been driven to it? Relationship breakdown, job loss, addiction. The big three which would have probably brought him to the woods whether by choice or not. She thinks about some of the places Elizabeth ended up, the smell of the soiled mattresses, the mess and the dirt. Would

Donna have preferred it if her daughter had chosen a tent in the woods?

'At the next junction, turn right.' The satnav's instructions break through Donna's musings. She refocuses on her route which takes her along a flat-bottomed valley. The trees disappear and Donna can see the sweep of the green hills to either side. There is the gleam of electric lights in the windows of the scattered buildings along the way. The sky above the rim of the hills is plum, its skin pricked by creamy glow-worms.

If it wasn't for the satnav, Donna would have missed the turning into a narrow road which crosses a stream and ends in a cluster of houses. Each in their own plot, they are built from the local golden sandstone, though as she gets closer she can see they are not very old. She parks outside one of them and gets out. She hears the *champ-champ* of a horse in the field opposite. Presumably Lynne Ritchie's steed.

Lynne's house is warm, bright and a muddle, with the obvious presence of several teenagers and a man. Lynne leads Donna through to the kitchen at the back, saying it will be the only place they will get any peace. It is a well-proportioned room with slate-grey and chrome cupboards, dark marble worktops and an Aga. Every available space is covered; it looks like possibly one meal has been eaten and another is being prepared. Lynne stirs something on the stove and then sits with a sigh at a small wooden table. She pours some white wine into a large glass and takes a sip. Then, as if remembering her manners, jumps up again. 'I don't suppose you can drink that – can I get you something? Coffee, tea, juice?'

'Water, a glass of water would be fine.' Donna begins to unlayer herself.

Tap water would have been fine, but Lynne pours some bottled water. She is a tall woman and muscular – Donna assumes from dealing with horses. Lynne has blonde-high-lighted hair scooped up into a big grip at the back of her head. Her heavy make-up gives her white skin a tawny palette. She is wearing a smart blouse over shabby slacks – half-in, half-out of her working mode. She's sitting again and drinks some more wine before saying, 'It was awful, you know, seeing him like that. I mean I'm used to seeing dead bodies, I was in the hunt before the silly bloody ban, but this, this was a man. It's different.' Another sip and the large glass is half gone. Donna wonders whether the whole bottle will go before bedtime. There's loud thumping as someone goes upstairs and into a room above, then a screech of out-rage. Lynne raises her eyes to the ceiling and her eyebrows form a perfect arch. 'Ignore it. I usually do. Have you found out who he is yet?'

'We're still investigating.' She has her notebook in front of her – writes the date, the names of those present and then she can begin. 'How often do you take that path through the woods, Ms Ritchie?'

'Lynne is fine. A couple of times a week, I suppose. I'm in insurance. I work from home on a Monday so I can be more flexible and do a longer ride. I often go that way on a Monday.'

'Always on your own?'

Lynne shakes her head. She normally goes with a friend and neighbour, but her daughter was sick yesterday.

'Yesterday? Was it only yesterday? It feels like it was an age ago. I dreamed about him last night.'

Donna makes a note of the woman's name and contact details; she will speak to her while she is up here if she can. 'It must have been a dreadful shock.'

Lynne nods, looks genuinely upset.

'Tell me what happened,' Donna says gently.

'I probably wouldn't have even seen him if Misty hadn't come to a sudden halt. I've been thinking, I bet Misty sensed he was there. Horses are very intuitive, they pick up things. Anyway, I wasn't really concentrating and I dropped my crop, so I had to jump down and retrieve it. That's when I saw him. Otherwise I'd have gone straight past, I'm sure, and he'd still be lying there, I suppose,' she says, sounding a little wan. Then she adds quickly, 'Oh no, someone would have found him, there's loads of walkers and dogs going through. Someone would have seen him.'

There's still plenty of noise off around the house. However, Donna is now more concentrated on the story being unfolded for her. She imagines they will do an appeal for those using Raincliffe to come forward, but she makes a note for herself anyway. 'You said you'd seen the tent for a while?'

Lynne nods. 'A week, maybe two. It's difficult to say. One week melds into another, doesn't it, at our age?' She gives a tentative smile.

Donna returns it to be encouraging. She's not sure she feels up to being bracketed with the fit, vigorous Lynne. 'Do you think you could pin it down a bit? It is rather important.'

'Oh well, let me think.' More wine appears to help her

thinking. She goes through her calendar for the previous month and then hits on a Wednesday, twenty days previously. She smiles more widely, as if she has just been told she has passed a test. 'And we were there the Sunday before that and it wasn't there. He must have moved in between the Sunday and the Wednesday.'

'You never spoke to him or approached him?'

Lynne shakes her head. 'I didn't see him, only the tent, until, well, until yesterday.'

They had been assuming the tent and the man were connected. Donna now wonders whether this is presumptuous. Forensics should tell them. And what if he'd been dead in the tent for some time and someone had moved the body? Or some animal had? The window for ToD could remain wide. 'And did you go to him yesterday? Or near or into his tent at any time?'

Lynne closes her eyes as a shudder runs through her. She opens her eyes and says, a tad defiantly, 'I could see he was dead. I thought it best to get on the phone to call you lot and an ambulance. I couldn't do anything for him. If I could have I would have.'

Would you? Then she reproves herself. Would she, before she became a special? Before Elizabeth? There is nothing more to be gleaned from Lynne. Donna asks if Lynne could organise for her to speak to her riding friend. Lynne says she'll give her a call straight away. Then Donna has to ask to use the bathroom. She finds it embarrassing. Lynne doesn't seem to mind, and she shows her a little cloakroom by the back door. There is no bin. Luckily Donna always carries nappy sacs. By the time she is back in the kitchen, Lynne has arranged for her friend to come round. 'She'll be here in a mo. She's pleased for an excuse to get her bloke to put the kids to bed – they are younger than mine.' Lynne's friend arrives soon after and gratefully accepts some wine. She can't add more to what Lynne has said. She didn't see the man, only the tent, but thinks the timing is right. When shown the photo, she doesn't recognise him. 'Poor sod,' she says, though Donna doesn't get the impression there's much depth of feeling in her tone.

Donna tells them she will type up the statements once she is in the office and then they will be asked to read and sign them. Donna leaves them chatting around the kitchen table. She realises how prickly she feels on the return journey. It is partly physical discomfort. The blood had leaked and, having been over-warm in Lynne's house, Donna is now very cold. She can feel a headache brewing. It is also partly thinking of Elizabeth and about all the people who stepped over her or stepped round her or didn't see her at all.

The phone call comes a few minutes after Donna has finished eating her baked beans on toast. She is sitting at her tiny kitchen table in her tiny kitchen staring at the square of night through the tiny window over the sink. She is enjoying the quiet. She is enjoying the thought that there are no expectations on her to be sociable tonight. She picks up the phone automatically without checking the number. 'Hello.'

'Hello, Mum.'

The voice immediately sends her back to before, to before it all went horribly wrong and Elizabeth was merely ringing to ask to be picked up from hockey practice. Donna remembers her daughter in her PE kit, already bigger than the other girls, stronger. Her clear pale skin pink from her exertions, she would have mud on her socks and up her stocky legs, and she would smell slightly sweaty as she leaned in for a hug. Her peanut-coloured hair in pigtails. 'Darling, how wonderful.' For a moment Donna can't think what else to say. 'How are you?' tumbles out to fill the void. *Was my daughter ever in pigtails?*

'How do you think I am?' The voice changes, is hard-edged, bringing back memories of the after, when nothing was right.

'I know, Lizzie, it must be awful.'

'It's not so bad.' Elizabeth will find a way of contradicting her mother, whatever she says. 'Regular meals. Methadone. Some of the girls are all right.'

'I am glad . . .'

'Oh, Mum, of course it's fucking shit.' There's noise in the background. Someone shouts. A door clangs.

Donna recalls prison visits she has made, for statements or to see Elizabeth. It has always been the continual racket which has put her teeth on edge. 'I'm sorry,' she mutters.

Elizabeth carries on as if she hasn't heard. Perhaps she hasn't. Her tone is ferocious. 'You left him then? Dad? At fucking last.'

'I haven't left him, I'm doing my probationary year here, to be close to you.'

'Don't know why you bothered.'

'I want to support you, Lizzie.' Donna feels herself straining. Straining to find the correct words. Straining to keep herself from crying. Straining to reach down the phone and hug her daughter close.

'Waste of time, Mum. I'm not worth it. Fucking piece of shit.'

'Don't say that about yourself, Lizzie. You are worth it. You are worth so much . . .' She runs dry of expressions. She loses conviction. She has said all this before.

'Whatever. Look, I can't stay on long, they count your minutes when you are a violent offender . . .'

'Don't . . .' Donna says quietly, too quietly to be heard by Elizabeth.

'I've put you on the visitor list. You can come if you like. You can book online. But I guess you can come whenever you want, being in the police.'

'I'll come, of course I will. When?'

'Whenever suits you. I'm not going anywhere, am I? Bye.'

And she breaks the connection. Elizabeth was always a bit like that. Even as a child, once she'd finished something, she wanted to be up and on to the next thing. Donna slowly puts down her phone and buries her face in her hands. Tears don't come. She's run dry. After a while she gets up and washes her crockery and saucepan. She goes to bed, thinking she will sleep. She is exhausted.

She does sleep for an hour or so and then she is wide awake, a headache chiselling at her right temple. She curses herself for not noting the warning signs and taking painkillers earlier. She crawls out of bed and dresses in jogging bottoms and sweatshirt. She takes her pills, two more than advised on the packet, uses the bathroom to clean off the blood again. Then she goes to the kitchen to make a cup of tea.

Rose had left her a bag of goodies as promised. Donna takes out the apples. They are slightly bruised. Donna nibbles into one. They are very tart. She begins to collect from the cupboards what she will need for apple cake. She stews the apples with a bit of cinnamon and then begins combining the sugar and flour with margarine and then egg. She can almost imagine a littler Elizabeth standing beside her on a footstool. She's mixing enthusiastically. Cocoa powder is rising into the air and then falling onto her apron and her sturdy feet in their silver-coloured sandals. She is singing along to the radio. They both are. Some daft 1960s number. They are both as tuneless as each other. 'Do you remember this song, Mum, when it first came out?'

'I'm not that old, I was only a baby then.'

'Anyway, they didn't have much pop in West Berlin, did they, Mum? You were crap at that quiz Stell's mum organised, you didn't know nothing. '

'I didn't know anything. Of course we listened to pop when we were growing up, it was just different, that's all. And don't use the word crap.'

'Well, you were.' Elizabeth has brought the wooden spoon full of cake mix near her mouth. She is watching to see if she will be told don't. Her quirky smile is so endearing, Donna doesn't have the heart. Elizabeth takes a big mouthful and beams. 'You were crap.'

Now under the bright light of the kitchen at 1 a.m. in the morning, Donna takes the apples off the stove and pours the puree into the bottom of a tin. Her hands shake, she can taste salt as she licks her lips. She drops the pan into the sink and it clangs satisfyingly. She stands leaning on the kitchen table, dry sobs raking at her throat. *I must have been more than crap, Lizzie. I'm so, so sorry I didn't do enough to save you.*

Chapter 5

Now

The apple cake is almost gone by the time of the briefing. Her colleagues appreciate it. Donna knows bringing it in will earn her a motherly reputation. On the whole she does not mind. Harrie and Theo are once again at the front of the room. They take the last two pieces of cake and eat it approvingly while everyone settles down. Donna only fell back to sleep an hour before she had to get up. Consequently she has cottonwool for brains. She sits at the back of the room, hoping to keep a low profile until she can wake up properly. It is not to be. The first sentence out of Theo's mouth contains her name. Her GCHQ enquiry has resulted in an ID. Henrich Grüntor. This brings Donna fully awake: their man was German?

Theo is glancing up, searching her out. 'Perhaps you could help me with the pronunciation, Donna?'

Eyes turn on her, not in an unfriendly way, more curious. Her smile is returned. On the whole. She says, 'You've got Henrich right, the ending like the "ch" in loch. The surname is a little trickier. The "u" has an umlaut, which makes it a kind of an "ew" sound, as in "mew" or "few". Then emphasis on the "or" at the end.' She demonstrates.

35

Theo repeats it fairly accurately, then looks round. 'Have we all got it? Let's show our deceased the respect of trying to say his name correctly.'

A few people quietly make some brave attempts.

She grins, drops her gaze to her notebook on her lap, draws a few doodles. She almost misses her assignment: she is to go with Theo to talk to personnel at GCHQ. The DI is going on to explain that GCHQ entering the picture has facilitated the PM and the forensics. They should have the reports by tomorrow morning. His tone suggests he recognises the hypocrisy, but is resigned to it.

Shilling then asks Trevor to give an account of his enquiries. He stands, opens his notebook unhurriedly and begins to talk. No one could accuse PC Trench of not being thorough, it's his summarising skills which are a tad lacking.

Eventually Harrie intervenes: 'So none of the rough sleepers from the South Bay had seen him and the volunteer at St Jude's said he hadn't either. What was his name?'

'William Bell.'

'However, you spoke to a rough sleeper there who did know Henrich?'

Trev nods. 'Derek Wyatt. He said Henrich had been in several times over the last month, at least once a week. He was a bit vague on time, but he was certain he had met him. They had spoken, Derek had explained how things worked and they had discussed the weather and a bit about the football. He was sure Henrich and William Bell had spoken too.' Trev looks at his notes. 'Derek said he thought Henrich sounded a bit posh, but then hard times could come to anyone. Well, he said it with a few more choice expressions, but that was the gist.'

'The gist,' says Shilling, her lips flirting with a smile. Those around Donna chuckle or roll their eyes. 'This Derek, is he a reliable witness?'

'I could smell cheap lager on him and it was ten-thirty in the morning.'

Donna notices Shilling doesn't enquire after the reliability of William Bell.

Shilling continues, 'Alcoholics need their drink to function. On the other hand, alcohol pickles your brain.'

'It's a discrepancy,' says Theo. 'One to bear in mind.'

Trev turns the page in his notebook. 'Derek says he last saw Henrich last Friday.' He closes his notebook and sits down.

'Which helps with the ToD,' says Theo.

'If true,' says Shilling.

'Let's assume it is for now,' says Theo. 'We've nothing better to go on. Donna, your discussion with Ms Ritchie didn't throw up anything useful?'

Donna struggles to push herself to her feet, her body is so fatigued. Despite this her mind appears to have caught alight. She gives a brief overview of her conversation with Lynne and her friend.

'Which means Friday late afternoon to Monday afternoon is still our best guess on ToD,' says the DI. 'Harrie, we need a team on to what CCTV there is around there. Plus let's plot a possible route from St Jude's to the woods. Also get an appeal on the local radio for anyone in Raincliffe during that time period.' He checks his watch. 'Meanwhile,

Donna and I have our appointment at GCHQ.' He looks over at her. 'Ready?'

'Yes, um . . .' She feels herself reddening. 'I just need to go . . . a minute to sort myself . . .' Her voice fails her.

Whether or not Theo understands, he says, 'Ten minutes by the garage.'

Donna is beginning to gain her sense of direction in Scarborough. She has always been quick at getting a map of where she is in her head. Besides, they are basically following the same route she had taken with Harrie not two days before, driving inland up a steep bank, known as Racecourse Road. She settles into the comfy leatherette seat and enjoys the smooth ride.

This time they take the tarmac drive up to GCHQ security where they have to stop to have their photos taken and passes prepared. They are told they must go straight to reception and follow the instructions of staff at all times. 'They don't want us wandering about,' says Theo cheerily. They have to leave the car and walk the last hundred metres up to the building. It is low-rise, grey metal. It wouldn't look out of place on any industrial estate.

The reception is as unexceptional. A woman is sitting behind a desk with a computer. The carpets and furnishings are muted browns. Donna instinctively looks up and sees several small cameras covering all possible directions. They don't have to wait long for Neil Murphy to appear and lead them down a short corridor to his room, which could also belong to the personnel officer of any company. Neil is probably in his late forties, his hair is thinning and his face has something of the hound dog about it. His trouser belt strains as he sits. He offers them coffee. Theo accepts, Donna asks for water. She takes off her coat. Neil has directed them to a low glass table around which upholstered chairs are grouped. Donna relaxes into hers. Theo takes the lead, asking Neil to tell them about Henrich Grüntor.

The natural cast of Neil's face assists him in looking suitably sad at the demise of a former employee. However, it is clear most of his information comes from files. Henrich was fifty-nine years old. He was single. He had worked for GCHQ since 1991. He was in the Russian section. He was an able and skilled worker. He liked jazz music and belonged to a club in town. Apart from that, as far as Neil knows, Henrich led a quiet life, living in Scarborough. He gives them the address and then looks up. 'We are incredibly distressed to learn of his death. How did it happen?'

'We are still investigating,' says Theo. 'When did he leave your employ?'

'Friday 22nd March.'

'Did he leave voluntarily?'

Just as Theo hadn't hesitated with the rote 'we are still investigating', Neil says, 'We came to an agreement.'

'Which was necessary because?'

'I'm not sure I can divulge the details.' Neil looks rather pleased with himself. Perhaps he is used to the spectre of national security being enough to put the majority of people off.

Not DI Akande. He is sat back in his chair, the lime-green jacket hanging open to reveal a dark green shirt and matching tie with a thin lime-green stripe. He takes in and releases a deep breath. 'We have a man found dead in the woods not half a mile from your door who turns out to be an employee who left six months ago. I think a judge would take a dim view of you withholding information which could assist our enquiries.'

Neil looks uneasy. Then he shrugs. 'You'll need to go higher up for permission.'

'I will.' Theo glances over at Donna. She's been taking notes. She now realises she is being given permission to ask a question if she has one. She has. She asks where Henrich was born.

Neil looks surprised. He searches in the file. 'Hamburg.'

Donna continues, 'Most Germans with a high level of proficiency in Russian come from the East.'

'We vet our employees very carefully, Miss, er, Mrs . . .'

'DC Morris. I'm sure you do.'

'Can we see where he worked?' asks Theo.

Neil gives a hint of a smile. 'That would need clearance. Anyway, there's nothing to see. When he left he took anything personal to him and someone else is working there now.'

'How about colleagues?' says Donna. 'Someone who knew him better . . .' she is about to add 'than you' then stops. Would Neil take this as a slight? She doesn't want to antagonise him more.

'I'll ask around. Tell them to get in touch with you.'

'You do that.' Theo stands. He's not tall for a man, only the same height as Donna at about five-seven, but he holds himself assertively. 'And we'll be back in touch with you for the information we need on how and why Mr Grüntor left the job he did ably and skilfully for over twenty years.'

'As you wish. I'll see you out.'

Theo suggests they stop at a café on the way back for a bite to eat. It is in a barn on a farm, there are heavy wooden tables and chairs which scrape across the floor when moved. Donna gets herself a herbal tea and a hummus sandwich. Theo has another coffee and a bacon and mustard roll. On the way in they had passed a byre of pigs, presumably relatives of those who had provided the filling.

'I don't like being stalled,' says Theo, taking a healthy bite.

'I suppose he's doing his job.' Donna is enjoying eating. The hummus has just enough lemon and garlic and has been combined with some carrot. 'Maybe there is a threat to national security.'

'A threat to him more like. You said you saw evidence of drug misuse on Henrich's arm. Neil's a personnel officer worried he didn't do enough to support an employee's mental health and now the employee has turned up dead, cause undefined.'

'He's thinking suicide.'

'It's not been ruled out.' After a moment of companionable chomping, Theo says, 'Tell me what your thinking is around whether Henrich Grüntor came from East or West Germany.'

'Nothing much, just surprised he came from Hamburg – my bet was on East Germany.'

'Because of the language?'

Donna nods. 'If he had been born in the former GDR then the first language he would have been taught at school was Russian. Plus he came to work at GCHQ in 1991, a year after German reunification. But he was born in the West, so it was a dead end.'

'Maybe.' Before taking another bite, Theo says, 'I think you need to give me a brief East–West German history 101.'

'Me? Oh, well . . .' She hesitates. Despite her background she could count on one thumb the number of times she's been asked to delve into this by anyone in the UK.

'It was post-Second World War, wasn't it, when the split came?'

She nods again. 'Under the agreements of the Potsdam Conference in 1945, the governance of Germany was initially to be split between the allies. Plus Berlin, which was slap bang in the middle of the Soviet zone, was split into four sectors. The British, the Americans, the French and the Soviets controlled a sector each. When it became obvious the Soviets were not going to give up their zone, the other allies consolidated theirs into the Federal Republic of Germany in May 1949, but they maintained their hold in Berlin. As the former capital, it was too important symbolically to just let go. So the city became a kind of island in a Soviet sea.'

'And the Soviets built the Berlin Wall?'

'No. That was the idea of a German, Walter Ulbricht. He'd spent the latter part of the war in Moscow and he wanted to build his own country into a communist state. He was a bit of a, what do you call it? A curate's sausage?'

'Egg, a curate's egg, I think.'

'Yes. The Soviets were happy about communist expansion, of course they were, but they were worried about annoying the British and the Americans too much. They were often trying to rein Ulbricht in.'

'Only he wasn't going to be reined in.'

She shakes her head. She is warming to her subject. She hadn't always understood all this – who has any perspective on history when they are living it? But she's read plenty since. 'He wanted the wall basically because his German so-called Democratic Republic was haemorrhaging people – young, skilled, educated people – through Berlin, into the western sectors. August 1961, the first barricades went up, with barbed wire and cement blocks. And the border crossings and underground lines which went from east to west were sealed. It was an enormous shock to the people. Ulbricht had said there would be no wall only two months before.'

'Never believe a politician when they promise absolutely not to do something.'

They smile at each other in shared cynicism.

'From then on, it just got more and more solid.' She pauses, then adds quietly, 'Frightening.'

'People still tried to escape though, didn't they?'

'Correct. It became increasingly difficult as time went on, but yes, people found ways. Some did. Not everyone wanted to go. Some people wanted to live in a socialist state, they believed in it. There were advantages – free childcare, full employment, housing. A sense of, I don't know, maybe all being in it together? Though in reality that wasn't true. Luxury and privilege no longer required money, for sure, but it relied on being a good party member. Then there were

43

the families who just kept their heads down and got on with it. Life could be hard. The GDR was a basket case, economically. The Soviets had walked off with a lot of the country's industrial infrastructure as reparations. And Ulbricht's policies were more ideological than realistic. There was a lot of petty corruption. Plus, of course, all the surveillance and the fear of being denounced for being a bad communist.'

Theo has finished eating. He is sipping from his coffee cup thoughtfully. 'My dad came from Nigeria in the 1960s. He was escaping political violence and corruption.'

She wonders if he is going to say more. When he doesn't, she responds, 'It must have been hard to pick up your life, move and start again.'

'It was. Though his brothers were here, he met my mum and they had me, and my sisters. There were compensations.'

She returns his smile.

He puts down his mug and sits back. 'It's what you did, isn't it? Move and start again?'

'I left West Berlin in my teens and went to be a nanny in Ludlow. Even that was something of a culture shock.'

'You came on your own?'

She nods.

'So you have family in Germany? You've been back?'

Thus far she has only been lying by omission. If he asks another question, she might have to tell one of her well-worn falsehoods.

He continues with his own thoughts. 'My dad has hardly gone back. We've an uncle and a few cousins in Nigeria who we've visited, but I think it always unsettles him. He doesn't quite belong there anymore.'

Torn between wanting to hear more of his story and wanting to avoid telling more of hers, Donna does an obvious time check by looking at her wrist.

Theo appears to gather himself, as if out of a reverie. 'Yes, we should get on. What say you and I go and check out the address Mr Murphy gave us as Mr Grüntor's home address?'

'Don't you have meetings to attend or detective-inspector-type things to do?' It slips out before Donna can censor it. She is relieved when Theo smiles.

'Probably, but they can wait.' He chuckles. 'I think I can justify some time with my new probationary DC, don't you?'

Henrich Grüntor's former home is a small terraced let on a main road. The decorators are in. They do not know anything about the previous tenant, only that all the rooms require sprucing up and the owner is putting in a new kitchen. They give contact details for the estate agent who is dealing with them. Donna calls the estate agent and is told Henrich had defaulted on his last two months of rent and had handed in the keys at the end of August. 'Meaning,' she says to Theo, 'he was probably sleeping rough for around six weeks.'

The neighbours on one side are a paint, wallpaper and carpet store. None of the staff recognise Henrich from the photo provided by Neil Murphy. On the other side the door is opened by a bleary-eyed youth. He explains the house is shared by students. He says he doesn't recognise Henrich, but will ask the others when they surface. 'We had a bit of a sesh last night,' he says. His grimace-grin reminds Donna of Christopher, in his late teens, before he got all serious.

'You'll let us know if they remember anything,' says Theo. 'Anything at all.'

'Sure bro.' He's about to close the door, then seems to have a thought. 'You could try Granny-Mare at number eleven, she keeps an eye on everyone and everything. That's not her real name, by the way, just what we call her' – again the slewed grin – 'but I think her name is something like Mary, yeah?'

Granny-Mare turns out to be a Marion, Marion Wicks. She is probably in her late sixties, and the photos in her bright, tidy lounge suggest she is a granny. She says she has a few minutes to talk to Donna and Theo before she goes up to the hospice for her volunteer shift. 'Apologies for not offering you refreshments, but I really do need to get on soon,' she finishes, seating herself in one of the armchairs. Beside it is a little table on which is piled several books and a copy of the *Telegraph* folded to reveal the half-completed crossword.

'We won't take up more of your time than is required,' says Theo, taking the other armchair.

Donna perches on the edge of the sofa. It is light coloured and, though she used the toilets at the café, she is always a little wary of a sudden rush of blood. She takes out her notebook and pen.

'We're enquiring about Henrich Grüntor, did you know him?'

'Henry? Yes, nice chap, quiet. What has he done?'

'Why would you expect him to have done anything?' asks Theo.

'Well, it's often the quiet ones.' Marion is sitting up straight, knees together, hands clasped on them.

Donna notices the titles of the books; they are all detective novels.

'Unfortunately,' says Theo, 'Mr Grüntor was found dead on Monday.'

'Dead? Goodness!' The shock is sprinkled with a pinch of salacious interest.

'So can you tell us anything about him?' prompts Donna, a tad snappily.

'Not a lot, he really did keep himself to himself. He said he was from Germany, worked at GCHQ. He liked his jazz, that I do know. I haven't seen him since he moved out at the end of August.'

'Did he say anything about where he was going, what he was going to do?' asks Theo.

Marion shakes her head and the low sun glints off diamonds in her ears. 'He said he had retired. I assumed he was moving somewhere for his retirement. Maybe back to Germany? Though, well' – she looks down briefly – 'I did hear from the agent that Henry had not paid his rent. And, well, he did start to look, um' – she pauses – 'a bit dishevelled.' She has ceased to look at them, her gaze resting on objects around the room. 'I met him on the street one day and, well, I was struck. I have to say, he did smell a little.' Again a pause and then she says, 'I did ask him how he was. He said fine.'

Fine. The English version of I'm really not OK. Donna notices Theo is watching Marion, but isn't about to ask a question. She follows his lead.

And Marion does continue. 'Then there was that odd night, when was it? Last year, end of last year, November sometime. I thought it was those students. Since nice Mr and Mrs Taylor had to – well, she died, of course, cancer, and he had to go into a home. Wasn't coping at all well, Mr Taylor, poor man, and now he's in one of those specialist places. Doesn't even recognise me when I visit.'

Donna is about to intervene to bring Marion back on track. However, her DI is remaining attentive and not interrupting, so she does the same.

'Yes, so, the Taylors' house was sold to – what do they call it? – an absentee landlord and it is always full of students. Henry never complained. Though I had to talk to the agent a few times about the noise and the mess. They could never get bin day right. They're at university and they can't put their bins out on the correct morning.' Marion gives a half sigh, half harrumph. 'So last November I thought it was one of them, carousing up and down the street at past midnight, high as a kite. Only it was Henry. He was half-dressed, I ask you. I thought about calling some of your colleagues. But then he went indoors and everything went quiet.'

After a moment, Theo asks, 'And did you ever find out what had been the problem?'

She stares at her hands. 'Not really. He came round to apologise. I understood from what he was saying that he had had problems with alcohol and this had been some kind of relapse. I believe it happens. Some people can't help themselves.'

Donna wants to contradict her, but finds herself unable to do so.

'How did poor Henry die?' asks Marion, her tone more tempered with sadness.

'We are still investigating the circumstances,' says Theo. 'Just to help us with our enquiries, Mrs Wicks, where were you at the weekend?'

'Oh.' She perks up. 'I was down at my daughter's in Sheffield. I can give you her contact details if you like.'

'Yes, please,' says Donna. She writes them down as Marion dictates them.

'I took the train, the ten-forty out of Scarborough on Friday morning and returned Monday afternoon. I am sure there will be CCTV?'

'I am sure there will be, Mrs Wicks,' says Theo.

She looks at the clock on her mantelpiece. 'I am sorry, I should really be going.'

They all stand in readiness for leaving, then Donna asks, 'When Henrich was shouting in the street, do you remember anything of what he said?'

'Oh no,' says Marion. 'It was all in German.'

Marion Wicks practically shoos them out the door. Once down her path and through her gate, Theo says, 'What are you thinking, DC Morris?'

'I am wondering whether anyone in this street understands German.'

He smiles. 'How about you do some door knocking and find out. Then see if you can unearth Henrich's jazz-club buddies. I really do have some detective-inspector-type things to do. Is it all right if I take the car back?'

You're asking me for permission? Donna beams. 'I like to walk.' It's true – it's a habit she developed when she was a teenager; it helps her think.

49

It takes Donna an hour to establish who lives in the street and that none of them understands German. She revisits the students, who are now eating cereal in a kitchen cluttered with unwashed cutlery and crockery. The pong of slightly sour milk would put Donna off consuming food, but the six lads appear to have no problems shovelling it away. Four are studying business, two are medical students. Marion Wicks's comment repeats in Donna's mind, *And you can't put your bins out on the right day?* They plead ignorance when asked about languages.

It is around 5 p.m. when she makes her way over to the pub which hosts the jazz club in its basement. She has rung ahead to discover the club will kick off properly later that evening, but there is a rehearsal going on. The organiser is in attendance. A flight of steps leads down from street level and Donna is in a large low-ceilinged space with a bar along the side. Lighting is more subdued than outside – it takes a moment for Donna to adjust. There is a stage at one end. Standing on it are a collection of people holding a variety of instruments. One is a small woman. Her very straight hair is dyed a bronze which flickers in the stage lights. She has a saxophone across her body; it is almost as big as she is. The guy picking out the tune on a guitar steps back and the others applaud him with some 'yeah's and 'way to go's.

Then the woman steps forward. She puts her lips to the saxophone mouthpiece. She doesn't even appear to blow, but the notes glide out. Donna is transported. She'd worked in bars and clubs in her late teens, before she met Jim. Some had been quite frankly dives, sticky carpets, sticky tables and loudmouth punters touching her bum. There had been one bar, however, which had live music. Leather and safety pins vied with sharp suits and even sharper haircuts, noisy guitars and drums with synths. It was the 1980s. But Donna remembers one man with his saxophone playing the solo from 'Baker Street'. She had slept with him. Once. No, maybe twice. He wasn't a quarter of the player this woman is. The notes draw tears to Donna's eyes. She wraps her arms around herself. Her hips begin to sway.

'She's good, isn't she? She's often out on tour, but whenever she comes back home she plays here. We're very lucky.'

Donna nods, unable to articulate much.

'I'm Floyd,' he says, holding out his hand.

She takes it, wondering if he is named, or named himself, after the band. 'DC Donna Morris,' she says, none too steadily.

'Mike – he owns this place – he said you were coming. It's about Henry? Shall we sit?' He leads her to a booth where there's a table and bench seats. Floyd takes one side, Donna the other. 'We haven't seen Henry for several weeks, which is odd because he never used to miss a club night. How is he?'

'I am afraid to have to tell you Henrich died at the weekend,' Donna says. She is beginning to be able to marshal her thoughts. The saxophone is being replaced by piano.

'What? Oh man, that's terrible.' Floyd is perhaps in his forties. Totally bald, he looks like he might work out. The sleeves of his black shirt are rolled up, revealing a tattoo of a stanza of music on his forearm. Donna wonders if it's a particular piece of music or merely random. 'How?' he asks.

'We are still investigating the circumstances.' Donna consciously parrots her DI. It steadies her further. She takes out her notebook, writes date, place and who is present. 'When did you last see him?'

'Oh man,' Floyd rubs at his forehead. 'I guess it's important to be accurate?'

'It would help.'

'OK.' He takes a moment, squeezes his eyes half shut. 'It was the night we had Charlie and the Rockin' Rackets playing, which was, yeah, 4 September, right after our August break.'

Right after Henrich had moved out of his house. 'How did he seem?'

'Fine.'

Donna waits.

'Oh man, he didn't . . . I mean, it wasn't suicide, was it?'

'We are still investigating. Did he seem any different to you?' The drums are now doing a solo. The thumping goes right through Donna.

Floyd hesitates before saying, 'Not quite his usual self, I would say. A bit subdued, but nothing, you know, nothing to suggest . . . oh man.' He looks glum.

Again Donna consciously holds back.

'He didn't used to drink – I mean alcohol. I think he said he had, you know, a problem. But he'd started drinking hard, last year sometime, know what I mean? One time one of the guys had to take him home. I remember that night – the last night I saw him – I had to help him up the stairs. I said, did he want me to take him home? He said, no, it was all downhill, he'd roll home.' Floyd gives a weak smile.

His hands are folded on the table in front of them. His fingers are long and sculpted. 'He did have a bit of a sense of humour at times, did Henry. But it was his love of the music – man, he knew everything, he appreciated everything.' The fingers twitch. Floyd looks down at them.

Donna waits.

Floyd says quietly, 'It wasn't only the booze, if you get my meaning. He took other stuff. Bit of hash. Bit of snow.'

Bit? Donna remembers the tracks on Henrich's arms. 'Did he get it from here?'

'No, no, no, man no. Mike wouldn't allow it.' He doesn't look her in the eye.

'Where then?'

He shrugs. Then he opens up his hands, showing his palms. 'Honestly, DC Morris, I don't know. My days of using are long gone. One pint's enough for me. I wouldn't know where to get gear from in this town.'

Does she believe him? Not really. 'It would help us to know.'

He leans in, his focus on her. 'I don't know and that's the God's own truth.'

She leaves another space, but he doesn't fill it. 'Where were you at the weekend?'

'Me? Mostly at the Spa. I manage the bar there over the weekends. Music doesn't pay.'

Someone shouts for him from down by the stage. 'Gotta go.' There's definite relief in his voice.

She hands over a generic business card on which she quickly scrawls her mobile number. 'Can you ask around about Henrich and drugs? You or anyone can give me a call, anonymously.'

He takes it and turns it over in his hands, halted in his flight from her. 'I'll ask around and we'll dedicate a tune to Henry this evening. He was a good bloke.' He looks up. 'What about his funeral?'

'We'll have to see once we track down some next of kin.'

He nods. 'If you don't – you know, if he hasn't anyone – we'll sort something for him.' Then he moves off, saying quietly to himself, 'Oh man.'

Donna sits for a while. The air has become close and stuffy and part of her is itching to move. Still she waits. After about ten more minutes she is rewarded. The woman with the saxophone starts up a mournful melody. Donna lets the tears drip down her face. For Henrich. For Elizabeth. For herself.

Chapter 6

Now

Donna knows from experience that each investigation has its own pace. This one has become glacial. The expected PM and forensics have been delayed because of 'complications'. Rumour has it that MI5 is becoming involved because Henrich was a Russian spy gone rogue or because he was 'one of ours'. Either way he was the victim of a Russian assassination. Alexander Litvinenko has been mentioned more than once.

Donna speaks to her CID colleagues who know about drug suppliers in the town to find out how Henrich might have bought his. They suggest he probably gave his order to any one of a myriad of kids who would go through to Leeds or Manchester and return with the stash. Weed can be bought on Scarborough's streets easily enough, but anything injectable is brought in by mules as young as ten. The officers say they'll show Henrich's photo around, though they aren't optimistic of anything coming of it. Could Henrich have suffered violence over some drug debt? Absolutely.

With nothing else needing immediate attention this

Friday morning, Donna goes down to the harbour with Trev to familiarise herself with it. The mellowness of previous days has been blown away. The icy blast, according to the forecasters, comes straight from the Arctic. Donna can believe it as she and Trev walk to the front. They take a route through town and then down a steep hill and then there . . . there it is: the expanse of blue framed by the tall metal arches of what Trev calls the Spa Bridge. For an instant, Donna is stilled. It's as if she has suddenly hit a barrier of noise, the churning of the waves which spin as if on wheels onto the flat expanse of ochre sand. Trev is a couple of steps ahead of her telling her that the bridge was opened in 1827 to take the lords and ladies to the 'Spaw'. Then he realises he has left her behind. He stops and turns. He smiles, perhaps at her expression. 'Stunning, isn't it?'

She can only nod. She follows him. It's not easy to get a word in on his commentary on the town – there's the Spa, here's the Grand Hotel, there's the lifeboat house – his pride in the place is obvious. But even if she wanted to, she thinks she would struggle to find words.

The iron railings which run along the back of the beach have, in places, their footings in the sand flung there by the weight of the sea. Some of the metal is rusted, as if chewed by some enormous canine. Small grey birds with awkwardly long thin legs run into the water and then out again, cheeping frantically. Trev tells her they are sanderlings, winter migrants from frozen Northern climes. He laughs at their antics. Donna joins him. The restriction on her chest eases. Nothing to prove. No one to please. Merely the moment to watch and enjoy.

PC Trench is in his element when they reach the harbour. He comes from a fishing family, but the boat had been sold during the downturn in the 1970s and Trev had joined the force. However, he still knows almost everyone they meet and fastidiously introduces Donna to each one as their new DC. He doesn't have to add she is recently moved to the town. They all know she doesn't come from hereabouts, and not because they catch a whiff of the underlying cadence of her accent. It's because they know everyone who does. They are friendly, though, warmly shaking her hand with their own work-roughened ones. They suppose, with satisfaction, that she finds life different here.

The harbour is enclosed by two breakwaters. They walk out onto the one Trev calls the West Pier. The smell of fish and salt hits Donna as soon as they step onto it. 'Scarborough is the second-biggest shell-fishing port in the country,' Trev says with satisfaction. There is a series of two-storey brick buildings along one side and a grey metal structure at the end. These are where the catches are landed and processed before being put on the distributing lorries. This had already happened many hours before, but there are still fish heads and crab pincers on the tarmac to be fought over by the gulls. Trev points out the different types – the turkey-sized herring gulls are the most prevalent. 'Scavengers by blood,' says Trench. 'And, of course, they're so used to our food now, those "Comforts" feeding them their fish and chips.' He smiles at Donna's puzzlement. 'Comforts,' he explains, 'come for t'day and then leave all their dross on the beach.' Then he points to the smaller birds flitting in for a bit of a meal while the herring gulls are looking elsewhere. 'The Little Gull, the Black-headed Gull – there's a common tern.' They all look grey to Donna, with black markings.

In between the two harbour arms, yachts are anchored to floating docks. The wind keeps up a percussion of cymbals as it blows through the rigging. Fishing boats and trawlers are tied against the quays. There is a strong smell of diesel. Trev points out how Donna can identify a Scarborough boat with its 'SH' registration and also that the other registration letters show how far some of the boats have travelled, mostly from further north and from Scotland. He does not have to point out how much bigger the non-Scarborough boats are. 'Trawlers,' he explains. 'Scraping every which way across the seabed, cutting through the lines on our pots.'

They get two hot chocolates from the café in the armpit of the outer sea wall and stand looking out over the charcoal water forming ever-shifting slate cliffs and valleys. Donna feels slightly dizzy watching. If Trev hadn't been beside her, she might have got slightly panicky. 'Did you want to be a fisherman?'

'Didn't have the choice once the boat was gone,' says Trev in his rumbling baritone. 'But I love it out there, even in weather like this.'

Donna can't credit it. She holds on more tightly to her china mug of steamed milk.

By the end of the afternoon, spent typing witness reports onto the system, she realises how invigorated she had felt earlier standing by PC Trench watching the tumult. Now her back and shoulders are stiff. Her head is stuffy. She looks at the time – she could go thirty minutes early and use up the lieu time she has accrued. The phone rings. It is the officer on the front desk – he has a call he has been trying to put through to the DI or to Shilling, but neither are at their desks. It is the German embassy, it's about Henrich Grüntor – would Donna take it? She agrees to.

A woman comes through on the other end of the line. She says her name is Sabine Barker, and she is desk officer at the German consulate in Edinburgh, the mission which looks after North Yorkshire. Her English is exceptional, though she still has an accent. An accent Donna knows her colleagues might term harsh. It unravels Donna for a minute or two. With its familiarity, it sends her back through forty years. She hears herself saying, *'Mein Name ist* DC Donna Morris.'

'Ah, Sie sprechen Deutsch?' Donna can hear Sabine's smile.

Donna explains she will have to call Sabine back.

'Of course,' says Sabine, 'to check I am really who I say I am.' She gives the number for the switchboard and says she will be waiting.

After breaking the connection, Donna leaves it long enough to be sure she is not being held on line to a scam number. During those minutes she does a quick internet search, locates the consulate in Edinburgh. Under 'Our Staff' she finds Sabine Barker, in post since October last year. There is also a photo of Sabine playing the piano at a benefit for the local hospice. The photo is not a close-up, however Donna thinks she recognises something about the face. On the other hand, it could merely be the classic Aryan features and blonde hair. She decides she has left enough time and makes the phone call to the switchboard number on the website. She is immediately put through to Sabine. The conversation is mostly conducted in German. Donna finds herself hesitating over some of the words like 'forensics' and 'post-mortem' which she has to deliver in English. Sabine laughs. 'I know,' she says in English, 'there are some things I can't translate either. For the moment, then, there is nothing to be done for the body? We can help repatriate if necessary. We can also look for relatives in Germany.'

Sabine sounds unphased by talking about the death of a fellow countryman. She hasn't expressed any sympathy or sadness. Perhaps this is her professional front. Donna imagines Sabine would have a different tone if talking to next of kin. 'Please keep me updated,' says Sabine. They exchange email addresses and direct phone numbers before ending the call. Donna is about to write an explanatory email to Theo and Harrie when her DS comes back in to the office and Donna is able to tell her what's happened. The DS appears tired and distracted, perhaps as dispirited as everyone about the lack of movement in the case. She tells Donna to continue with the email for Theo and then to get on home. 'Doing anything nice this weekend?' adds Harrie, as she turns away.

'Nothing special,' Donna lies.

During the evening, Jim calls her. Apart from sporadic texts, Donna has not communicated with him since she arrived in Scarborough. He is petulant. Fed up, Donna deduces, with cooking his own dinner. 'I thought you were coming back for the weekend,' he says.

'Sorry, work.' Donna lies again. Only Jim knows his wife better than her colleagues do – he sniffs out the untruth.

'You're going to see her, aren't you?' His tone is now edged with a righteous anger. 'I don't know why you are bothering.'

'She's our daughter.'

'And have you forgotten how she cheated and stole and lied? What she did to that poor woman? Your daughter assaulted you, for heaven's sake.'

'She pushed me.'

'You fell over and bruised your elbow. I had to take time away from work to take you into A&E, as you thought it might be broken.'

Elizabeth didn't mean to. She was desperate. The words form but are not said. Donna knows it is pointless. They have had this argument too many times before. She asks instead about Jim's plans for the weekend. Golf, watching the rugby with the lads, golf again on Sunday and lunch at the club-house restaurant with his golf buddies. 'Sounds like fun,' Donna says, appeasement coming into her voice. She cringes. She pictures her husband sitting in their lounge; he might be gazing through the conservatory into the garden. The garden they both planned and tended together. Jim will be relaxed in his capacious armchair, out of his suit, in joggers and the chunky cardigan she'd bought him. He will be slumping, his slight paunch will be more obvious than when he is standing. He is not tall, on the stocky side, but oh she thought him a looker when they first met. Dark hair, blue eyes, a kind smile. This was during her peripatetic years. Nannying in Ludlow left far behind, the bar she was serving in was near Epping Forest. He and his mates had come for a Friday night out. A bit clichéd, but he had asked her out properly, not just gone in for a grope. He had invited her to a meal in a good restaurant. She had been impressed before she was smitten.

Jim grunts. 'You'll be back next weekend, then.'

'I'll have to see – it depends on the investigation. We've got a big one on.'

Jim doesn't ask about it. Even when she can talk about her work, he never wants to hear about it. Though he is quite happy to entertain her, as he puts it, with tales from his property development business. 'We agreed, Donna, you'd be back at weekends.'

'Did we?' Jim had said it was what he expected. Donna had said nothing.

'There's the golf club dinner next weekend. You'll want to be back for that,' Jim says before saying goodbye.

Will I? Donna sits on her two-seater sofa staring at the mobile in her hand. She's eaten, showered and is in her nightdress, wrapped in her towelling dressing gown, thick socks on her feet. The house is quickly warming up, being so small and hemmed in on both sides. She is comfortable. The bleeding and the aching has eased.

Will I? The thought of the golf club dinner brings waves of boredom and lethargy. She once enjoyed dressing in her evening clothes and being shown off on Jim's arm. But really, they have the same conversations every time, only everyone gets a little older and has more medical complaints to talk about. However, Donna isn't allowed to mention hers. She's hardly allowed to talk about it to Jim. 'Menopause,' she whispers now. Then louder and louder and louder, until she is screaming it: 'Menopause!' She howls once, then thinks about the neighbours.

She draws her knees up to her chest and clamps her mouth shut against them. *I will have to tell him I'm not going,* she decides with resolution. A resolution she is aware is unlikely to survive the night.

Chapter 7

Then, thirty-six years ago

Unexpectedly the lake loosens its clutches and tosses Erika to the surface. She breaks it. Gasping. Gasping in air and water. Choking. Gasping again. Finally oxygen reaches her lungs and she is breathing. She lies on her back as her panting slowly quietens. The sky above is a sparkling azure. Serene. Erika has the impression of it being a hard dome, keeping her in. Imprisoning her. Stopping her being her.

Her body's automatic reactions had fought to save her from drowning. But does she want to be saved? What is ahead of her? She sees herself moving down a narrow track of education, training, work. She is constricted on all sides by eyes, critical eyes. Eyes ready to report every step out of line, every word she might want to say that questions the validity of this track she is on. Every time she wants to challenge these eyes and their reports.

Now her body is calmer – she can hear the breeze rattling the tree branches. A small animal plops into the water. The lake licks at her exposed skin. She is cold. She is getting colder. A slackly strung bow of geese flies across her frame of vision. They are heading north after wintering in the south. They are free.

She remembers something a teacher told her about geese, how the one at the head of the flock is constantly being replaced, so none get tired and all of them take responsibility for getting everyone to their destination. The teacher had meant it as a metaphor for the GDR. Erika had liked it at the time. She had even repeated it at her Guide group and had received approving glances from the adults who encouraged the other girls to clap. She had glowed in the appreciation. However, now she realises how foolish she was. There are only a very few geese who are free to roam, to do as they please, and they do not relinquish their places. *If I lie here for long enough, I will get so cold I will not be able to move*, she thinks. *I will sleep and I will not wake up. It will serve everyone right.*

Chapter 8

Now

The woman in front of her is new to this, Donna can tell. She is not like the others. Women and some men, but mostly women – mothers, sisters, partners, cousins, aunts, friends – bustling in, hiding their fear and sadness behind brashness and humour. The woman in front of Donna is elderly, perhaps in her seventies. She is slightly hunched and walks incredibly slowly – Donna can feel the impatience of the others in the line. She leans forwards and says gently near the woman's ear, 'Is this your first time?' The woman glances back. Her expression is stricken. In her work Donna has seen many a face rendered by utter sorrow and desperation and unable to reform itself for the usual social interactions and niceties. This is one such face. Donna smiles, places her hand lightly on the woollen sleeve of the woman's coat, near her elbow. 'Don't worry,' Donna says. 'It takes a long time, but we all get through it in the end. Your daughter?'

'My granddaughter,' the woman whispers. 'My daughter was – well, she didn't cope very well with, with life I suppose.' She says it as if it is a higher maths question she is never likely to comprehend. 'She died a few years back.'

For die read overdose. Donna understands this from the woman's lowered gaze and closed-in stance. She doesn't want to be questioned about it.

'I tried my best,' the voice wobbles.

Ah, the cry that binds us all in this room. 'I'm sure you did,' Donna says kindly.

The queue shuffles forwards. By now, the process is as familiar to Donna as making a cup of tea. She helps the woman in front of her present the correct documentation, gives her an encouraging squeeze on the shoulder before she is searched, and sits with her in the anteroom. Finally the woman brings out a photo. It looks as if it has been folded and screwed up several times. It is of a young woman in her early twenties – she is smiling broadly, cuddling a toddler dressed in a fancy, frilly dress with bows in her fine hair. The woman talks a little about the bright future her daughter once had. 'She could have been a lawyer,' she says, suddenly bristling. 'She could have been anything she wanted.' Her quick haughty scan of the room tells Donna the woman is thinking, *Not like this lot.* Donna feels the sadness course through her. She had thought this once. She had thought her family was different. She had thought, *It's a minor infraction before Elizabeth, we all, get on with our lives.* She doesn't think this anymore.

She tries not to think too much. On the drive over she'd had the music turned up and had sung along. Her voice had cracked during the ballads and her vision had blurred. Still she had kept the thoughts at bay. The *Why?* questions. The *Could I have done better?* questions. The *Where did it all go wrong?* questions. And, worst of all, the looking into the future questions. She had asked all of them in the past and it had got her nowhere.

The road wound itself into the middle of the moors. Donna could imagine it being a bleak place. This morning, however, the sun had shone. The purple of the heather blazed in amongst the brown ferns and bracken. The few trees stood together for company – dark pines and red-pocked hollies in with spindly birches, their leaves bronzed. HMP North Yorkshire, built in the 1980s of red brick, sits in a slight hollow almost in the centre of the moor. Its nearest neighbour is a farm which is run by the prisoners. Elizabeth has been moved here to see out the latter part of her sentence. As Donna parked she decided she prefers Elizabeth here than in some of the places she had been: the outdated, the poorly maintained, the squeezed into the rundown parts of cities. She breathed in deeply, the air fresh with a tang of vegetation and of manure from the farm. Yes, on the whole, Elizabeth is better off here.

At last they are allowed into the visiting room. Bland and austere. Tables with chairs on either side are set in rows. The high-up windows let in a glint of the sun which reflects off the metal. The elderly woman's granddaughter comes in. There is hardly any resemblance left of the toddler in the photo. Her very short hair is inexpertly dyed bright green. Her sallow face is full of piercings. Below the neck she is huge in ill-fitting jogging gear. Her mouth twists into disgust as her grandmother weeps silently.

Donna knows not to cry, not to laugh, not to overly express any emotion. Staying neutral is best. Elizabeth appears well.

She is tall like her mother, stocky like her father. Her frame has filled out. Her brown hair has regained its shine. Her pale face has a peachy tint to it. She has spent some time at the farm. She talks about it. She even admits to enjoying it. 'On the whole.' She chuckles. 'That's your favourite saying, isn't it, Mum?'

'Is it?' Donna finds joy in English idioms. It is a joy she keeps to herself.

Elizabeth is continuing, 'Nothing too excessive, yeah, but on the whole.' Then she stops smiling, she asks after Christopher. 'I've tried phoning him to tell him he is on my visitors' list.'

Elizabeth's brother is screening his calls, of that Donna is certain. They had been close as children, enjoying playing together, keeping secrets for each other as they went into their teens. The final straw for Christopher was when Elizabeth stole money from his in-laws at his wedding. Since then he has joined his father's camp. Elizabeth is past saving. 'He's very busy,' says Donna. 'You know he's setting up his own architectural practice now, it's taking all his energy.'

'None left for his big sister anymore,' says Elizabeth without rancour. 'He's given up on me. I would have done.' She fiddles with her fingers as if they had rings on them.

'Give him time. He'll come round.'

'I don't suppose so.'

For a moment Elizabeth sounds wan. Donna wants to reach over and hug her. Elizabeth would not tolerate it. She looks up. 'You OK, Mum? Your face has gone a funny colour, sort of raspberry.'

Donna can feel the heat rising through her as if she is sitting on a radiator. 'It's my age,' she mutters.

'The menopause,' says Elizabeth loudly, smiling when they get a few people glancing over, as she had intended.

Donna refuses to let the embarrassment slay her. She sits up straighter. 'Peri-menopause. I'm still bleeding.' *And how.*

'You should see your GP, get HRT,' says Elizabeth. She's losing interest.

'HRT doesn't help with bleeding,' says Donna quietly. The wave of discomfort is abating. Though an ache has snagged to her temple and in this tomb to body odour it will only grow.

Elizabeth asks for news of her brother and his wife and kids. Donna supplies what she knows. Her son doesn't tell her very much these days. After a slight lull, when Donna becomes aware of the others in the room, Elizabeth says, 'They've said I can go to this Buddhist thing, to help with my addictions.' The clasping and unclasping of her hands is the only sign of nerves. 'They come here to start with but if I'm a very good girl I get to go to their centre in Scarborough.'

'Sounds good,' says Donna cautiously.

Her response hasn't misfired. Elizabeth smiles. 'Yeah, should be a laugh. How about you, Mum? How's the new job?' For all her faults, Elizabeth is the only one to be even remotely interested in Donna's work. She maintains eye contact and nods as Donna gives her a brief summary of her first week. 'Wow, a dead body on your first day. Can't be many of them in Scarborough if you don't count the alkies and the druggies killing themselves, which most people wouldn't.'

'I think it is rather unusual.'

'And a decent crew to work with?'

'Yes, they are.'

'Being by the sea must be nice.' Elizabeth doesn't notice her mother's hesitation. 'I quite like it up here, at least I can breathe, but I'd like to see the sea. Maybe I can come and visit you, Mum.' She pins Donna with her stare. She has cornflower-blue irises. Donna had almost forgotten.

'Once you get day release.' It's why Donna had moved here. On the other hand, her stomach feels like she's going up in a fast lift. The last time Elizabeth had visited it had been a disaster. Of course, she had argued the whole time with Jim. But she had also been rude and aggressive to Donna. Plus she had emptied both her parents' wallets before leaving early one morning.

'If I promise to be nice, yeah?' She smiles a genuine smile before looking down at her chewed fingernails. 'I do want to get it right this time, Mum. I do.'

'I know you do, love,' says Donna, touching her daughter's hands. The skin is dry and hot.

'Only you don't believe I will.' She moves her hands away. Her tone is harsh. 'Well, maybe I'll prove you wrong, yeah?'

I hope you do. Donna doesn't get to say this, which is probably a blessing. Visiting time is over. She watches her daughter go. It's as if there is a jagged elastic band attached to Elizabeth which is being pulled out of Donna's chest. Like many women she has folded away most of the memories of her children's births. She has not forgotten them. And suddenly she remembers the red-hot hoops of pain around her abdomen, the tearing, the sense of being completely in

71

the grip of something beyond her control. Then, at last, the feeling of pushing out from under a flow of lava. Surfacing. This tiny being skin to her skin. Her daughter. She could not believe this human had somehow been created and grown inside her, distorting her body, until finally released and there – there lying between her breasts, her mouth puckered fish-like.

'You'll have to be getting along.' The prison officer addresses her firmly.

Donna stands and walks as if an automaton. It is only once outside, taking in a gulp of tart air, that she puts both her hands to her sodden cheeks and tastes the sea on her lips.

Chapter 9

Now

Donna lets Sunday unwind and herself with it. She gets up with *The Archers'* theme tune, puts on some washing and decides the cleaning could wait. She sets up some standing orders for bills, works out whether she can manage on her salary and decides she can.

As she is enjoying her second cup of tea sitting on the sofa, Rose comes round and invites her to the allotment. They walk together to the hill behind Falsgrave Park, where garden plots colonise the slope and valley. Donna has not been to an allotment since she was a child. She recalls mostly regimented rows. Rose's is anything but regimented, however it is fruitful. They pick apples and pears from small trees. They pull up some leeks. Then Rose shows Donna how to turn over a bed with a spade. It is hard work, but satisfying. Rose is not much for chitter-chatter. They work to the rhythm of birdsong, which Rose identifies as a robin and a blackbird. Donna sees them flitting from bush to ground, pulling up worms.

At a brief break for a cuppa to warm their hands and rest their backs, Rose talks about sea swimming. She invites

Donna who shakes her head. She feels the need to explain she had half-drowned once; it makes her fearful. 'I would take care of you,' says Rose. Donna believes her.

She leaves after a couple of hours. Before she does, Rose gives her a small bottle. 'It'll help,' she says, 'though you should go to your GP for more advice.' Donna wonders what Rose has heard through the walls dividing their houses. Back home she takes a teaspoon as instructed, with her herbal tea. On the label it says it contains motherwort, balm and mint, and it tastes of the latter. In the afternoon, Donna falls asleep over her book. She treats herself to a delivery curry for an evening of TV, and the next morning goes into work feeling revived.

Twenty-four hours later, Donna is a tad more jaded. She is in a meeting in the DI's office with Brian and Harrie. They are almost knee to knee, having barely managed to squeeze the extra two chairs in. They have all been reading the PM and forensics reports and have come together to discuss them. It is the first time Donna has seen the raw reports for real without them being assimilated by senior officers. She has found them more dense and difficult to decipher than the ones they had for roleplay on her first tranche of DC training.

She is thankful when Harrie says, 'Right, let's start from the beginning. What have we established?' Then answers her own question. 'We have established the ID for Henrich Grüntor. Neil Murphy, personnel at GCHQ, provided a visual and there were also fingerprints and DNA on Mr Grüntor's file. Derek Wyatt saw our vic on Friday

27 September at St Jude's Community Kitchen at approximately three p.m. At approximately one p.m. on Monday 30 September, Lynne Ritchie found the body. In the post-mortem report, our Prof Jayasundera's best guess is Henrich had been dead sixty to twenty-four hours. Which puts the ToD window at approximately midnight Friday 27 September until midday Sunday 29 September.'

Donna recalls the smell as she bent towards the body. Her best guess is Friday night or Saturday. Though she knows the body had been attacked by some animal or bird post-mortem. A fox or a crow, the prof had said. She sees again the birds congregated in the trees. Waiting. Now they seem to her to have been waiting. On the way to the allotment, Rose had looked up at a flock of the birds in nearby trees. She had explained the Celtic tradition that Morrighan the warrior goddess appears as a crow when she's deciding whether a person lives or dies. 'Most people say it's a murder of crows,' she said. 'But I prefer a wake of crows. They favour their meat dead.' *Poor Henrich.*

Harrie is continuing. 'OK, what about cause of death?' She sighs. 'Well, our Prof Jayasundera is hedging his bets more than usual. We have: indications of long-term heroin use, though an overdose is not indicated. The presence of amatoxins is suggestive of ingestion of *Amanita virosa*, a close relative of the Death Cap mushroom. Symptoms onset after ingestion is six to fifteen hours, up to forty-eight. There is a black eye and bruising around the abdomen, indicative of punching and kicking up to twelve hours before death. The spleen is ruptured. And, inevitably, there is the general condition of the body which was emaciated and hypothermic.'

'Take your pick then,' says Brian.

Harrie shrugs.

'What about this?' He indicates a paragraph in the PM report. 'Puncture wound at back of neck which could indicate a hypodermic needle or very slender blade.' He is sitting with one ankle resting on the other knee, which is bouncing slightly. 'Everyone is talking about it being a Russian elimination. Polonium-210 or some poison we haven't even heard of yet.'

'We can't rule it out,' says Theo. 'But that's not really our bag currently. That's being passed up the chain and decisions on whether to do further toxicology will be made in conjunction with MI5. We need to be focusing on everything else. We need to know more about Mr Grüntor's movements. So far CCTV hasn't given us anything. Brian, I want you to take the lead on that and redouble efforts.'

Brian nods, though hardly enthusiastically. 'It might not even be a suspicious death. It could be accidental or suicide.' He sounds a tad grumpy.

'On the other hand,' says Theo, 'the black eye, bruising and ruptured spleen suggests an attack, whether it led to death or not. And we need to investigate that. Harrie?'

Harrie looks down at her notes before continuing. 'OK, well as we all know, the forensics for a victim who has been sleeping rough for over a month in a makeshift tent in the middle of a wood is not going to be the easiest to process, especially as we have had some wet days. There's still a lot to be done. There's some camping-type crockery and cutlery which might yield something. The fingertip search uncovered a wealth of items, the majority of which probably have nothing to do with the case and have most likely been discarded by users of the wood. What comes out will be of more use once we have suspects.'

'Donna' – Theo turns to her – 'what can we say about Mr Grüntor? His background, his recent history?'

She's glad to have something useful to contribute and straightens a little in her seat. 'Fifty-nine years of age. He worked for GCHQ since 1991. From West Germany initially—'

'Though you sound like you still have a question mark there?' interrupts Theo.

'Do I?' Donna gives a frown. 'I can't imagine GCHQ got it wrong.'

'Can't you?' Theo smiles. 'Well, I think we should hold that possibility.'

Donna feels pleased at being taken seriously.

'What difference does it make?' says Brian flatly.

She turns to him. 'Well . . .' She presumes that, unlike his DI, Brian does not want a potted history of post-Second World War East–West relations. She says simply, 'It could add to the spy theory. Someone from the former East Germany could have been more than just a casual or pragmatic communist, they could have been working for the KGB. But also—'

'Yes?' asks Theo.

'Well, anyone hiding something from their past . . . well, it might come back and bite them,' she finishes.

Theo nods.

Donna feels herself redden. She looks down. *Why did I say that?*

'Anything else, Donna?' asks Harrie.

She fumbles over her words until she regains her stride. 'OK, um, he was let go or fired or retired in March of this year. But it appears he had begun drinking again and upping his drug intake from around the November before. Is this drug related? A debt to a dealer? I have shared information with the drug squad.' She revels in her DI's look of approval. 'He left his home end of August. And was found dead end of September,' she finishes, a sad tinge to her tone.

No one speaks for a moment. Then Theo says, 'I think we need to know more. You've had contact with Ms Barker at the German consulate, can you see what she can find out about his background? And we certainly need next of kin. Harrie, we'll have to lean on our Mr Murphy to talk to any colleagues of Mr Grüntor.'

She nods and makes a note on her pad.

Theo continues, 'Brian, check whether Mr Grüntor sought any medical help on the 27th; in fact, go back over the last month or so.'

He nods, but nothing gets written down in his notebook.

'Donna, work with Trev on finding more people who use the woods for walking and cycling, especially at the weekend. You're not busy next weekend, are you?'

She shakes her head. The golf club dinner will have to be cancelled. She grins.

Chapter 10

Then, thirty-six years ago

Erika's young body is not prepared to give up. It won't let her sink. It won't let her sleep. It won't let her fade away. Her arms propel her nearer the shore, where it is shallow enough for her feet to find the bottom, and she staggers to the bank. She is shivering. She is crying. She slumps down onto the sandy ground, wraps her arms around her knees and curls over. She hears her name being called. She does not think she has the strength to lift her head. Only she does. She lets out a scream which is more of a thin wail. It is enough for her mother and father to find her. They ask questions. 'What happened?' 'Where have you been?' They do not expect answers. The others exclaim and ask for explanations when she is carried back to the house. She does not speak.

'Erika, are you OK?'

It is Ralph.

She closes her eyes.

'I think we will take her home now,' she hears her father saying. She is enveloped in blankets. She is carried once more, this time to the car. During the drive back she unthaws. She begins to feel safer cocooned in her blankets.

Lying on the back seat, she watches the street lights come on and stretch across the darkening sky as the car passes. She hears her parents murmuring in the front. She cannot make out any words. They live on the outskirts of the city, in a block of apartments built by the Soviets to replace housing destroyed in the war. Her father parks outside. Erika is able to walk across the pavement, into the mustard-painted entrance hall and up the stairs to the third floor. Home. Two rooms. Her parents sleep in the living room. There's a separate kitchen and a bathroom. At least they have their own bathroom, her mother always says. Tonight there is not enough hot water for Erika to have a bath. She lets her mother sponge her clean of lake water, wash her hair and comb it out before wrapping it in a towel. Her father has prepared some warm milk with nutmeg. In one corner of the sofa, which is also her parents' bed, she tucks her legs and feet under her. Her mother sits beside her. Her father sits on the only chair. There's soft violin music coming from their neighbour's record player and outside a Trabant *chuck-chucks* by.

'You need to tell us what happened,' says her father.

'Ralph, he followed me . . .' she begins. Then she sees the look which passes between her parents. She knows the look, it mixes fear with a big 'no'. Then it's as if a wall goes up. Their features remain neutral, merely unlistening, unresponsive. When they don't want to hear something they won't. Like when Erika tells them it's not fair that Sofie's father has been arrested again.

Now her father says, 'Ralph was with us all the time. He never left the house.'

Erika's mother moves to put her arms around her daughter. 'You slipped, didn't you, darling? Slipped into the lake. Well, it doesn't matter now. You are safe now.'

Erika wants to scream and shout and kick at her mother, *No, it wasn't like that at all. Why don't you ever listen to me?* Instead she swallows it all down. She knows the Stasi can cause more pain than a fall in a lake. She lets herself be held. Only there's a fissure beginning to open up, deep down, between the little girl she has been and the young woman she is becoming. Erika can feel it, like a bruise.

Chapter 11

Now

Raincliffe Woods cover one side of the steep valley. The straight path cuts a swathe through the middle of the trees. The land rises precipitously on one side and falls equally abruptly on the other. The track is, however, relatively level and wide. The dark green conifers tinge the air with their resiny scent. Beneath them, shed needles rust the earth. There are also beeches, sycamore and birch, the leaves a banner of reds, burgundies and yellows in amongst the oxidised copper.

The woods form a junction with Forge Valley. There had been iron forges here in the fourteenth century, fuelled by charcoal made from the trees. Donna finds it hard to imagine such industry as she strolls with Trevor Trench and a young PC, Nicky Fletcher. All three of them are kitted for the walk. They could be friends out for some exercise, if Nicky and Trev were not in uniform. Donna didn't expect to miss the uniform. Now she does. She realises it had given her a sense of belonging. And a sense of authority. It strikes her forcibly that today, because of her lack of uniform, she is the senior officer. She is in charge. It shakes her for a moment.

Luckily PC Trench has taken on the role of instructor to Nicky, which in turn is shaping their approach. 'Stop everyone, get name and contact details first off. Ask them about how often they come and what they do here. Ask if they have seen anything unusual in the last month. Then focus on the weekend in question. Call me if anyone gets lippy.' He turns. 'You too, DC Morris.'

'Donna, please. And thanks.'

They start by working the main path. It being a Saturday, as mid-morning approaches there is someone to talk to every few minutes. Walkers, with or without dogs. Family groups, the children rushing here and there, sending their whoops up into the treetops, with the occasional teenager tagging on behind, earbuds in, deep into their own reality. Then there are the cyclists. Trev tackles them mostly as they prove hard to wave down. Donna's notebook begins to fill up with names, phone numbers, observations. Nothing leaps out at her as being important. But she takes it all down. It will be in the rereading and cross-referencing of what all three of them gather that something will pop out. *Hopefully.*

Trev insists they don't stray too far away from each other, so there comes a moment of calm while the other two are talking to witnesses and Donna is waiting for them. She sits on a log by the side of the path. She tunes into the birdsong and thinks she identifies a robin sounding like a manual typewriter in the defence of its territory. Certainly one hops down and regards her quizzically before flitting off again. A squirrel flings itself from one swaying branch to another until it lands on the ground across the path from Donna. It stands on its hind legs, its front paws clutched to its chest.

Donna giggles to herself – it's doing a perfect impersonation of Les Dawson in drag at the garden fence. Reruns of his comedy always made her laugh, however often Elizabeth told her it wasn't funny and it was degrading to women.

Trev and Nicky come up to her. 'Must be time for a cuppa,' says Trench, checking his watch. 'There's a seat further up.'

The bench is in a clearing, a meadow with a pot-bellied oak at the centre. Its bark is heavily grooved, one fat branch droops to the ground. Donna thinks that it must have seen many things, this old oak, and three police officers sitting under it would be the least of it. They've each brought flasks. Donna has a box of flapjacks she has made which she passes round. PC Nicky Fletcher eats hers with relish. She is on the plump side which isn't helped by being short. She has a pretty round face, white but not pasty. Her dark hair is in a topknot; it has a flash of blue dyed through it like a kingfisher's wing. Donna chats to her and discovers she is local and has been on the force for three years.

'My uncle was a sergeant,' she says. 'You remember him, don't you, Trev?'

'Yes.' Trench says no more. His silence tells Donna more than words.

Nicky continues, 'I thought it would be a good career, from what he said, interesting, worth doing.'

Donna notices the past tense and the slight droop of the shoulders. 'How are you finding it?'

'Oh' – Nicky's eyes open wide as she looks round – 'fine. Yes, good. Only sometimes, you know, it's hard.'

Trev grunts his assent.

Donna nods. She wonders about probing more, then sees the time. They've done two hours and they have another one and a half hours to do. This is her moment to show some leadership. She begins packing away her Thermos. 'I think we should head up to the top path – it's nearer to where Mr Grüntor had his encampment. We'll talk to anyone we meet on the way, like before.'

They follow the main path until it intersects with one which shoots straight up the slope. It is something of a scramble, with mud and thorny bushes making it more difficult. They are all puffing by the time they reach the top. Here the woods end and farmland begins, the dark earth ploughed into lines stretching across the crest, tramlines merging to a point. *Henrich would have had this view. Is it a comfort?*

Donna pauses to orient herself, then says, 'We'll go left first, towards the crime scene, then we'll have to retrace our steps and go this other way to loop down to the car. Is that right, Trev?'

'It is.' He sounds impressed.

Donna is pleased with herself. The track is narrower, muddier, less well used. There are tangles of blackberry bushes, nettles and sweet-smelling broom encroaching on the path. Donna had not approached Henrich's camp from this direction before, so they are almost on top of it before it has really registered. It is the beech tree she recognises with its contorted trunk. Then she hears the caw and sees the crow. She stops, the others brought to a halt behind her.

'Are you OK?' asks Trev from the back, in a whisper.

'Yes, sorry. Just getting my bearings.' The uneasiness settles in her stomach like an undigested lump of gristled beef.

Foolish, Donna, the crow didn't kill Henrich. She moves slowly forwards. There is nothing to see. Except for a small glade in the woods. Everything has been cleared away. Yes, she can detect perhaps a slight flattening or browning of grass. Was that where Henrich's tent stood? Was that the bush which was his final shroud? Her eyes dart around. They fix on a bunch of flowers. Yellow daisies, blue harebells, red herb Robert, white clover. All picked from the surrounding area, but nonetheless brought together into an untied bouquet. *Someone is remembering Henrich?*

A twig snaps. Donna is shaken out of her reverie. She can see nothing. Maybe it was a bird or an animal. But no. There it is again.

'You little tyke.' Trev pushes past Donna and Nicky is paces behind him. All Donna sees is the back of a hoodie emblazoned with a squawking seagull standing on a football, which disappears through the trees at the edge of the glade. Donna hears Trev and Nicky crashing through the under-growth, then she hears Trev calling Nicky back: 'It's too steep. They've gone.' The two return. Nicky's round cheeks glow pink. Trev has his hands on his hips as he regains his breath. They both agree the runaways had been from Westfield.

'Little ruffians,' says Trev. 'But probably only come up here for a look-see.'

Donna nods. 'OK, let's walk back to the car park. We're meeting the afternoon shift there in twenty minutes.' A few suspicious youths. A bunch of flowers. A pad full of names and notes. Will any of it prove to be significant?

Chapter 12

Now

The holding cells are full of sullen youths. Theo has told Donna to take a break. It is going to be a long night and he wants her to join him in one of the interviews.

Donna has walked to the South Bay before she thought about what direction to take. She turns down the little road which becomes a path past the Spa buildings, Victorian Gothic in honey-coloured stone. It is the dog hours of this Monday afternoon. The Spa's suncourt, reminiscent of the lower tier of a wedding cake, is not filled with sun, rather a claggy fog. Donna had seen it earlier banked up on the grey sea. It has toppled over and coated the shore like a mudslide now piled into the cliffs. It creates a different world of many tones of grey, softening the edges of buildings, making them appear as if they are sketched rather than solid. The air smells of socks damp from the wash.

Donna continues on past the Spa and the cliff lift, where the path dips below the beach huts, their brightly coloured doors muted behind the shifting toile. She can hear the *lap-lap* of the waves, cats' tongues against the concrete sea wall. Then the doleful call of the foghorn.

The previous week had been full-on, searching for potential witnesses: talking to people, checking and rechecking the scraps of information being brought in, trying to piece everything together to create a less fractured picture of Henrich and the last days of his life. Sunday had been a repeat of Saturday, roaming the woods with Trench and Fletcher, speaking to all and sundry. What had they seen? What had they noticed? The smallest thing. The most insignificant thing. There is a mound of detail Donna and Brian still have to go through and put on the system. It makes Donna feel anxious as she walks, the weight of the undone swirling around her shoulders like the fog.

Jim has not phoned her since she told him she could not come back for the golf club dinner. He is sulking, and she has only had the time to text him. There have been intermittent pangs of guilt, though as she showered on Saturday night and then sat on her sofa to watch TV, she would not have said she regretted being where she was. She had sent a card with a short chatty letter to Elizabeth. The picture on the card was of the sea at Scarborough by a local artist. She thought it would either please her daughter because it showed her mother listens to her or she would tear it up as it reminded her of what she cannot have. The freedom to walk along this concrete path bordered on one side by cliffs and on the other by sea, as Donna is doing now.

She stops. Ahead she can see only a few metres to a bulge which she has been told is an open-air swimming pool, filled in within the last decade. She has seen a copy of a 1930s railway poster with a stylised image of the pool, depicting a gloriously sunny day. There was a figure in the background diving from a high board. In the foreground a curvaceous woman wearing a brightly hued full-skirted dress with a floppy hat hung on the arm of a well-turned-out man. In contrast, today is inconsistently bleached. The damp is seeping through Donna's hair to her scalp. A winged creature, the colour of a fossilised dinosaur, glides down to land without a sound on the swaying water. A wave glugs the wrong way up one of the drain holes through the sea wall and splashes onto Donna's boots. Donna is suddenly aware she is alone. She feels as if she could disappear, become fog. She tells herself not to be ridiculous, and turns round.

The police station is full of heat and activity. Donna pulls off her jacket and scarf. Rose's concoction is helping her deal better with temperature, still she's glad she has layers and can divest herself of her pullover too. Brian tells her about the breakthrough. The tips of his prominent ears are the colour of flamingo feathers and there's a shine to his eyes. A spot of blood on a jacket and an ill-judged social media post. He licks his lips. 'We've got 'em.'

The group of five lads had been brought in after a phone call to Crimestoppers giving a name, a place, a date and time. Someone had a conscience. However, it is unclear whether this caller is one of the group, and whether he may now be regretting his lapse. Stirred by the intelligence from the anonymous informant, Brian had got on with trawling some relevant CCTV footage. It had revealed the young men running like the clappers away from the top end of Peasholm Park. A crime scene manager had been sent to scope out the area. There were several shadowy and hidden corners where the park becomes graveyard, possible sites for an attack on a vulnerable rough sleeper who one of the attackers may know has money enough for drugs. But without more certainty on a locale, the CSM decided a forensics sweep would be wasted.

All the youngsters live on Westfield. Nicky and Trev had already filled in Donna on its poor reputation. Initial chats with the individual boys – really they are no more than boys – had not revealed anything. They were just messing about. They hadn't seen Henrich. They hadn't seen nothing. Clothes were seized from their homes. The DCI, scenting a closure to the case, had agreed to paying the extra for speedy forensics, providing the result the officers need as they prepare for the interviews.

Four of the youths come from families known to the police. One does not. Indeed, his mother is considered a linchpin for the community, an organiser with indefatigable energy for improvements in the neighbourhood. 'He's the one who will break,' says Theo. He says it with sadness, as if he takes no pleasure in it. He and Donna are to interview this youngster, Calvin Davidson. Theo goes on to wonder aloud whether they should talk to him in the family suite rather than in an interview room. Harrie says they will get further faster by putting the fear of God into him. Theo agrees, it appears with some reluctance. Harrie and Brian will speak to Jordan Smith whose leather jacket has the incriminating drop of blood, Henrich's blood, on its lining.

As Calvin Davidson is sixteen years of age, he requires an appropriate adult with him. He has refused to have his mum or aunt – they are both currently sitting in reception being plied with tea by the desk sergeant. Instead it is an appropriate adult from the rota who comes in. Donna doesn't need to be told the woman, Jean, is a retired school teacher, though of the friendly and encouraging incarnation. Alongside Calvin and Jean sits the solicitor Reggie Harvey, a portly gentleman with a taste for vibrant bow ties. 'He may look benign,' Theo had warned her, 'but he's sharp, very sharp. He won't let us get away with anything.' He sounded like he approved of, even admired, Reggie Harvey.

With all five of them in the room, it is stuffy. Although painted a soothing green, the walls are unyielding, and the high-up narrow oblong windows do not open. It has been agreed Donna will take the lead. She explains who everyone is for the tape and what the charges are. Jean makes sure Calvin agrees that he has understood everything thus far. Then Donna invites Calvin to tell them what he had done during Friday 27 September.

He looks at his solicitor, at Jean, then leans forwards, his elbows on the table, blows out some breath. He's not a small sixteen year old. He's chunky, could pass for older. His skin is florid, especially over the chubby cheeks, becoming more so as he sits there. His hair is very short, a very pale mouse. He has on a collared shirt under his hoodie. Donna suspects a maternal intervention. 'From the beginning?' he asks.

'If you like,' says Donna, with the sense she is being played.

She is. Calvin describes his day with particular attention to every toilet break and every meal. Donna lets him carry on, appears to take notes, does not let her frustration show on her face. On the whole Calvin is relatively likeable, even at times humorous, but then she remembers Henrich reaching his skeletal hand towards her.

Finally, they get to the meat of the matter. After school Calvin meets up with mates and they have a bit of a lark around in the park. He wants to gloss over this bit. Donna won't let him. She takes him through it. Who did he meet with? Where? How did they travel to the park? What were they talking about? What were they doing? How did Calvin feel? Where did they enter the park? Who did they see? What did they see? Then what happened? And then? And then? Calvin's answers are becoming more and more vague and terse. His head nods forward. His voice goes quieter.

'You know, Calvin,' Donna says gently, 'I was very impressed with your memory for your school day, for the detail you went into. I'm just wondering why you can't do as well when talking about what you and your friends did in the park?'

After a pause he mutters, 'No comment.' Then, lifting his head, he glances from Jean to Reggie. 'I can say no comment, can't I?' They nod.

Donna can see the desperation in his face.

A firm edge to his voice, Theo says: 'You can say no comment now, Calvin, but it won't help you when this goes to court and, indeed, it may damage your defence not to speak here.'

Silence; the head drops forward again.

Donna says, 'Do you know who Henrich Grüntor was?' She keeps her tone soft, though a wave of anger and upset rattles up her spine.

Calvin shakes his head.

'He was a fifty-nine-year-old man who had lived in Scarborough for over twenty years, quietly going about his business, hurting no one. He worked for GCHQ. Do you know what GCHQ is, Calvin?'

'We had a school trip there,' he mutters.

'Then you'll know how important their work is. What did Henrich Grüntor do to deserve to be beaten up?'

'I didna—' Calvin clamps his arms around his chest.

'You didn't what?' asks Theo. Donna can feel his steadying presence by her side as he leans forward.

Calvin peers up through his fringe. 'We didna do nothing, OK?' he says with determination.

'You rang Crimestoppers,' says Theo.

Calvin jerks backwards. 'How—?' Then he catches himself and firmly shuts his mouth, his top teeth tearing at his bottom lip.

Reggie Harvey says genially, 'Is that a question, Inspector? A judge might take a dim view of trying to lead or even confuse someone as young as Mr Davidson here.'

Jean checks with Calvin whether he needs a break. He does not respond.

'Did you know your mum and aunt are sitting out in reception?' says Donna. 'Our desk sergeant is doing his best, but I bet it's not very comfortable and when the front door opens there's a blast like you—'

'Is there a question, DC Morris?' Reggie interrupts.

'Everyone wants this over, Calvin, and all we want is for you to help us. Did you and your mates meet Henrich Grüntor on 27 September at the top end of Peasholm Park?'

'No comment.' He's slumped back in his chair.

'Did you assault him?'

'No comment.'

'Did you kick him so hard his spleen was ruptured?' Donna can feel the heat rising in her. She hopes her face has not gone the raspberry hue.

'No comment.'

'Did one of you know he had money for drugs on him?'

'No comment.'

'Did Jordan know? Had he done a drugs run for Mr Grüntor in the past?'

'No comment.'

'Did you steal that money off him?'

'No comment.'

'Did you leave him for dead and run off and spend that money getting blathered on cheap lager bought from the Drinks an' Stuff offie on Falsgrave?'

'No comment.' His chin is on his chest. He growls into his locked arms. Then with a swift movement he divests himself of his hoodie and Donna sees the emblem on the back, a squawking seagull balancing on a football. She now knows this is the badge of the local footie team. 'Where were you on Saturday 12 October? Last Saturday?'

Theo gives her a quick glance. This is not in the prepared script. She sees he won't stop her, is indeed curious to know where she is going.

This change of tack also wrong-foots Calvin. 'Jus messin about, jus hangin,' he says cautiously.

'Just hanging in Raincliffe Woods?'

He blinks several times. Shakes his head. Less of a denial, more of an attempt to clear his mind.

'Did you want to see where Henrich Grüntor had died because you knew you had killed him?'

'No!' His jaw goes slack. He presses his fingers into his eyes.

'Ghoulish tourists, were you?'

He doesn't respond. He has gone quiet.

She recalls the flowers. 'Or did you want to put a bouquet there? Perhaps you were having second thoughts, regrets about what you had done?'

'Huh?' He glares up at her.

The tribute wasn't from him then.

'DC Morris,' says Reggie, 'it's difficult for my client to have second thoughts about something he is not confessing to doing. Is this diversion taking us anywhere?'

Donna shrugs. She nods briefly at Theo. He takes his time appearing to peruse his notes, though Donna knows he is already clear of the next move. He gives out a dramatic sigh. 'The problem, Calvin, is we have something called joint enterprise. If we have an attack by a group of people and we can't be sure who did the damage, then everyone gets charged.' He gives a quick look at Reggie. 'I am sure your solicitor will explain it to you better than I can, but that's the basics. And we know Jordan Smith attacked Mr Grüntor. We have found Mr Grüntor's blood on Mr Smith's jacket. Leather jackets are very difficult to launder.' He sounds truly sorrowful about this.

Donna knows it is theatre, they all do, apart from perhaps Calvin who has gone the colour of slushy snow.

Theo continues, 'Also we have this from Mr Smith's cousin.' He pulls out of a folder a screenshot of the Facebook post. 'Why would Mr Smith's cousin, Jayson Smith, be claiming he had been paid by Jordan with Jerry money? Why would he say his cousin had, and I quote, "given a dirty fucking immigrant a good hiding" the night before? This was posted on 28 September.'

'I didna . . .'

'What didn't you do, Calvin?'

Silence.

Theo sits back. 'Mr Smith is being questioned at this very moment by my colleagues DS Shilling and DC Chester. What do you think he is saying, Calvin?'

Silence.

'I imagine to begin with he'll stick to your agreement, say nothing or no comment. But when he hears about the blood, do you think he's going to take the fall for all of you? Maybe he's saying he was merely a bystander while a certain Calvin Davidson put the boot in?'

The wail which came out of Calvin tore at Donna's heart. She wanted to put her arms around him. *Poor sod. Poor fucking sod.* Then she remembers Henrich and her heart is split. She is glad, nevertheless, to see Jean put a comforting hand on Calvin's arm, and that Reggie suggests a break for him to speak to his client.

The three of them file out. Donna and Theo sit for a moment. The noises outside invade: the traffic at the road junction, the shutting of doors down the corridor, someone shouting a name on the street. 'Well done, Donna,' says Theo. 'A good job done.'

She nods. Henrich already damaged, broken by such young lads greedy for money and fuelled by bravado. She is overwhelmed by weariness.

Chapter 13

Now

Donna is less anti-paperwork than some of her colleagues, it would seem. Certainly than DC Brian Chesters. She is well aware he has left her with the bulk of the sorting still to be done on the Grüntor case. Brian believes it is closed. With Calvin's testimony, him and his mates have been charged variously with GBH and manslaughter. Brian thinks it should be attempted murder or murder. Donna has pointed out the PM report would not support this. She doesn't even think they will get manslaughter. Theo agrees with her. He also agrees with her that there is more to be done for Henrich, even though Brian is all too ready to move on. He has found an excuse to leave her with updating the case file on the system. She has the observations garnered from the users of Raincliffe Woods to do, plus more from the forensics on Henrich's improvised campsite.

Taking a break from the screen, she calls Sabine Barker. She is put straight through.

'DC Morris, any news?' asks Sabine.

Donna hardly knows the woman, so she is guessing at nuances in her voice. Is there a tinge of anticipation? A slightly fearful one. Like the time Donna rang a mother about her missing child when the mother knew where he was – dead in the back shed, because she had put him there. Donna shakes away the memory. She makes an effort to keep her tone neutral. 'We have arrested several young men who mugged Mr Grüntor and in doing so ruptured his spleen.'

'So the case is closed,' says Sabine. 'Well done, DC Morris.'

Again Donna is surprised by the other woman's lack of sentiment, but then it could be just her way to hide her feelings. 'Not exactly. We are continuing with our investigations.'

'Oh? In what direction?'

Why does that mother keep coming to mind? She does a physical shake of her body. 'I'm not at liberty to say.'

'You will keep me updated, won't you, DC Morris?'

'Of course. Have you been able to trace any next of kin?'

Is there a slight pause or is it merely the phoneline. Then Sabine says, 'No, unfortunately not.' She hurries on, 'Well, DC Morris, I am afraid I do have a rather important meeting. I wish you good day.'

The connection is broken. *Maybe she is in a hurry.* Donna stares at her phone. Something feels askew. Then she ponders Henrich Grüntor lying in the morgue. Perhaps he really does have nobody in his birth country: unmarried, an only child to only children, parents dead. It is possible. It may be left up to Floyd and his friends to bury him. *And that could be the best thing, the right thing. I expect Floyd would put on a good show.*

She gets up for a wander to get herself moving, decides to do a vigorous walk up and down the stairs rather than go outside where it is grey and raining on and off. It is in one of the turns of the stairwell that she finds PC Nicky Fletcher. Standing there, leaning into the corner. She tries to give Donna a cheery smile, but her big eyes are pink and brimming. One tear breaks free and rolls slowly, treacherously, across her feverish cheeks.

'What's up, Nicky?' She rests a hand on Nicky's upper forearm, resisting the temptation to go in for a full hug.

Nicky shakes her head. 'Nothing.'

'You're hanging out, is that it? In this stairwell?' Donna forces a grin and a lightness of tone. 'You've got a thing for magnolia paint and bleach?'

Nicky shakes her head again, swallows hard. 'I'm fine.'

'Not.' She's picked the terminology up from the kids.

Nicky lets out an exhalation, half chuckle, half gasp.

Donna rubs Nicky's arm. 'Tell me.'

'I thought he was nice, he said he'd help me, show me the ropes . . .' Nicky runs out of breath. She hangs her head.

Donna can guess the rest. She waits for the confirmation which she gets.

Nicky goes on, rushing the words, 'He – he asked me out for a drink. I didn't want to go, but he'd been so kind, so nice, I thought why not. He tried to – at the end of the night – tried to . . . I said no, I had to push him off. He did go away and I thought, *OK, misunderstandings do happen*. But now, now . . .' Tears are dripping down her nose. She rubs furiously at her red eyes. Even in this day and age, no one wants to be caught crying at work.

'Now?'

She clams up. 'Nothing.'

'It can't be nothing, Nicky.'

'Nothing I can put my finger on. Paperwork, more paperwork than I know what to do with. And, and he said something the other day . . .'

'What?'

Her voice lowers to a facsimile of a young man's: "'I'll remember this, PC Nicky Fletcher.'" She looks up, her eyes wide. 'What does he mean? What can he do?' She sounds panicky.

Donna gives her arm a squeeze. 'Nothing. He can't hurt you, Nicky. I won't let him.' She silently laughs at herself for this comment. *Coming on as the battle-weary lioness. Didn't help Elizabeth.* 'You must tell DI Akande.'

Nicky's eyes turn almost circular. 'I couldn't possibly. You don't bitch, you don't tell tales. My uncle says it's the first rule of being on the force.'

'Does he? Well, he's wrong. The DI will handle it sensitively—'

'No, no, no.' Nicky pulls away. She searches in her pockets and finds a crumpled tissue which she uses to mop herself up. 'And don't you dare say anything,' she says fiercely.

Donna does an indeterminate wobble of her head.

It seems to satisfy the younger woman. 'I've got to go.' She does some more ineffective patting of her face. Her mascara has run. 'Do I look OK?'

'A trip to the ladies might be advisable. Do you want me to come?'

'No.' She begins to walk away, then stops. 'Thanks, Donna, for listening, but please, please don't say anything.' Then she strides off down the stairs.

'Nicky?' Donna calls after her. She doesn't turn.

Donna waits for several minutes to see if Nicky will return and also to calm herself. Part of her understands Nicky's reluctance. She's always loved the camaraderie she's found in the police force. The downside is you don't snitch on a colleague without consequences. It's an environment she found she naturally navigated. Another part of her is boiling. *Are we living in the twenty-first century? Are women still a body first and a co-worker second?* She stomps up the stairs.

To curtail her revengeful thoughts, Donna focuses on the statements she, Trev and Nicky collected in Raincliffe. Many of the habitual users of the woods knew each other by sight. Donna makes a list: woman with lurcher, man with mountain bike and yellow helmet, running man in dark sweats, and so on. The majority then turn up as people they had questioned and, for one reason or another, on the whole discounted. She cross-references and finds only three who don't. A woman running in pink Lycra. A man who looked like a long-distance walker with a large pack on his back. Another woman who had caught the witness's eye because she was blonde and smartly dressed in a high-end jacket and knee-length boots. Trev had faithfully written down what the witness had said: 'I remember her because we're most of us dressed as if we've fallen from a charity shop through a hedge.' Donna smiles for the first time since talking to Nicky at the accuracy of this statement. She wonders whether it is worth putting out an appeal for the three people who appear anomalous. She will ask Harrie.

She fetches herself a lemon and ginger tea. The coursing of her adrenaline has eased, but she still has the energy to tackle the supplementary forensic reports which have come in. The snippets she teases out of the report give her a further insight into Henrich's life. The list of cutlery, crockery and cooking pots is paltry. There was some pasta, a tomato and a banana kept off the floor in a string bag. There was his drug-taking paraphernalia stowed carefully in a carved box. There were a few library books. Donna imagines him seeking refuge in the library, allowed to sit in a chair with a newspaper and nod off, everyone politely disregarding his malodour. There were a few bits of paperwork. Bank statements going back, buoyant at one point, gradually becoming parlous. There were several programmes for concerts with jazz musicians Donna has never heard of. The images, once vibrant with colour, are spotted with mould and damp. Kept because they are reminders of more vital times? It's all rather pathetic and Donna has to stop typing for a moment as her vision blurs. She takes a deep breath and carries on. They did find a passport, place of birth confirmed as Hamburg. Most of the fingerprints which have been lifted are Henrich's. There were two sets on a mug which don't match – his, each other nor anything on any database. She thinks about the unribboned bouquet. Perhaps he did have visitors, chums who kept him company for a while? Fibres and hairs aplenty have been collected from his clothing and from the tent. Only one sample appears out of place. Cashmere, perhaps from a sweater, found at the entrance of the tent. High-end, the forensic scientist has noted.

The phone on Donna's desk rings, breaking into her

concentration. She looks round. She is alone in the CID office. She remembers murmuring responses to various fellow officers saying goodbye on their way home. She picks up the receiver. It is the desk sergeant – there is a man called Derek, a rough sleeper, in reception. Initially he wanted to talk to PC Trench who isn't in today. Now he's becoming distressed, shouting about friends of his being murdered. Donna is the most senior officer in CID available.

Great. She closes down the computer, determined to be off home once she has sorted this out. She goes downstairs. She assumes this is the Derek who had been the last to see Henrich. It does cross her mind he might be interesting to talk to if only for this reason.

She enters the reception. A man is sitting on one of the benches by the door and keeps anxiously glancing out of it. The desk sergeant indicates him with an incline of the head and a roll of the eyes. The man is rangy, his beard is dark and shaggy. He is wearing a woollen bobble hat. His clothes are none too clean and Donna can smell the sweat on him from where she is standing. She goes over and introduces herself, suggests they go through to one of the interview rooms. He points out of the door, 'I can't leave me things.' He has a strong Liverpool accent.

She sees a shopping trolley piled with plastic bags, bits of cardboard and blankets. She goes out and pulls it in. 'We'd better take it with us then.'

Derek smiles; several of his teeth are missing.

'You want something to eat?'

Derek nods. 'Breakfast.'

Donna makes no comment on a late-afternoon breakfast,

perhaps it is Derek's first meal of the day. She asks the desk sergeant to arrange it to be brought down with some tea for Derek and water for her.

'Veggie,' says Derek.

'Pardon?' The desk sergeant pauses with the phone receiver partway up.

'I'm veggie, no meat in the breakfast.'

'Right.' A small word. Donna can hear the full commentary behind it: 'Who does he think he is? He's lucky to get anything.' She leads Derek away. They manage to manoeuvre the trolley into the corridor outside the interview room which she takes him into. Once they are seated either side of the metal table, she asks him what he wants.

'I wanted to speak to Trev, he'll listen to me.'

'I'll listen to you.'

He takes a moment to assess her, then he puts his clasped hands on the table. His nails are thick and grimy. 'It's Til, I don't know where she is. I think he's murdered her.'

'OK, let's start at the beginning.' She opens the pad she has with her and picks up her pen. 'Tell me who Til is, when you last saw her, who "he" is and why you think he has murdered her.'

Derek then begins his tale. He is relatively succinct and the arrival of the breakfast hardly interrupts him, as he talks as he eats and he eats fast. Til is a woman probably in her forties who Derek met when he arrived in Scarborough about eighteen months previously. Til leads a life which includes sometimes rough sleeping, sometimes going to hospital to dry out, sometimes staying in hostels, sometimes working. Over the last six months she had managed

104

to stay alcohol-free, had found herself a small, rented room and work as a cleaner. She still meets up with Derek at St Jude's every week on a Wednesday for lunch, never misses it. Only she did this week. She didn't turn up this lunchtime. 'I waited and waited, then I went round to her house. It took me ages to persuade someone to come to the front door to let me in. I went up to her place, the door was locked. I banged on it but she didn't answer.'

'Maybe she's gone away.' *Or gone back to her old habits.*

Derek shakes his head. 'She's in there, I know. The lights are on, there's music playing.'

'Maybe she's sleeping.' *Got falling-down drunk and is out of it.*

'I know what you're thinking. She's drunk, she can't get up to let me in.'

Donna feels herself redden.

Derek goes on, ''Til had made it past that. She wasn't going back there.'

'You know sometimes, Derek, it's not that easy to stay—'

'How do you fucking know anything!' Derek is suddenly agitated.

Donna wonders if she will have to hit the panic button.

Maybe he sees her glance at it. He calms himself, taking deep breaths and telling himself quietly that everything will be OK. Finally he says levelly, 'With all due respect, DC Morris, you don't know Til.'

I know my daughter. She turns back to her notebook. 'And you said "he" had murdered her? Who?'

'William Bell.'

'Tell me more.'

'He's giving out crap about how to forage for yourself from hedgerows and stuff.'

'Sounds like it could be useful to some?'

'Yeah, but one bloke told me William's been giving bum advice. He's got poisonous mushrooms on his foraging leaflet.'

Henrich? 'You saw this leaflet?'

Derek shakes his head. 'Heard about it. Til said William had given her it. I told her to be careful, but she wanted to be more healthy, more green, taking walks in the country, picking stuff for herself. And now she's dead.' He screws up his face and clenches his fists.

'We don't know that,' Donna says calmly.

'No, cos we're fucking sitting here instead of going to take a look.'

Again the forcefulness causes Donna to wince.

'Sorry, sorry,' Derek mutters. 'I don't mean nothing. Wouldn't hurt a fly.'

'OK, OK. Tell me where Til had a room and I'll see if we can raise a landlord to check this out.'

'Can't you break in?'

'One step at a time. Let's see if we can find a landlord first.'

She gets a PC to come and bring Derek the dessert he's requesting and sit with him while she goes off to do her research. It proves surprisingly easy to get someone with a key to Til's room. She rents from a social housing association and they have twenty-four-hour cover. The night warden will meet Donna and Derek at the building in twenty minutes. Donna persuades Derek to leave his trolley and they make good time to a once-grand house on a steep street in the shadow of the castle. Close up, Donna can see it has had better days and it is now very much multi-occupancy. As they wait for the keyholder, Donna asks Derek whether mid-afternoon on the 27th was the last time he had seen Henrich Grüntor.

'I said so, didn't I? To Trev.' Derek sounds surly. It's chilly out here and he only has a thin jacket on. Donna wishes she had thought to bring one of his blankets with them. He continues, 'I tried to ring him, like, on the Saturday.'

'Ring him? He had a phone?' They hadn't found a phone.

'Yeah, no answer.'

'Do you have his number?'

'Yes.' He doesn't appear keen to give it to her, but she convinces him to key it into her phone. 'I miss him,' he says quietly. 'We did the crossword together.'

She thinks about the flowers. He tells her without her having to question him, how he had gone up to the encampment and wanted to leave a tribute. 'No one else'll bother 'bout him.'

'You knew where he stayed?'

'Been there a couple of times' – caution comes into his voice – 'and no, I didn't visit him on the 28th or 29th. I know how you lot work.' His tone gets louder. He clamps his mouth shut when the night warden drives up.

The three of them troop up a wide staircase. It's shabby, but Donna can imagine women in crinolines once floated down it. Til's room is up in the eaves, perhaps where the maids would have been. The door is cheap MDF. It would probably have given way if Donna had leaned on it hard enough. However, she allows the warden to unlock it with a key from the large bunch on his belt. As soon as the door to Til's room is opened, Donna can smell the vomit. As soon as she sees Til lying on the bed, she can tell the woman is dead.

Chapter 14

Now

'You've had a full-on week, Donna,' says DI Akande, smiling. 'Two deaths in two-and-a-half weeks is unusual for around here.'

They are seated in his office with Harrie and Brian. As ever it's a bit cramped.

'At least this one is accidental and we have arrests for the other,' says Brian.

Theo rests his elbows on the desk, his chin on his clasped hands. 'Harrie, you don't look convinced.'

After checking for vital signs, calling an ambulance and securing the scene at Til's spare little room under the eaves, Donna had alerted the DS on duty who turned out to be Harrie. It was close on eleven by the time Donna had given her report to Shilling. Donna then had to persuade Derek to return to the station for his trolley. She rang up for a room in a shelter for him for the night. However, she suspected he wouldn't use it and would instead bed down near the morgue at the hospital. It was inching towards 1 a.m. She was exhausted. Harrie told her to go home. 'You look done in. And take some lieu time.'

Donna had taken her DS at her word. She had slept into the afternoon. She'd eaten, watched some TV. Then she'd gone back to bed and slept some more. This morning, only thirty-one hours since she was last at her desk, she nevertheless feels as if eons have passed. On arrival, Harrie had filled her in. Patricia, known as Til, Shearer had been poisoned with mushrooms, *Amanita virosa*. There was no evidence that it was anything more than an accident. There is to be a documentary inquest before her body will be released to her family, of which there appears to be a legion, mainly from Redcar. Donna wondered whether she can persuade them to be welcoming to Derek. She'd asked about the statement he had given and William Bell, and Harrie had said, a tad sharply, that she hadn't forgotten. 'It appears Brian didn't follow up with the hospital on Henrich as he'd been requested,' she'd said. 'I will be having a word with him about that. Sometimes he thinks he knows best. Meanwhile can you give them a call, ask about Henrich and mushroom poisoning in general. We have a meeting with the DI in twenty minutes.'

Donna had nodded. She had also decided she would not want to be on the other end of 'a word' from DS Harrie Shilling.

Brian, however, appears uncrushed. He is sitting back in his chair, one leg with an ankle on the knee of the other. He is tapping his pen against his closed notebook.

Harrie is responding to Theo's enquiry. 'There is the statement from Derek Wyatt about William Bell. Plus Donna gave the hospital a ring. They had no records of seeing Henrich in the last three months. However, in the last six months they have seen three cases of poisoning by *Amanita virosa* amongst rough sleepers. None were fatal. And in the twelve months prior they had none.'

'*Amanita virosa* only appears in our woods between July and November,' says Donna, checking her notes to be sure she is accurate. 'One case occurred in February, the other in April.'

Theo leans back. 'They could not have been found in the wild then. They must have got them from another source.'

'That's the implication.'

'I don't suppose the hospital kept records of how the victims got their supply?'

'No. I get the impression that, once they were off the critical list, they were swiftly handed over to the rough sleepers' team. However, on two occasions the handover was more nominal than actual. On the other, the rough sleepers' team found the victim, a Clive Wallin, a bed for the night. He then moved on, away from Scarborough by all accounts. No further questions were asked.'

'And we didn't find one of those leaflets Mr Wyatt was talking about in Ms Shearer's room?' He turns to Harrie, who shakes her head. 'But you want to talk to William Bell.' She nods. He takes only a minute before assenting and telling Harrie to take Donna with her. 'Frame it as a friendly chat, following up on the statement he gave Trench. Anything else?'

'Donna has been through all the statements from the canvasses at Raincliffe,' says Harrie.

Is Donna imagining the emphasis on her name?

Certainly, Theo glances over at Brian, a quizzical expression on his face. Brian does not see it. He is looking down.

Harrie is carrying on. Whether she notices the exchange, or non-exchange, is unclear. She is asking whether an appeal can be put out for the three unaccounted-for people noticed rambling through the woods on 28 and 29 September.

Theo nods. 'Right, we're done. Let's—'

'Um—' It escapes from her throat before she has time to think.

'Yes, Donna?'

Six eyes are on her. She hopes she is not reddening, but fears she is. She had been prevaricating over bringing this to Theo's attention. But she knows she must. She starts with the easy part. 'Henrich had a phone, Derek told me. I've got the number. It wasn't found, so I'll get tech forensics on to it?'

Again Theo nods. He waits.

She has to go on. 'And, um, Derek knew where Henrich's encampment was. He had visited it a couple of times.'

'On the 28th or 29th?' shoots in Brian, immediately alert.

'He says not.'

'Of course he does,' says Brian.

Harrie says, 'We need a statement from him and his fingerprints for elimination. We've got the prints on the crockery.'

'I think you'll find,' says Donna, 'he's already in our system and has been eliminated.'

'Violence?' says Brian.

'Drugs,' says Donna.

'There you go,' says Brian.

'There you go nothing,' snaps Harrie.

112

Theo glares at both of them and they close their mouths. 'Donna, ask Trench to get a statement from Derek – they seem to have something of a rapport. Brian, once you've got this, search for the CCTV to corroborate where Derek says he was on the 28th and 29th.'

Brian nods and actually makes a note.

'OK,' says Theo, 'we're done.' This time it is more of a command than a question.

Brian and Harrie manoeuvre out of the room with their chairs. Donna stands to go. Then she stops. Theo is on his way to turning to his computer when he realises. He asks her if there is a problem. She hesitates, not sure if she is doing the right thing.

'Donna, it's best to tell me and I can then take responsibility for deciding what the correct course of action might be. Is it Elizabeth?'

She shakes her head. 'I was, er, I was approached by a colleague, a female colleague. It appears, well, it appears she is being harassed by, er, another colleague.' She sits back down, deflated again by Nicky's story.

Theo is now giving her his whole attention. 'Are they both at this station?'

'Well, the young woman is. I'm not sure about the other officer, but I think so.'

'Names?'

She confesses, feeling sad. 'I said I wouldn't say anything to you and she didn't tell me who it was who . . .'

There is a pause. Then he stands. It's as if an energy strike has run through him and brought him to his feet. He sounds angry. 'I won't tolerate bullying. It's not going to happen on my watch.' He strides the few paces to the wall and back. 'When I arrived it was rife. My predecessor was a bully.' He sits again, forward, arms on the desk, focusing on Donna. 'He created an environment where he made it appear as if it was OK, part of the game even. Unfortunately, people will take advantage of this, either because they enjoy the sense of power or because they are afraid not to be part of the team – because if they stand out, they too risk being bullied.'

Donna nods. She knows how the system can warp behaviour.

'I thought I had changed all that,' he says gloomily.

'I am sure you've done your best,' she says quickly.

'Thank you.' He chuckles. 'I always try to do that.'

'I didn't mean . . .' She is suddenly concerned she has overstepped a mark she didn't notice. She can feel the heat rising. She remembers she forgot to take Rose's concoction this morning.

He waves away her concern. 'You've done exactly the right thing, Donna. Thank you. I can't act until I know who. I understand your reticence and won't push you now. However, please rethink it. Or – better – persuade your colleague to come and see me. Assure her I will support and protect her.'

'I'll do what I can.' She supposes her cheeks are scalded.

If they are, Theo does not notice. 'Are we done?'

'Yes,' she says firmly, before heading for the door.

William Bell turns out to be at his day job, visiting a print shop, part of the large franchise he manages. He suggests they go to a café next door. The café is busy. There is a particularly sizeable group of young women with prams and babies who have colonised the tables and space by the windows. William finds a table wedged between the serving counter and the toilets. He gets a coffee for himself and Harrie and a fruit tea for Donna. The hiss of the barista machine, the hum of conversation and the squeals of delight or cries from the children rise and fall around them like a tide. Harrie starts by asking Bell about his involvement in St Jude's. He explains he had been dealing with some issues in his life and had started to volunteer some hours at St Jude's to make amends. Donna knows at once what William Bell's issues had been. Elizabeth had tried the twelve steps, only had balked at the use of the word 'god' or 'higher power'. She was never good at accepting hierarchies. William is, Donna guesses, in his forties. He has an impressive head of hair, dark with threads of grey. He is smartly dressed in a suit and tie and looks like he does enough exercise. His skin is tanned, whether from a booth or a late holiday in the sun. He has slipped into his response that he is married, has a daughter and goes to the local evangelical church. He explains he encourages all his employees to take time off to volunteer in the community.

'Do you know who this is?' Harrie brings out a photo of Henrich, a recent one from his GCHQ file, better than the one Trench would have had to show.

Bell shakes his head.

'And yet he came to St Jude's on Friday 27 September when you were there.'

'I would have been there. But I don't remember him. Sometimes we have quite a crowd.'

'You were seen talking to him.'

Bell picks up the photo to study it. Then shrugs. 'I try to talk to as many people as I can. I want them to feel welcomed. I want to meet them on a human level, so to speak. I don't always remember everyone. They can turn up next time and act as if we know each other and I've forgotten them. Of course I hide it, I wouldn't want to hurt anyone.'

'How about Derek Wyatt?' asks Harrie. 'Do you know him?'

'He's a regular, everyone knows Derek.' Bell smiles, he has an appealing smile. 'He can get a bit confused, because of his problems, but he's a good bloke. Had some issues in the past, of course, too quick to flare up, use his fists, but I think he's been getting some help with anger management.'

'Have you heard about Til Shearer?' asks Donna. When Bell looks blank, she explains that Til is dead.

'Oh poor thing. How did it happen?' He seems genuinely uninformed and concerned.

Harrie asks, 'Do you forage, Mr Bell?'

He brings his mug up to his mouth and takes a sip, then puts it down again. 'I'm sorry?'

'Do you forage? Do you go out into the countryside and pick things to eat?'

He sits back, hands flat on the table. 'Sometimes me and my daughter pick blackberries.'

'What about mushrooms?'

At that moment there's a screech and all their attention swivels to a child who has slipped over and brought a plate of cake down to the floor with him. The young women clatter around, picking up the boy and any other who has decided

116

crying is a good idea, then trying to salvage the cake. Finally, Donna and Harrie turn back to William. He is watching the chaos with a rather wolfish grin. 'Mushrooms,' Harrie says again.

He rotates his focus, finishes his coffee, says solemnly, 'I am very sorry to hear about Til. I believe she has family in Redcar, I am sure they would want to know. Are we done? I need to get back.'

'You didn't encourage people at St Jude's to go foraging, perhaps distribute a leaflet?' asks Donna.

'No. The only leaflet I've had to distribute was about our church services, and then I only gave them to people who asked. I know nothing about foraging, or mushrooms.' He pushes himself to his feet. 'I really have to go. It's been good meeting you ladies.'

He leaves. Donna watches his confidence. A man in his prime who knows it. Who probably knows she will be watching. She snaps her gaze back to Harrie. She is also watching Bell. Once the door of the café is closed behind him, Shilling takes a deep breath and lets it out slowly. 'Nothing useful there then. Shall we get out of here? Bit too much like a kindergarten for my liking.' She grins.

Donna scurries to follow her out, pulling on coat and scarf as the chilly outside air hits her.

'You've got kids, haven't you, Donna?' asks Harrie, as she eases the pace to a saunter.

'Two. Elizabeth and Christopher. They've both left home.' She hopes Harrie won't ask what jobs they are doing. It appears she is not among the few 'need to knows' who have been told about Elizabeth.

'How did you manage? I mean, career and kids together?'

'I didn't. Kids came first, then career. I started out as a special when both of them were at school and built on from there.'

'Oh.' Harrie sounds disappointed.

'I never really thought I was having a career as such,' says Donna. 'I saw some young people out, so drunk they could hardly walk, and I thought about how vulnerable they are. That's what took me into being a special. I didn't expect to enjoy it or stick at it, but it just sort of happened. The opportunity to become a PC came along and I took it, then someone suggested I could try out as a DC. I didn't have a plan.'

'No.' The disappointment is still there.

Donna wants to say something to rally the younger woman. 'I imagine it can be done, though, having a career and kids. Other women do.'

Harrie grunts her assent and quickens the pace.

Chapter 15

Then, thirty-five years ago

Sofie isn't coming back.

All summer Erika's parents had been keeping her from seeing her friend. Sofie's family is anti-revolutionary, they are anti-socialist – they are capitalists. Erika considers the way her mum and dad talk about Sofie's parents, you would imagine them with horns and tails like the devil no one is supposed to believe in anymore. But Erika has always enjoyed going to Sofie's. Sofie's mother likes to play board games and doesn't always let the children win. Sofie's father sings and makes the best biscuits. However, he is often absent from the house. He is a writer. Erika comes to understand that what he writes is not acceptable to the government. Sometimes he is in prison. Sometimes he is just gone.

And Erika loves Sofie. She loves walking arm in arm with her, and talking and talking about everything and nothing.

Erika's mother sometimes asks, 'What do you talk about for so long?'

Erika is vague in her response. She won't tell her mother

about the conversations she and her friend have about travelling beyond East Germany's borders. Not east, but west to France, to the UK, to Norway, to America. At first Erika had been dismissive of the idea of actually wanting to go to capitalist countries. But Sofie had laughed. 'They are just like us,' she had said. 'Only more exciting.'

So little by little they had dreamed up fantastical journeys. Travels Erika's mother would not approve of even whispering about. Nor can Erika tell her mother how she feels when she talks to Sofie: cherished, absorbed and, best of all, listened to. Since the Ralph incident it's as if Erika's parents listen to her less and less. So she is bursting with things to tell Sofie when she hurries to the first day of the new autumn term. She expects to find her friend waiting for her in the playground. She is not there. Neither does she come into the classroom in time for registration. Erika doesn't let anyone sit next to her in case Sofie is merely running very late. Some of her classmates give her sideways glances, as if they know something. She keeps her spine straight, her gaze forwards. At the end of registration, the teacher says, 'Sofie won't be joining us.' She snaps her folder closed. She is not open to being questioned.

During the first lesson, Erika cannot concentrate. It is double maths. She normally finds it easy. She makes stupid mistakes. The teacher glares at her. 'Where is my star pupil?' she asks crossly.

Still the possibilities spin through Erika's mind until she is dizzy. *Is Sofie ill? So ill she has left the school? Is she dead? No. No. Perhaps the family has moved away? Yes. Yes. Perhaps* – and here she allows herself a secret smile – *Sofie and her parents have gone to the West.* Sofie had whispered this once: they were going to get out. Then she had refused to be drawn further.

'What are you grinning at, Erika?' barks the teacher. 'Have you finished? Have you got them all right this time?'

Erika dips her head and applies herself to the calculations. Her breathing comes more smoothly now. The figures on the page begin to make sense. Everything begins to make more sense.

Her contentment lasts until lunchtime, when she meets Ralph and his mates coming out of the canteen. She tries to sidestep them. Ralph plants himself in front of her and leans forwards. 'Your little friend Sofie,' he says quietly, 'a deserter. *Pow-pow-pow.*' His hands take the position as if he is holding a gun and then as quickly drop to his sides. He goes off laughing.

Erika is shaken. She is about to rush off to the loos to hide the threatening tears. Then another girl she knows beckons to her, come and join them. They are laughing. They are chatting. Erika allows herself to be taken into the swirl of their good humour. *Sofie is not dead*, she tells herself firmly.

She keeps telling herself this to get herself through the coming days and nights. She asks her parents if they know anything. They say they do not. However, Erika is getting better at recognising when they are lying. She turns away from them infuriated. She wonders at what age a child realises their parents are not perfect and whether it is inevitable.

At the end of the week she goes to the apartment where Sofie's family lived. It is in a house built in the 1930s, cut up into several dwellings. Despite this, and despite the degradation of the years when little has been spent on it, it retains some of its former elegance. In particular it has one long window which lights the length of the staircase. This used to be all stained glass. Now much has been replaced by plain. Erika remembers sitting at the turn of the stair with Sofie, the sunlight filtering through coloured panes turning their hair and skin red, gold and green. The building stands in a garden, now communal. Sofie's mother had planted a small flowerbed. It looks unkempt.

An elderly woman is sitting beside it on a canvas chair. She is wrapped up as there is an autumnal chill in the air, even with the sun. 'Are you looking for your friend?' she says.

Erika nods.

'She's not here. They've all gone.'

'Where?' Erika crosses her fingers.

The woman closes her eyes. 'Best not to ask.'

Erika is about to turn around, then she stops. 'Please,' she says hoarsely.

The woman does not respond. Maybe she is asleep.

Erika creeps closer. She could touch the woman on the shoulder, wake her up. Erika does not dare. 'Please,' she repeats.

The woman remains motionless, only her lips move, but almost imperceptibly. The words seem to be coming stealthily with the breeze: 'They went to the Strandja Grenzzone. They were betrayed. The father went over. The mother is in prison. The child . . . the child is dead.'

'What? How? Please . . .' Erika stutters her requests for more information ever more desperately. The woman remains still and quiet as if truly dormant. She gives out a loud snore for good measure.

Erika turns and walks away. She continues to walk and walk and walk. The streets become city streets with taller buildings. She walks through a park. She walks past trams, past lorries, past people and more people, ordinary people about their ordinary business. But nothing is ordinary for Erika anymore. The words Strandja Grenzzone have a mythic quality to them. A never-never land which few reach. She has a vague idea it is in the south-east of Bulgaria, on the border with Turkey. She has heard stories that it is easy to hop over the border there, as easy as taking this one step on one paving stone and then this other step onto another. But the official line is of an impenetrable forest with heavy fortifications within. No one comes out alive. The bodies are hung from the barbed-wire fences as if they were crows hunted and displayed by farmers. For a moment Erika sees Sofie strung across a fence, her skin pierced and bleeding, her hair tangled into the wire. Erika stops. She is almost sick. She sits on a nearby bench, crumpled over. She thinks she will never move again. She will stay on this bench until she starves and freezes. *It will serve them all right.* She considers her parents tearful at her funeral and is glad, for a moment. Then she is cold and hungry and crying.

A couple of women carrying wicker shopping baskets half-full with packages stop and ask her if she is unwell. She nods. The hopelessness, the grief, feels like an illness seeping into her bones. The women take charge. They lead her to one of their homes. They feed her and give her warm milk to drink, wrap her in a blanket on a sofa. They then go to a neighbour who has a telephone and contact her parents. Her father drives over to pick her up. The women are impressed he has a car. He takes Erika home and her mother puts her to bed, much as she would have done when her daughter was five. Erika is aware all this is happening. It is as if it is happening to someone else.

Chapter 16

Now

'I'm telling you it sounds like my sister. She was wearing white, right?'

'Right. And your sister's name and current address are?' Donna has her pen poised over her pad.

'Oh my sister's dead, love. Dead these twenty years. But she haunts them woods.'

'Why? Was it a special place for her?' Donna can't help herself, though her stomach clenches against the other words threatening to spurt out: *Another time waster.* After all, it's unacknowledged grief which compels the woman at the other end of the phone line.

'My sister go walking in the woods?' The woman laughs, rather an extravagant, artificial, laugh. 'No, love. Never had a heel less than two inches on them shoes of hers. But my nephew has heard her there. Never seen her. I've told him about the radio appeal. He'll be there today. He'll be glad to see his mamie again.'

Will he? Donna assumes he must be a young man now, maybe late twenties, early thirties. Had he taken refuge with the trees in the early years of his bereavement? That she could understand. She would weep for him if he is still searching for a glimpse of his mum in Raincliffe now. She thanks the woman and puts down the receiver. She types up a log of the call. She's answered thirty in the last three hours.

Relief makes her want to bury her forehead in her hands when Harrie comes over. 'You look like you could do with a break. Want to come out for a drive? I'll show you a bit of our patch.'

When she had first arrived, Donna had followed the A road from York along the valley between two expanses of hills: the wolds to the south; the moors to the north. Harrie now takes her onto the eastern edge of the moors, heading north towards Whitby. It is the road Donna had used to see Elizabeth, though she doesn't mention this. She and Harrie swap updates on the case. Donna says she hasn't heard of anything useful coming from the radio appeal. Harrie says Trench has Derek's statement. 'Brian is on with reviewing the CCTV,' she adds. Then mutters, 'He'd better be.'

Donna watches the landscape slide by. At this time of year the moors are purple with the heather and rusted with the withering bracken. There's still green in the fields where sheep in clotted coats graze. She casts an eye to the seam of dark blue which folds in the raw edges of the land. What it is when half your patch is water and the other half a sea of bracken and heather. The narrow road swings up and down and loops like a roller coaster. Donna rests her head back, watching the sky. Grey clouds are crowding in from the west, as if they are eager day-trippers. As they gather, they become darker, and then let loose a scattering of needle-sharp rain which clatters onto the windscreen. The police call handler suddenly breaks into the silence between the two women. There's been a report of a theft, she gives the location. Harrie nods at Donna. She picks up the radio and says they'll attend.

They turn off the main road, heading east. The road narrows further, lifts up to a crest and then looks as if it is going to peter out. Donna is reminded of what Trench had said, *The only roads out of here go west, north or south; if you go east, you'll need a boat.* The track does, in fact, end, in front of a stately home, now a hotel, plonked improbably on the rounded clifftop. It has massive bay windows, terraced gardens with walls which remind Donna of some Victorian man's idea of a medieval castle. Its revolving doors lead into a dark-panelled reception straight out of a 1930s movie. The young lad at the desk calls the manager who doesn't look much older. He tells them the robbery was reported by a couple of guests, Trixie and Lex Benson, who had been staying in one of the holiday cottages in the grounds. They are now being served complimentary drinks in one of the lounges. 'I've had the lodge sealed off waiting for you to arrive,' he finishes proudly.

One good thing about crime dramas on TV, thinks Donna, *everyone fancies themselves a forensic scientist.*

The lounge has a stunning view over the bay. Under a louring sky, the sea is indigo. It sweeps below crumbling cliffs to the next hamlet which spurts houses to the shore. Donna inwardly gasps. Maybe something of her appreciation shows on her face as the manager says, 'Breathtaking, isn't it?'

Trixie and Lex Benson look to be in their late twenties. Both are bronzed. Both are blonde, though probably not entirely naturally. They are enjoying a bottle of champagne and had been doing the chatting-while-scrolling-through-their-mobile-phone-data thing which Donna associates with the young. She's not bad at multitasking, but this skill still eludes her.

She and Harrie sit in the spare armchairs at the table and accept a tea and a coffee offered by the manager. As Donna anticipates, these are served in silver-plated pots with bone china cups, plus a side plate of buttery shortbread. Harrie begins with asking questions, however Trixie seems eager to tell their story, so they allow her to get on with it. Donna notices how cogent she is in the telling. Some people are good at being observant and accurate. Trixie punctuates her tale with frequent glances at her husband and the phrase: 'Isn't that right, Lex?' To which he nods ardently. They had come from Malton for a couple of days to celebrate their wedding anniversary and to get away from their busy professional lives as entrepreneurs (of what, she doesn't elaborate). They had just taken a turn around the hotel gardens and were wandering back across the lawns to their lodge when they noticed a trail bike parked by the front door. In that moment someone dashed out, leaped on the bike and took off across the lawns. 'Of course, we ran then, didn't we, hun? And we got indoors and at first we thought, phew, nothing's been taken, but then I looked in my little vanity case and, oh, it was gone.' Trixie dabs at her eyes. Lex reaches over to squeeze her hand.

'What had gone, Mrs Benson?' asks Harrie, her tone neutral.

'My, my necklace. Diamonds and rubies, from my grandmother.' She takes a steadying swig from her champagne flute.

'And you had left the doors unlocked?' asks Donna.

'No, of course not,' says Lex. 'Bastard must have forced the lock.'

'The door was literally off its hinges,' adds Trixie.

'Do you have a photo of the necklace, Mrs Benson?' asks Harrie.

Trixie picks up her phone. 'As a matter of fact I do. For insurance purposes.' She finds the picture and shows it to them. To Donna it looks like something someone would bring to the *Antiques Roadshow* and not show surprise if it were valued in the several thousands. Trixie confirms this. 'Worth in excess of five thousand pounds,' she whispers reverentially.

'Well, we'd best take a look,' says Harrie, standing. When Trixie and Lex look as if they are going to do the same, she tells them to wait here. 'Need to preserve the crime scene.'

They nod and relax back.

'Do you believe them?' asks Harrie, once they are out of earshot.

'What's not to believe?' asks Donna.

'I don't know,' says Harrie. 'Maybe I'm just getting cynical in my old age.'

They step carefully through the front door of the holiday lodge. Not off its hinges, but there's no doubt somebody has taken a jemmy to the lock. They are in a beautifully appointed kitchen-diner. Walking through they get to an equally ravishing sitting room with patio doors revealing the gorgeous view. To one side is the en-suite bedroom, in which they find the vanity case. Donna would hardly describe it as 'little', with its two tiers, one for a selection of make-up a professional model would be proud of, the other for jewellery and scarves. The case stands on a dressing table. Its drawers are open. So are the wardrobe doors. Apart from this there's no disorder.

'Whoever it was knew exactly where to come.' Harrie sniffs, as if scenting something.

'They had a root around a bit,' says Donna, indicating the drawers and doors.

'Did they?' Harrie arches an eyebrow. 'Or are Mr and Mrs Benson just a bit messy?' She looks into the vanity case again. 'Her granny's necklace may have been worth a wad, but everything else in there is costume. The thief knew what he or she was after.'

Donna follows her out to the porch. The clouds are scattering pins from the freezer. The breeze is stiffening. 'Go and find out whether any of the hotel staff or guests saw anything, will you? I'll get forensics up here. Oh, and ask Mrs Benson which direction our thief took off in.'

Donna does as she is bid. The receptionist says he thinks he may have heard the bike, but none of the other staff have anything useful to report. They were all too busy cooking, cleaning or serving to notice anything. The manager is reluctant to allow Donna to question any of the other guests, he doesn't want them worried. But anyway, most were out on trips of one kind or another. The few that were in were right the other end of the hotel and are not able to add anything. Donna returns to find Harrie welcoming the CSM. The two other lodges are empty, so no witnesses there. Trixie Benson had indicated the assailant had driven off in the direction of Scarborough. 'Right then,' says Harrie, 'let's see what we can find.'

They discover what looks like a tyre print from what could be a trail bike. It is in the muddy edge of the lawns of the hotel, and the earthy globules on the road suggest the bike had continued towards the cinder track which would take it to town. 'Well, something in their story checks out,' says Harrie. She sounds a bit chirpier.

The cinder track is the remains of what used to be the Scarborough to Whitby railway, victim of the Beeching axe in the early 1960s. It is now used as a walking and cycling route. Today, given the inclement weather, Donna and Harrie meet no one as they follow it some way south. There are tyre impressions aplenty, a couple of which could be from a motorised vehicle. Harrie grumbles that it'll be difficult and costly to tease out any usable evidence. They come to a lone house standing stoically in the centre of an overgrown garden behind what must have once been a station platform. The building is made of the same mellow sandstone as most of the buildings hereabouts. The window sills are of the creamier dressed York stone. But the wooden frames are sagging. There are a couple of slates slipped on the roof and a bush growing out of a gutter which has come unclipped. The paint on the front door is peeling. Donna is certain she sees a curtain in the upstairs window flick when Harrie rings the bell and then gives the door a good thumping. However, no one comes. They are halfway down the path when a woman's voice shouts from behind them, 'I don't fucking care about any god you are selling.' They turn and walk back.

'We're not selling anything,' says Harrie. 'We're police officers.'

'At last,' says the woman. 'You'd better come in.' She leads them through a dark hall into a sitting room. What a contrast to the one in the lodge. The furniture looks like it has come out of a skip. There's a musty smell. It doesn't take long for Donna to identify the patch of damp going mouldy in the corner above the window. Another broken or blocked bit of guttering no doubt. The woman sits in the one armchair and waves vaguely at the sofa which groans uneasily as Harrie and Donna sit on it. Donna gets up and pulls over an upright chair from a nearby desk. Though her limbs are stick thin, the woman is heavily pregnant. Perhaps it is the embryo which is keeping her warm in this cold room. Or maybe not. She is wearing layers of jumpers, a fleece, a scarf and fingerless gloves. She is pale, under her eyes are pouches the colour of bruises and her hair has been inexpertly chopped short. She looks surprised when Harrie asks for her name. 'Fleur Greene. Isn't it on the file?' Then she narrows her eyes, her nose reddens, she crosses her arms. 'You're not here about that, are you?'

'What?' asks Harrie.

'The fucker who poisoned our water source by dumping his crud on our land. June it was. Tyres, an engine, an oil heater, all sorts of crap, oil and chemicals leaked, and I had lambs dying and they were nearly ready for market. I made a full report to . . .' She puts her fingers to her forehead. 'What was his name? A town of Roman origins,' she says, as if puzzling over a crossword clue.

'DC Chesters?' supplies Donna.

'That was him. Then he came back when . . . well, what I'm saying is, it wasn't as if he didn't know the way here. He seemed competent enough, but I haven't heard from him since.'

'I'm sorry, Ms Greene, we're not here about that, but I can assure you I will check up on what is happening on the investigation and come back to you,' says Harrie.

'Yeah, right.' Fleur sinks back. She looks exhausted. Donna remembers feeling the same in the last few months of pregnancy.

'I promise,' Harrie says with conviction.

Fleur shrugs. 'So what do you want?'

Harrie explains about the trail bike coming by and asks if Fleur had heard it.

'Heard and seen it. I was with Lily and Freddy in the field, got them right riled up.' She starts to dig around in her pockets. 'Took the number down too. Was going to report it, but then thought what's the point?' She bares her teeth in what could be a grin.

'If you could find the reg number for us, that would be very useful,' says Donna encouragingly.

'Well, here it is.' She finds it in her fleece pocket and holds it out. Harrie takes it. 'Now you'll be on your way, I expect.'

Harrie had been about to stand but sits back down again. However, it is Donna who speaks. 'Are you on your own, Ms Greene?'

Fleur rakes at her bottom lip as if this is difficult to answer. Finally she nods. 'Sid left,' she says abruptly. 'You should have a file on that an' all. Now' – she heaves herself to her feet – 'I've got to get on.' She walks out into the hall. Harrie and Donna follow. Fleur has the front door open.

Donna thrusts her card into the woman's hand as she passes. 'If you need anything,' she says quietly. Their eyes lock for a moment and Donna sees a spasm of desperation which is gone as quickly as it came.

'I'm fine,' says Fleur as she firmly shuts the door, unsettling Donna further.

'What are you thinking?' asks Harrie. They are standing on the cinder track where it passes the field next to the house. Incongruously, against the grey-blue North Yorkshire seascape, a chocolate-coloured alpaca is contentedly cropping grass next to a donkey. Lily and Freddy perhaps, or Freddy and Lily.

'I'm thinking,' replies Donna, 'that Sid Greene is a bastard. You?'

'Aha, what a surprise,' Harrie says, not sounding surprised.

Donna turns to look at her colleague. She's been doing the tapping-on-her-mobile-while-talking thing.

She looks up and smiles. 'Trail bike registered to one Jayson Smith. Cousin to the lovely Jordan Smith. What a fucking surprise.'

Built in the 1950s, with its inside bathrooms and fitted kitchens, Westfield was a welcome haven for those who moved there from the slums around the harbour in town. However, years of under-investment and a lack of jobs or training opportunities for the residents has taken its toll. There are houses where the front gardens are strewn with rusted cars and broken kids' toys, where windows are broken and patched with cardboard, where curtains are made of sheeting. Not so the Smiths' home. The front garden holds more gnomes, in varying poses, than Donna has ever seen before, not to mention an actual working waterwheel in a miniature stream. The window frames are new UPVC. The door has a splendid horse's head as a knocker. And the doorbell chimes sound a bit like the 1812 Overture. On the way over, Trev had filled her in about Jayson Smith. He had first got into trouble as a sallow youth, shoplifting and the like, which escalated with each birthday reached. A spell in prison had given him some brawn and new tatts and, Trev had thought, a new direction, an apprenticeship in plumbing. 'I'd reckoned he'd given up the thieving.' Trev had sounded disappointed.

Jayson answers the door. The slickness with which he admits to owning the trail bike puts Donna on her guard. He then goes on to say it had been nicked the night before. He even has an incident number. He then invites them in to have a look around the whole house if they like and Donna knows they won't find anything. They don't. Jayson plies them with cups of tea. He says how sick it is for anyone to lose their gear and he hopes they've got the forensic boys in. Which suggests to Donna he knows there won't be anything useful at the lodge. He's got a story to cover everything. At the end of a couple of hours Jayson waves them off with an affable grin.

Back at the station, Trev says he will write up the visit,

such as it was. Harrie has asked Donna to follow up on the case of fly-tipping on the Greenes' land and she settles down to do so. She finds the comprehensive first report from Brian and also evidence that he did take some action, interviewing a possible suspect. Then nothing. Either he did nothing further or he logged nothing further. Donna's searches bring up another file. When she reads it, she becomes even more concerned for Fleur Greene.

Chapter 17

Then, thirty-five years ago

How long Erika might have stayed in her lethargic stupor is anyone's guess. Her grades begin to fall. She still hangs out with the group of girls, only it's as if she's looking at them from the inside of a goldfish bowl. She spends most of her evenings lying on her bed staring at the ceiling. The hours pass. The days pass. The weeks pass. Then her form teacher pulls her aside and whispers tersely, 'Sofie wouldn't want you to fail, she would want you to live.' This brings with it another juggernaut of mixed emotions. *What does it mean to live?* she wonders. *To be alive is to breathe. But to live?*

She starts to apply herself to her studies. She forces herself to smile more. She finds she can laugh at her friends' jokes. Still it lingers, the question, is she living? Every day she sees another flaw in the glorious fabric of the social-ist state. Her father is a minor functionary in the Deutsche Post. He never talks about his work, he says it is too boring. When he comes home he rubs his eyes as if he has been reading too long. Her mother is chief cook in a hospital can-teen. It was her job which brought them to Berlin. Their family has a car. They have good health and dental care.

Why? Because her parents are good party people. More from fear, she's beginning to realise, than through conviction. Fear of all they have to lose, for themselves and for her.

She tells them she has taken up running. She does run, through the nearby park, but she also uses the time to range further into the city, by bus and tram and then on foot. She walks street after street after street. Searching. She comes to comprehend she is looking for something. What, she cannot entirely define. Perhaps some tiny proof her parents' actions are worth it, are contributing to a greater, collective good.

One evening, dusk is upon her as she walks and the plummeting temperature makes people hurry past her. No one notices as she slips off the main thoroughfare. She is not entirely sure where she is going, though her sense of direction is sharpening. Obviously, this part of the city is not on any map. The alley squeezes between two high stone buildings, their windows bricked up. These were once apartments before the government requisitioned them. Heaven only knows what they are used for now. She wonders if she is being watched from above. She presses herself further into the shadows.

A sudden movement brings her to a halt. Her heart pounds at her throat. She is ready to turn and flee. There is a pile of rags on the top step leading to what was once a doorway. She is mesmerised as it suffers a mini earth tremor then reforms into a human being. A man who utters a string of expletives, as shocked as she is to have been found out. The effort brings on a fit of coughing. She quickly assures him she means him no harm and asks him if this is where he lives. 'What do you think?' he says. 'Now scram.' She quickly moves past, the foul smell of him getting into her nostrils pushing her into a run. Another state lie: full employment and housing for all. Erika's mother would have said the man could have had both if he had only asked. Erika doesn't believe it. *No one chooses to live in their own shit.*

She is out of breath by the time she reaches the end of the alley. There is a roadway which used to be a busy street. She can see a few of the buildings still retain their shop signs above display windows. Then a couple of steps and she would be in front of it. The blank concrete face, twelve feet high, with the rounded top, belies what lies behind. It could have been the backside to a sports hall or a school. Beyond it could have been grass or a racing track or class-rooms. Instead of sharpened dragons' teeth, watch towers, spike mats. The death zone. The Anti-Fascist Protection Rampart. It is the first time she has been so close she could touch it. She had overheard her father one evening drunk-enly, proudly, declaring his daughter was conceived the night the Antifaschistischer Schutzwall came into being. She wraps her arms around herself to stop shaking. She clamps her teeth together to prevent them from chattering. She is tiny before this monolith. Forgotten. Disregarded. A mouse to be trapped and despatched. She turns. She runs. Her feet pound on the paving stones. It is the only sound she can hear over her own panting. A badly timed kick grazes the back of her leg. She stumbles. She picks herself up again. She runs and she runs towards the streetlights and the scur-rying people. *Mice, all of us mice.*

Chapter 18

Now

It is interesting how quickly something out of the ordinary can become a kind of normal. The drive over the moors, with the music on the radio at top volume, gives Donna the space to file away work worries and unwind. Even in drizzly rain, the landscape is awe-inspiring. *Awful. Awesome.* She plays with the words in her mind as she taps the steering wheel to Taylor Swift telling her she knew he was trouble the moment he walked in. The magnetism of a bad man. Donna had known it once, before Jim. Well, the bad man wasn't bad, she admits to herself. Just misleading to an impressionable teenager. *Was Sid Greene trouble from the moment he walked in?* She really does have to put that one down, at least until she can get to talk to Brian and hear what he has to say.

She turns onto the side road which brings her to the prison car park. There are members of staff she recognises now and she makes a point of giving them a friendly greeting. She knows what a tough job they have and has no illusions as to how her own daughter might contribute to their difficulties if she feels so inclined. The process of getting in runs smoothly enough and Elizabeth is waiting for her at the table. As soon as Donna sits down she senses an atmosphere and the line from Swift's song replays in her head with the gender changed. She decides on a direct approach.

'You seem down.'

She can tell immediately it has misfired, but then any opening would have. Elizabeth needs to be angry with someone. Anyone, apart from herself.

'Yeah? No shit. What d'ya fucking expect? It's not exactly a fucking kindergarten in here, whatever the *Daily Express* might want people to think.'

'Has anything specific happened?' Donna keeps her tone level.

'Life. Fucking life happened. That specific enough? And that's on your head, Mrs James Morris.' Elizabeth looks like she's bitten into something foul.

'I guess your dad has something to do with it,' Donna says. Even as she feels compelled to try to lighten the tone, she knows it is a bad idea.

'My father? He's an arsehole. You couldn't even get that right, providing me with a decent sire.'

'He loves you. He always has loved you two children,' says Donna, suddenly feeling defensive of Jim. Elizabeth frequently brings this out of her. She nevertheless marvels at her daughter's scorching rage.

'Chris, maybe. Me? I don't think so. Didn't he say he disowned me, the last time he threw me out?'

'He didn't mean it,' says Donna quietly. She lowers her head, a supplicant before the mighty.

'Well, he shouldn't have said it then. And if I'm not to

believe him when he says that, how am I to know when to trust what comes out of his mouth?'

A good question. Donna doesn't have an answer. Despite everything he has done and said, she remains convinced Jim loves his daughter. It's a faith, much like a religious one, which is difficult to share with a nonbeliever.

'I don't know why you married him. Why you've stuck with him all this time. Why, Mum, why? Why choose him over me?'

'I'm here, aren't I? With you,' snaps Donna. Elizabeth will never acknowledge what it cost her mother to defy her husband. Donna suddenly has the impulse to try and make her, even when she knows it is useless.

Elizabeth won't be diverted. She's listing off all the things about her mother which she thinks are indicative of Donna's failings. They include: wasting her life on being a wife; golf club dinners; floral tiebacks for curtains; an upright freezer with water dispenser . . . She ticks them off on her fingers as she goes.

Donna wants to cover her ears. *Yes, yes,* she wants to shout. *But don't you see? When you've never had anything nice, nice things matter.* She nails her hands to the table top and waits.

Elizabeth finally runs out of steam.

'I never had a matching bath and toilet pedestal set,' says Donna. She greets the slight quiver on Elizabeth's lips with a proper smile.

'Oh, Mum,' says Elizabeth, letting her chin fall to her fists clenched against the grey metal counter. 'You could have done so much better. You're not unintelligent.'

'Thank you.'

There is quiet between them. The conversations of those around them can be heard. An excited child talking about her birthday outing. Murmurings, perhaps of love, perhaps of hate, perhaps of something in between. A chair leg screeches as someone abruptly gets up to go. Donna asks a few questions about Elizabeth's week and gets monotone, monosyllabic answers. Then she asks about the Buddhist training, holding back on the quip that it doesn't seem to be having much impact.

But Elizabeth catches her mother's thought and verbalises it. 'Yeah, yeah, you've noticed I've not become a Zen master.'

'Not yet,' Donna says quietly.

Elizabeth lets out a snort of laughter. 'Probably never.' After a pause she goes on with some intensity, 'I do love it though. And it helps me stay quiet and calm, for a while. Only . . . only I can't hold on to it, that feeling. I want to but I can't.' She slaps the table.

'Give it time, you've only just started. You can do anything you put your mind to.'

She shrugs, then shakes her head. 'Maybe. Maybe, you know, Mum, I'm just not good enough.'

Oh Elizabeth. 'I don't think it's about goodness, is it? It's not about being perfect. We're none of us perfect.'

'Ain't that the truth.' Elizabeth looks her directly in the eye.

At what age do you realise your parents are not perfect? Donna thinks she must have been around sixteen. Elizabeth was an early starter in this, as in much else.

Elizabeth yawns and says she is off. Donna wants to say something to make her laugh. She wants to hold her, grab her hand at least. Instead she watches her daughter shuffle away, knowing she couldn't ever get it right.

Donna stops at a village café for a strong coffee and a doorstep of a cheese and chutney sandwich. She has a seat by the window looking out over a pretty green, a pond and a weeping willow in the centre. She drinks and eats slowly. She has the urge to nourish herself and orders a chocolate brownie with further coffee. Not only does she want to taste sweetness after her latest encounter with her daughter, but she also has a long way to travel today. Not just in distance. Forty-eight hours with Jim, it's as if she might be travelling back in time, to a self she has left behind. *Ridiculous,* she tells herself. *It's not even been a month. Twenty-seven days, to be exact.* It seems a lot longer.

She sets out towards Kenilworth. Reaching the motorway she takes the direction to 'The South'. Last night, when she and Jim talked about the coming two days, he had sounded eager and she too had felt pleasure in the anticipation. He'd said he was preparing some treats for her, her favourite dinner tonight, a walk tomorrow. She hadn't even minded that one of the treats will be lunch at the golf club. However, as the miles add up she begins to turn over things in her mind. She refutes entirely Elizabeth's judgement of Jim as an arsehole. In some ways they are all too similar. At times dogmatic, liking things clear cut, not tolerating not knowing or a lack of decision. 'It's not "either/or" it's "and",' a counsellor had once said to Donna. This was when they had been left staring at each other after Elizabeth had stormed off. The counsellor (*What was her name?*) had obviously thought the hour could be usefully spent delving into Donna's psyche. *After all, the mother is always to blame!* 'We can have rain and sunshine,' the woman had said with a toothy grin. 'Then we get a rainbow.' Donna had wanted to throttle her at the time, but it had struck a chord somehow. *I'm not a good or bad mother, I'm both.*

The drizzle turns heavier, the skies darker. Donna turns on the windscreen wipers. Artics thunder past throwing up spray. Their drivers are probably dismissing her as another useless lady driver, even though she did exceptionally well in her police driving test. She hunches over the steering wheel. *Why, Mum, why?* Elizabeth's words come back to her. In recent years she's become more strident in her incomprehension over why her mother ended up with her father. In truth, though Donna has never told her daughter this, she had needed some convincing. She'd been drawn to Jim, a handsome young man with such confidence. She'd found his jokes funny. He wasn't what you might consider successful then, but he wore the smell of future success like an aftershave. He came into her life at the moment when the disjointed years – that's how she characterises them now – were beginning to pall. Yes, there were the parties and the endless round of new people to meet, the places to go, the new experiences. It was the early 1980s, there were plenty of marches to be on and women's groups to join. None of which Jim had ever understood. Not really. He had endured them until he and Donna married, then quietly suggested she was too busy for them. But before Jim there had been the constant moving on from squat to a friend's sofa to a tent in a field (which should have been perfect for the summer except for the inconsistencies of the British weather). Jim had been something to cling to. He'd led her into a different world. And, probably the clincher, he'd had a family who welcomed her in. She hadn't even realised she missed a family until she'd met his.

Donna stops briefly at a service station. She's no longer certain she wants to reach her destination, but she wants to be able to stop driving and it's too far to go back. She sets off again. She tries to use the radio to distract her from her thoughts. It's not often her parents enter them, but they do now. Jim's parents are still alive and still (according to him) wonderful. They have never lost their patina of perfection. She remembers how hers catastrophically fell from the pedestal she had built for them; she has more empathy for them now. Elizabeth has taught her this, if nothing else. *It's not either/or, it's and.*

She automatically takes the turnings which bring her to the home she has lived in for the last twenty-five years. Jim had always said they would have this kind of house, sitting central to its plot, a paved drive, bay windows, gardens to front and back. She hadn't quite believed him at first. However, six years into their marriage he had brought her and the children here. He is a man of his word. She pulls to a halt in front of the garage and turns off the engine. She sits, only hearing the rain pelting on the roof; she is not sure she can move. Yes, she is tired from visiting Elizabeth and from the drive. However, it's more than that. She is not sure she wants to re-enter her life with Jim. She is not certain she can.

Then the driver's door is pulled open and he is there with an umbrella. He is grinning. It's a long time since she's seen a grin such as this one on his face. It makes him look younger. She recalls the day when he first brought her here and stood grinning on the driveway and told her it was theirs. She had laughed and hugged him. She could not fathom her good fortune. Now she steps out of the car with less grace, her body stiff from being held too rigid for too long in the driving seat, and she steps into his embrace. She rests her forehead on his shoulder. It feels comfortable. It feels safe. *This is why, Elizabeth.*

Donna creeps downstairs so as not to wake her husband. It's early morning and still night outside. She's finding it hard to sleep in the once-familiar bed. She has on pjs and a dressing gown. However, she has forgotten to bring socks and doesn't want to risk returning to the bedroom for any. Her feet are freezing. She roots about in the under-stair cupboard and finds long-forgotten wellies belonging to her daughter. Inside are some woolly socks. They are musty smelling, on the small size and there is a hole on one heel, but she remembers buying them with the ten-year-old Elizabeth and for a moment she is undone. A sob escapes as she has to sit down on the bottom stair, a sock half pulled on and the other gripped in her fingers. Even then Elizabeth had known exactly what she wanted in terms of texture and of colour, a swirl of rich browns and reds. They had walked home together afterwards, hand in hand, Elizabeth skipping every few steps, excited by her new socks. Donna has to lean over to stop another louder sob being ripped from her.

It takes more than a few moments to compose herself enough to pit-a-pat into the kitchen to make a cup of tea. As she waits for the kettle she glances around the room. She and Jim had extended the whole of the back of the house out into the garden. The result is a huge space with skylights and large glass doors. The furnishings are of the highest spec, chrome, grey and black, the only splashes of colour two vintage posters on the wall advertising golfing holidays. Donna remembers poring over the plans and brochures with Jim to build their dream kitchen. She had been as involved as he was. She was particularly proud of the posters which she had sourced herself and were her gift to him.

On her arrival yesterday, he had hurried her in, saying she mustn't get wet. There had been a bouquet of flowers. He had cooked an aromatic and tasty thali which they ate by candlelight. He had taken her hand frequently, kissed her, said how much he missed her. And it had all felt good. Why, then, does she now feel out of sorts?

There's a door from the kitchen into the garage. She goes through into the cool space, mostly filled with Jim's car. Squeezed into one corner are some metal shelves. On the lower ones are boxes of tools and a can of oil, some rags, though Jim rarely does any car maintenance himself these days. She has to bring the steps from the kitchen over to reach the top shelf. Here are old bits of crockery which never quite found a place in their new house but Donna was loath to discard. Plus, stuck between a bowl and a jug, a metal box. In it are various bits. Here's the plastic bracelets from the hospital for Elizabeth and Christopher when they were born. There's an envelope addressed to Mr and Mrs James

Morris, probably the first she received with her married name. Here's a library card in her maiden name, Donna Newhouse. There's a hair slide with a butterfly on it, one of Elizabeth's. Here's a little metal shield Christopher got for swimming the width of the baths. Finally, Donna unearths it. An envelope containing one photo. She knows what it is, though she hasn't seen it in years. She came in here purposely to get it out. Yet she cannot. Instead, she shoves the unopened envelope into the pocket of her gown, puts the box back and hurriedly returns to the house.

She takes her cooling drink into the lounge, a huge corner room which also has a view over the garden. Curled up on the sofa with a blanket over her she sips her tea. 'Welcome home,' Jim had said. It doesn't feel like home. There was a time when she had luxuriated in its substantial dimensions, now it feels too big. Once upon a time, she would never have thought of leaving Jim for any longer than a day. She's been apart from him for almost a month and does it bother her? Really? When had Jim's embrace begun to feel imprisoning? When had she begun to chafe at the ties which bind? She knows she has been pulling away. *It's me*, she decides. Leaving is something she knows she can do.

The morning is flushing the dark with pink when Jim comes downstairs to find her. She's been asleep, is slightly disoriented. He puts his hand to her forehead. 'You not feeling well, my love?'

The use of the endearment, the gentleness of his voice, reminds her of how it was when they first got together. She was hardly twenty, he was twenty-five with a job with prospects and a car. He was spruce and charming. Donna was, eventually, bowled over. The hair might be receding and his chin sags, however he's still trim. Donna wonders what she could have been thinking of, just a few hours previously. They were muddled middle-of-the–night thoughts. She and Jim had their pearl wedding anniversary last year. 'I'm feeling fine.' And she is. She lifts her head so their lips meet. She puts her hand to the back of his neck to draw him in closer. They hold on to each other for a long moment. Then Jim straightens. 'One of my full Englishes?'

She nods.

He wanders off to the kitchen humming.

Chapter 19

Now

Donna had not had to feign her pleasure in her Sunday walk with her husband and even in meeting their (his) friends at the golf club for lunch. She had felt more than a pang on leaving Jim Monday lunchtime. Her 'miss you' and promises to be better at keeping in touch were genuine. However, as the miles stretched under her wheels, it was as if Mrs Jim Morris was unravelling, being shed along the motorway. Donna arrived at her own little house on the little cul-de-sac pleased to be alone. She was happy to be where she was, wife to no one, to be where the only sounds were the ones she chose to make. As she prepares her supper, she thinks, *It's like I've left a part of me behind.* No, she corrects herself, she's done that before in her life. She's not a snake discarding its skin this time. *I'm a chameleon, adapting to the environment I'm in.*

Now she's DC Morris sitting at her desk catching up on emails, hoping this next one she opens will bring some good news. It does not. Last week she had attempted to track down Henrich Grüntor's phone. However, Calvin and his mates had all denied taking it and it had not turned up in extensive searches of their homes. Donna believed Calvin would tell the truth at this stage, nevertheless she had tried to find out if any of them had sold a phone recently. None of her enquiries unearthed anything. She then asked IT forensics what they could do. This is their response. The phone had been a pay-as-you-go, consequently there were no records available from phone companies. All IT forensics can tell her is it had not been used in the North Yorkshire area since 27 September. To find out whether it had been used anywhere else would take the investigation and cost to another level. Donna passes the request up to Harrie.

She notices Brian Chesters is now resident in the CID room and, for once, the rest of the desks are empty. She goes over to him. He blanks his screen and turns in his seat as she approaches. They do a quick exchange of greetings and comments on their respective weekends. As a way of explaining why he had not gone out Saturday night, Brian says, 'I'm waiting for my sergeant's exam results. Then there's going to be a pa-ar-rty. And then' – he makes a gliding motion into the air with his hand – 'outta here. This time I've nailed it, I know I have. Last time there were questions which weren't supposed to be on there. Everyone said it was a hard one.'

Yet Harrie flew through it, Donna has heard. Harrie and Brian had started out as DCs together. The banter has it that they are the best of mates. Donna hasn't seen it, not so much. After a pause, Donna begins slowly, 'I was wondering—'

'Coffee would be great,' he interrupts, grinning. 'The place across the—'

'No,' she says firmly. 'I was wondering if you remember

a case of fly-tipping on the Greenes' land? Sid and Fleur Greene?'

Brian stretches, his hands clasped behind his head. He is no longer making eye contact. 'Remind me.'

'June 3rd, you went to the Greenes' farm up at Ravenscar. They reported someone had dumped rubbish on one of their fields and it had contaminated a water source. You investigated, you spoke to a suspect, it was a thorough investigation . . .'

'Why thank you, DC Morris,' his tone is light. There's a tautness in his features.

'Only there's nothing further on the log and you didn't report back to the Greenes.'

'Is that what Mrs Greene says?'

She nods.

'There wasn't anything *to* report. I couldn't bring any charges.'

'We're still supposed to keep victims informed.' The more laid back he appears, the more cross she becomes. 'And you attended on August 23rd, when Sid Greene committed suicide.'

He nods.

'What about Fleur Greene? Didn't you think to flag her situation up?'

'We're not social workers,' he growls, standing, his arms folded.

They are nose-to-nose now. 'No, but Fleur is bereaved, pregnant and drowning in debt.' Her voice rises in volume and up the scales.

His goes down. 'She's an adult.'

'A vulnerable adult.'

'So flag her.' He turns abruptly and strides towards the exit.

However, his way becomes blocked by Harrie coming in the other direction. She looks from one to the other, draws her lips together in a thin line. 'OK, you two, you're off up to GCHQ.'

Brian glances sharply at Donna. 'I'm busy.'

'No, you're not,' says Harrie, equally pointedly. 'One of the members of staff has agreed to talk about Mr Grüntor and you are going with Donna. Now.'

Donna drives them both to the listening station. After several minutes of frosty silence, Brian starts to expound on what a waste of time this interview is. As he talks he strokes his tie – striped in candy colours – and runs his fingers down his suit lapels. Neither are expensive, though probably more costly than Brian can really afford; however they are new. He wants Donna to exclaim over them. She doesn't oblige.

Once through security, Donna parks and they walk to the reception. The sun is low in the sky, glinting off the other-worldly aerials and masts which stride across the sheep-chewed grassy slopes surrounding the base. Inside, Donna is again struck by the blandness; this could be the entrance for any kind of offices. She is itching to see beyond. It is not to be – the receptionist ushers them into a side room. It has a low table and several comfortable chairs. The side wall on to the reception area is glass. They are offered refreshments. Donna accepts a herbal tea and Brian says he'll have a coffee. He sits, his legs wide apart. His glance grazes over the young lass as she leaves and then again later when she returns with their orders. Brian is being so obvious it makes Donna cringe. The receptionist gives him an awkward smile. Donna wonders if she is really comfortable with the attention or doesn't know what else to do.

'I think I might be in there, what do you think?' says Brian, when they are on their own.

'I think you should keep your mind on the job,' Donna snaps.

Brian stiffens. It's as if his gelled hair bristles a tad more. 'I'll remember that comment, DC Morris.'

He mutters it so low, Donna cannot be sure she has heard it right. She recalls what Nicky Fletcher had told her.

Genevieve Lawrence walks in. Short and plump, in what looks like a M&S skirt and blouse, Genevieve does not live up to her name. She is probably in her fifties. The white skin around her neck is less than firm. Her carefully coiffed hair is grey-brown. She gives each of them a swift handshake and a warm smile before sitting, neatly tucking her skirt under her. She places her bag next to her; peeking from it is a brown folder. Her quick glance at it tells Donna of its significance.

Brian had said he would lead the questioning and Donna had acquiesced. After all, he is her senior and also the local. However, she has to grit her teeth as he begins. He sounds so bored. Genevieve responds precisely and succinctly. She had known Henrich since she started at GCHQ fifteen years ago. They had been work colleagues, good work colleagues, but she had never seen him in his home environment. He had been a good listener when she had spoken about her family life, though had rarely said much about his own. 'Except for the jazz club. He loved his music. He would talk about all sorts of people I had never heard of.' She smiles, then continues for the first time without a question being asked, 'He was a kind man, a good man. I really can't understand how all this has happened to him.' She places both hands onto her lap and looks down.

Donna would have left space for her to go on. Brian cuts in: 'He let his alcohol and drug addiction get the better of him; it unfortunately left him vulnerable to being mugged.'

'I didn't know he was addicted to drugs,' Genevieve breathes.

Again Donna waits for Brian to pose the question which presents itself. Instead he asks, 'What about his work here, could that have put him in any danger? Could he have been a target for any Russian spies?'

Back in her practical tone, Genevieve says, 'I thought you said it was a mugging?'

Brian nods. 'And we have the culprits.' He looks as though he is about to pack up.

Donna says quickly, 'Mr Grüntor was certainly attacked probably twenty-four to forty-eight hours before his death. We cannot be sure what finally killed him.'

'Poor Henrich.' Genevieve glances down again and perhaps sideways at her bag. Then she turns her attention to Donna. 'You speak German. I can tell by the way you pronounced Grüntor.' Genevieve's lips tip upwards from the frown they had formed.

Donna nods. 'You mentioned you did not know about the drugs. How about the alcohol?'

'We have our social outings and clubs like any other workplace. Henrich would come out with the rest of us occasionally. In the early years, he did get very drunk. I had to take him home once. But then he seemed to get himself sorted. He didn't drink at all when we went out. He told me he had stopped entirely. Like a lot of addicts, moderation wasn't an option.' Genevieve is tapping her fingertips together.

'And then?' asks Donna.

After a pause, the other woman appears to make a decision. 'And then he must have started again. He came in drunk several times. In the end I – we – Neil Murphy could no longer ignore it.'

'He was offered support?'

'Oh yes, I'm sure. That is, Henrich probably . . .' All the preciseness in Genevieve's diction deserts her. Her posture deflates.

'When was this?' Donna ignores Brian's restlessness by her side.

'I'm not sure. End of last year – November maybe?'

'Did Henrich say whether anything was wrong?'

Genevieve shakes her head.

And no one asked. You didn't ask. Donna leaves it unsaid, though she has the feeling the phrases are being echoed in Genevieve's mind.

'I did once say, you know, if he wanted to tell me anything he could.' She sounds sad. 'But Henrich was a very private person. I didn't want to pry.'

Achso. Prying, the greatest of crimes for the English. Donna holds her frustration in check. 'But you think maybe the

157

drinking had started again because something had happened to upset him?'

'Yes.' Genevieve too looks upset. Her gaze is wandering again back to the folder.

'And you don't know what?'

'I was terribly worried to hear he had lost his house and was living in the woods, in a tent. He could have come to me. I would have put him up. He'd been so kind to me when I first started, I thought he knew he could have come to me.' The words topple and wobble out of her. She looks at Donna as if for absolution.

'Genevieve,' Donna says gently, '*wissen Sie warum er sich aufregte?*' Do you know what had upset him?'

'You have a lovely accent, so like Henrich's.' In a moment the folder is out of the bag and in Donna's hands. 'Before he was, erm . . . before he left here, he gave this to me. He said I would know what to do with it, but I didn't.' She's shaking her head as if she has been accused of something.

Donna lets the thick brown A4 file wallet drop to her lap as she pulls latex gloves from her pocket and puts them on. She studies how it has been carefully sealed with staples and a sturdy elastic.

'I didn't open it,' Genevieve says quickly. 'It says "Only open upon my death" – Henrich's, that is.'

Donna is impressed by Genevieve's rectitude. Donna knows she'd have had the folder open before Henrich left the building. Jim always said her curiosity would exterminate a slew of felines.

'Can we take it, Mrs Lawrence?' asks Brian. He sounds a bit tetchy.

'Yes, yes, of course.'

Brian too has put on gloves. He carefully places the file in an evidence bag, seals it and gets Genevieve to sign it. 'Well, if there is nothing more . . .' He stands.

'Is there anything else, Genevieve?' Donna asks, remaining seated.

'No, no, nothing.'

'If something occurs to you, please get in touch.' Donna hands over a card on which she has scribbled her mobile number. She promises, at Genevieve's request, to let her know the date of Henrich's funeral. She and Brian say their goodbyes and leave. When Donna glances back she sees Genevieve Lawrence through the glass wall, still sitting, hands on her lap, head bowed, almost in an attitude of praying. It seems Henrich Grüntor will be kindly remembered by at least one person at the place he dedicated most of his working life to.

Brian insists on driving back to the station, accelerating and braking too abruptly. He says he will get the folder to forensics. Donna knows it is the right thing to do, even though she is impatient to have a peek inside. 'So you're conducting interviews in German now,' says Brian. He takes the corners too fast as he turns into the road behind the police station. Donna's elbow is caught painfully by the armrest. She doesn't respond. Once in the garage, he parks, slamming on the brakes. He faces her. 'Yes, I attended Sid Greene's suicide. I helped cut him down from where he was hanging in the barn . . .'

'Brian—'

He holds up his palm. 'And I chose not to tell Fleur Greene her husband had accepted payment for the crap tipped onto his land. Money he then spent on gambling, instead of on his energy bills so his pregnant wife could have a warm house to live in.' He gets out and slams the door.

'Brian . . .' Donna calls uselessly after him. She sits for a moment. Seen as a motherly, mature figure, more often than the other specials or PCs, she has 'assisted' in several suicides. *It rips your heart open*. She puts her fingers to her own to check it is still beating.

Chapter 20

Then: thirty-four years ago

Another birthday. Erika is seventeen. Erika insists on no party. She wants a dinner with her parents instead. 'My little girl she is growing up,' her mother says. Erika is seated. Her mother kisses her daughter on the top of the head. The only time she can still reach that once-favoured kissing spot. She goes back to her cooking. The smells emanating from the pans are delicious. She continues in her sing-song voice, 'And excellent school reports too. Our girl will go far. Our move from Dresden has been good for her. For all of us.'

It is the first time Erika comprehends that there was some risk in the move. She had come to lament the day her parents had made the decision to relocate. Now she is grateful. She sees the possibilities it opens up for her. They are not the ones her parents are thinking of, or even would approve of, if they knew. Which they don't, so all is well. Erika smiles broadly. She relaxes into her role as daughter: chatting about nothing; laughing; joining in with the board game her father has bought her. Tomorrow – tomorrow she will be Erika.

***

The next day, she goes out at lunchtime. It is one of those bright April days with a chill wind. Her parents think she is going to meet some school friends in the park and they will go to a local café to celebrate Erika's birthday. Her father makes sure she has enough GDR Marks to buy a hot chocolate and a *Kuchen*. She will add most of it to her hoard when she gets home. Money she is collecting for her escape, though to where, and when and how, still elude her.

She has to use some of it to take a tram to Kollwitzplatz. She walks down a shabby residential street with tenement blocks on either side to a shadowy corner where an unassuming brick building stands. Only the modest spire gives it away. She enters through a side entrance and takes the flight of steps down to the crypt.

Here she finds her friends – her new friends, her new tribe. She had stumbled in here one February evening. Out on one of her running/walking expeditions, hopelessly underdressed with only a light jacket, she had been caught in a torrential downpour. She had taken refuge in the doorway. A young woman who had been hurrying to get out of the rain and down the stairs had invited her in to warm up. In the crypt she had found light and warmth and had been plied with hot tea. She had even been given a dry pullover from a box of lost property. She had stayed, sitting on the outskirts of the circle to listen. What she heard brought up images of Sofie, hanging from the fence, barbs piercing her flesh. She sobbed quietly and the woman who had invited her in put an arm around her.

Erika has been going back regularly. There are discussion groups. There are pamphlets to be printed off. There are art and singing workshops. There is lots of tea, coffee, *Kuchen*, laughs, chat and, best of all, a shared understanding. A shared understanding that those in power are not creating a fairer society where everyone benefits. Then there's the radio. Erika almost loves this more than the *kuchen*. On it she can hear the BBC World Service. She has begun to learn English at school, but, with the radio, she perfects her accent and expands her vocabulary. 'Camaraderie', 'prevalence', 'snitching' – she rolls these words around her mouth, enjoying the taste of them.

Today there is a speaker at the little group. A man, a student, from West Berlin. He is in his mid-twenties, not over-tall, a little stout. He has dark hair to his shoulders, dark eyes and a dark moustache drooping around his mouth. He is in jeans and a jacket of thick blue material with leather patches on the elbows. After his talk on what student groups in West Berlin are doing to help the democracy movement in the East (Erika barely hears a word) she goes up to him, desperately trying to think of something to say. In the end what blurts out is, 'I like your jacket.'

He smiles. 'It's a donkey jacket,' he says in English with a glimmer of an American accent. He smells of a mixture of cigarettes and aftershave.

It is a chilly April day. It is the day after her seventeenth birthday. Erika is in love.

Chapter 21

Now

The beach at the base of the cliffs is already in shadow even as the feeble sunlight glistens off the York stone frontages of the tall Edwardian terraces which grace the Esplanade above. Donna has taken to regular walking after work. She thinks of it as good exercise, more appealing than an hour in the gym. However, there's more to it than that. She frequently finds herself here. She follows the path as it winds past the Gothic Spa buildings. Beyond are beach huts with their brightly painted doors of red, green and blue. This evening she takes the steps down to walk on the sands below the high sea walls hung with seaweed – bladderwrack, gutweed, sea lettuce. They had all been seaweed to her before Rose told her the names. She recites them in her head as if they were a poem.

Before leaving work she had rung Sabine Barker. The promise to keep in touch, given at the beginning of the month, had not materialised. Indeed, Donna had left several messages and not heard back from her. She'd wondered whether Sabine was busy or whether she'd been so anglicised that 'I'll get back to you' had lost its true meaning. This time

Donna was put through, although Sabine had sounded as if she'd picked up the phone by mistake. Immediately, she'd said she was in a hurry. 'I have not been in touch because I have no news. We have not been able to find a relative of Herr Grüntor. The embassy will, of course, help with the expenses of the funeral. There is a form, I will send it over to you. It is better the funeral is done in Scarborough now, I think.'

Donna agreed, saying there were friends here who would rally round.

'Good,' Sabine interrupted. 'You will tell me the date and I will see the embassy is represented. It will be soon.'

It had been an opinion, not a question. However, Donna had responded, 'Not quite yet, the case is not closed.'

A brief silence. 'It is not? I thought you had the culprits?'

'We have some youngsters who we have charged with grievous bodily harm. Their trials won't be for a few months. But there are some things to tie up.'

'There are?'

Donna had felt like, for the first time in the conversation, she had the other woman's full attention. 'Yes.'

'Like what?'

'I'm not at liberty to say.'

'No, of course not.' Again the pause, longer this time. Sabine appeared to be less worried about running late. 'I imagine we could request a report, from your superior? There may be something we can help with. Who should I contact?'

Donna gave her Theo's name and then was asked to spell it.

'I will contact him,' she'd said. 'Thank you, DC Morris. I must go now.' And she had gone.

The exchange has left a peculiar taste in Donna's mouth. In fact, she always finds her head is fairly buzzing at the end of her work days. These walks help to settle her and sometimes, just sometimes, whatever it is that has been gnawing at her rattles free. There has been something nagging at her since her interview with Genevieve Lawrence. The wallet file she gave them has met a logjam at forensics. The DCI has ruled out spending further funds on releasing it. He and Brian appear to be of the same mind: they have the solution for Henrich's death and the culprits, Calvin and his mates. Donna pauses. Frustrating as this is, it's not what is currently vexing her.

The sea has retreated, leaving an expanse of brown sand. It holds the memory of the rippling water in hard ridges. A clawless crab lies abandoned in one of the hollows. Donna can hear the ceaseless murmur of the waves. She can smell the frost on them. But they have hunkered down, a mere dash of white on the edge of what could be a parachute of air-force blue silk gliding towards the horizon.

Genevieve had said something, now what was it? Donna continues walking, her strides easy and relaxed. Far out, several metres above the gently billowing parachute, white hyphens tilt and lean. Then they roll themselves up to drop like tennis balls into the water. They too are aiming to grasp at something which keeps flitting just out of reach. Donna takes the path which zigzags up the cliff. By her side, short stumpy hazels and hawthorns bend themselves double to hold their footing. Though she has to slow right down with the incline, her breath remains steady. She notices she is not feeling tired or weighty. She gives a silent cheer. *Gut gemacht, Donna*, she says to herself. And it comes to her, the tiny grain of information which had almost slipped through her mind.

Chapter 22

Now

Given she had only seen her after she died, Donna had not expected to see any family resemblance when she meets Til's sister and niece. However, there's something in the shape of Nat and Lou Shearer's faces which reminds Donna of their dead relative. But the mother and daughter's cheeks are plumper, their eyes are clear, their noses are neat. Their healthy visages reveal how Til could have been without the ravages of addiction. And, according to her sister, how Til once was.

Donna meets Nat and Lou in the lounge area of the B&B where they are staying. It looks out onto a little yard filled with plant containers of all descriptions – buckets, a bath, even a tea pot, as well as the more conventional varieties. Though the flowers have gone, there are enough ferns and other greenery to give Donna the sense that she is looking into a tiny patch of wilderness. The smells of breakfast still linger. She can hear Radio 2 playing and people moving about the kitchen which juts into the yard. They occasionally sing or hum along with the tunes. The room is a compact square with an impressive marble fireplace suggesting it was once more commodious. Dried flowers and lavender now sit in the hearth. The walls of the room are a light grey and there is one painting, a colourful abstract of the moors. There are books, magazines and puzzles contained in a light wood, glass-fronted sideboard.

Donna is in the one easy chair. Lou and Nat are seated on the sofa. It is small. Their thighs are touching. Neither seems uncomfortable, it merely echoes an innate closeness. It's been a long time since Elizabeth has voluntarily allowed Donna in such close proximity.

Til was Nat's older sister by several years and by another relationship. Nat is talking about her with warmth. 'She always looked out for me. I don't think me mam was very well when I was born – it was Til who made sure I was taken care of. As she got older, she would get me stuff, little treats, new clothes, stuff we couldn't afford.' She twists her pretty mouth, it is coloured a battle red. 'Not always entirely legally.'

She and her daughter are short, the mother stouter, perhaps with the years. Not that she is old, mid-thirties Donna guesses, which would mean she had been teenage when she got pregnant. Donna recalls Til as diminutive in stature and rail-thin, her skin dry rice paper, not glowing with health and make-up like Nat and Lou. They are sombrely dressed, though not, Donna guesses, in the outfits they will have carefully picked out for the funeral later in the day. These would be more black, more elaborate.

'I didn't notice, you know, when Til wasn't doing so well.' Nat's eyes turn glassy and then spill over; she brings a screwed-up tissue out and dabs at her cheeks.

169

Lou pats her mum's arm. 'You were too young,' she says gently.

Nat blows her nose. 'Yes, I know what you say, Mam should have, well . . .' she pauses. She finishes harshly, 'Mam was good at having kids but not at raising them.'

'She did all right with you.' Lou kisses her mum on the cheek.

'Thanks, love.' The two of them glance at each other.

Donna feels washed over by the affection passing between them. Then she reflects on Lou's age, recognises the swapping of mother–daughter role, and wonders what it was in Nat's life which allowed it to happen. Maybe addiction hadn't just trapped Til, but she was the one who didn't escape. Donna gathers herself, she had asked permission to visit the Shearers to ask this question. 'I didn't know Til when she was alive unfortunately and I know she had a very tough life here. But she did have friends. I don't know if you have managed to contact any of them to come to the funeral? There is one in particular, Derek?'

Lou nods. 'She did talk about him. Ex-forces. We would like him to come. Can you get hold of him?'

'I can call him.'

'We've told William Bell,' says Nat. 'At St Jude's. Til spoke very highly of him.'

'Oh?' Donna says encouragingly.

Nat doesn't need to be egged on, she appears to enjoy chatting, especially, currently, about Til. 'She said he was such a lovely man – kind, generous. Do you remember, love?' She turns to her daughter. 'He persuaded her to come back for my birthday that time, and helped her get the money together. Not that she didn't want to come . . . and it wasn't just the money, we'd have given her that . . .' Nat comes to a halt.

Lou immediately picks up, 'You have to understand, Detective Constable Morris—'

'Donna, please.'

'Donna. Til had an illness. Addiction is an illness, but not everyone sees it that way. People say it's all the individual's fault. They wouldn't say that if the person had cancer, would they? Society shames the person with addiction, even though it's not their fault . . .'

Not entirely their fault.

'It was shame that kept Aunty Til away from us.'

'She's doing psychology at college,' Nat says proudly. 'None of the rest of us passed our CSEs.'

Her pride burns into Donna's heart.

'Though Aunty Til probably could have done. She was smart. Had to be to survive.' Lou's voice wobbles a little. Aunty Til had ceased to survive.

Donna can see how the young woman forgets and then it hits her like bricks falling from a wall. She refocuses on the thread which intrigues her. 'William Bell was good to Til then?'

'Oh yes,' says Nat, relief in her voice, perhaps at the thought that someone had been. 'He was a bit religious for her, but he wasn't the sort to keep shoving it down someone's throat.'

'He took them walking, didn't he?' adds Lou. 'He believed being out in nature is good for the mind as well as the soul and he's right, there's loads of studies showing it.'

171

Nat chuckles. 'Til didn't know her oak from her, oh you know, whatever . . .'

'Horse chestnut,' chimes in Lou, like it's a game they are playing.

'Yes. But with William she even went picking blackberries once, made some jam she gave me. It was tasty too.' Nat's eyes fill up again.

Her daughter gives her a quick hug. 'It's all right, Mam,' she whispers. 'You did your best.'

'And mushrooms?' Donna says it as if it isn't foremost in her mind.

'Mushrooms?' Nat and Lou look at her, their foreheads furrowed in unison.

'Did William Bell tell her about foraging for mushrooms?'

'Foraging?' 'Oh no, she got her mushrooms from Tesco's,' mother and daughter say in unison. Then they both sigh and ask if Donna would like some tea or coffee. She shakes her head. Nat begins to say they really ought to be getting themselves ready, and both are on the verge of rising from the sofa, when Lou stops, turns to her mother. 'Didn't Til say one of her mates got food poisoning from some mushrooms?'

'I don't remember, love.'

'Yeah, I think . . .'

Donna can feel herself stiffen, instinctively lean forwards slightly. 'Do you remember their name?' She tries to keep the keenness out of her voice; however, Lou picks up on it.

She turns. 'Is it important? Til died of food poisoning, didn't she?' The inquest had been a documentary inquest so no family or witnesses attended. The coroner merely reviewed the reports and came to his conclusion. 'Are you saying it was mushrooms and, and . . .' She thinks for another moment. 'It's happened to other people so may not have been an accident?'

Damn. The last thing she wants is a family clamouring for an investigation until she has something more concrete to go on. She says soothingly, 'Til's death has been ruled as a tragic accident and the police see no grounds to investigate it further.'

'Clive Wallin,' Nat says triumphantly. 'I remember we thought his surname was funny, funny-appropriate I mean, because he came from Wallsend. I think he was sweet on Til—'

'Barking up the wrong tree, then,' says Lou, still keeping an eye on Donna.

Nat sighs. 'Til'd've gone with anyone for her fix.'

'Mam,' says Lou outraged, turning to her mother.

'Well, it's true, love, and you know it.' Nat dabs at her eyes with the disintegrating tissue. 'Til was a mess a lot of the time.'

'Oh, Mam.' Mother and daughter embrace and hold each other.

Donna feels her inutility. Involuntarily she moves her legs and this breaks the intimacy which has pervaded the air between her and the sofa, making it hard for her to breathe. Lou looks at her, her expression not unkind, more curious. Donna asks for more information about Clive and is given an estimated age plus a possible address where he was brought up. Armed with these, Donna thinks she can probably track him down. She begins to take her leave. Lou stands and takes her hand to shake it. She holds on to it. She grips Donna with her gaze as well. 'If there is something funny about Aunty Til's death we want to be told,' she says.

'You'll be the first to know,' Donna promises, relieved when she is released to hurry out of the house.

Chapter 23

Now

Detective Sergeant Gary Horne, North East Counter Terrorism Unit, is a big man. One of those big men who get bigger because a mainly desk job means they do less exercise than they should and who seem bigger because they insist on wearing ill-fitting crumpled shirts. Donna wants to whip off the current one he is wearing and give him one the next size up, freshly laundered. One with a small pattern. One which doesn't show sweat so much. Horne has already been nicknamed Horny by those officers who knew he was visiting. *Why must they be so obvious?* Donna wonders. Besides him, DI Akande looks even more dapper. He is wearing a dark grey suit over a light-grey shirt. The burgundy stripe in his light-grey tie matches today's frames on his glasses.

Horne and Theo have done the round of the incident room, stopping to talk to several officers. One is Brian. Donna notices how he perks up at being picked out. Then, to her surprise, they come to Donna's desk. She automatically brushes down her chest, hoping there aren't any remnants of her lunch lodged there. Theo asks her to join them in his office. She feels several pairs of eyes locked on her progress through the room and she prays her skirt is neither bunched up nor stained.

Gary Horne occupies a lot of space in Theo's office. Donna squeezes in beside him. Theo sits behind the desk and begins: 'Donna, as you know Gary is here because of the Henrich Grüntor case. He has read the reports we've collated so far, but why don't you fill him in on things from your perspective, particularly what you told me yesterday.'

Donna takes a moment to collate her thoughts, then begins. 'Henrich Grüntor was found dead in Raincliffe Woods on 30 September. A previous employee of GCHQ, he had been dismissed in March, after having turned up at work drunk several times. He defaulted on his rent and left his home at the end of August. He had been sleeping rough for approximately four weeks. There is still some lack of clarity over CoD. He was attacked on 27 September and probably suffered a ruptured spleen. It looks like he ingested *Amanita virosa*, poisonous mushrooms. There's his obvious alcoholism and drug habit. And finally the unexplained puncture at the back of his neck. It could have been a combination of all of them. We recently talked to a colleague of Mr Grüntor. She indicated he started drinking heavily again in November 2012. What isn't clear is why.'

'Perhaps he just did,' says Horne. 'Once an alcoholic, always an alcoholic.'

Donna flinches inside. *Don't define him by his addiction.*

'All this was in your reports on the case. What's new?' The DS is sat back in his chair, relaxed, unhurried.

Donna suddenly feels exposed. She dips her gaze to her notebook. What was she thinking of, telling Theo her idea?

176

He now gently prompts her. 'Something else came out of the interview?'

'Yes.' She determinedly refuses to speak to her own lap. She turns to 'Horny'. 'It was something the interviewee said when I spoke some German. She said I had an accent like Mr Grüntor's.'

She falters, then continues, 'I have an East German accent. It is very distinctive.'

She is positive Theo had picked up on the discrepancy between what is in her HR files and what she is now saying. He misses little. However, he had not commented.

Gary looks mildly more interested: 'You are saying Henrich Grüntor is from Eastern Germany?'

'Yes. And given his age, it means he was a citizen of the GDR, not, as he said on his GCHQ application form, of the Federal Republic of Germany, West Germany.' She finishes feeling triumphant, before adding quickly, 'Or it's a possibility.'

'The Iron Curtain went a long time ago,' says Horne. 'I'm not saying Russia isn't of interest to us. But Germany is an ally.'

'Yes, I realise that,' says Donna, a tad tersely. 'Many of . . . most of the population of the GDR got on with the regime because they had to, until they didn't. People are like that. They do what they have to do to survive. But some were Altkader. The Old Guard. They were trained in the Politburo. They didn't change their minds just because a wall came down and a border moved. They would have been easy to recruit, they wanted to be recruited – by the KGB I mean.' When she finishes she feels out of breath.

Considering Henrich in this light has made her think once again about those she had left behind.

Theo adds, 'We've always had concerns about the puncture at the back of Mr Grüntor's neck, which is why we alerted you right at the beginning.'

'You think Mr Grüntor was a KGB operative assassinated in a stretch of woodland on the outskirts of Scarborough?' DS Horne manages to infuse his statement with a dollop of incredulity while remaining polite.

Theo smiles winningly. 'It must be one line of enquiry.'

Gary shifts his head which could indicate agreement or not.

Knowing she is supported emboldens Donna. 'Then there is the folder. The one left with our interviewee by Mr Grüntor and passed on to us. You'll have seen it mentioned in the case report. It might have something useful to add.'

'Where is it?' asks Horne.

'Languishing in the forensics lab.'

'The least you could do, DS Horne,' says Theo, 'is make some enquiries with MI5 and expedite the examination of the folder.' Horne huffs a little, but then agrees.

As he gets up to take the DS to the reception, Theo mutters to Donna, 'Good work.' She sits for a while in the empty office, thinking about the Altkader. She's avoided such useless ruminations most of her life. Keeping herself busy as a wife, as a mother, as a police officer, it was easy to file it all away. Now Henrich Grüntor has brought it all back to her. Unusually for her these days, she feels cold.

She is still sitting there when her DI returns.

'Is there something else, Donna?' he asks, surprised.

She had not meant to stay, however now the query forms itself. 'Have you heard from Sabine Barker from the German consulate in Edinburgh?'

'My DCI has. She's requesting a report on our investigation. I understand he is minded to give her one. Is there a problem?'

Is there? Donna casts her mind back and cannot quite work out when she began to feel uneasy about Sabine. She prevaricates over what to say.

Theo sits. 'What's concerning you?'

'I can't say exactly. I got the impression she was relieved when we made arrests.' *And why shouldn't she be? The death of a compatriot explained is reason enough for relief.* 'And when she heard we were still holding the case open, she appeared, I don't know, unnerved?' She realises how thin this all sounds. When keeping secrets is almost in your DNA, it's all too easy to be driven by suspicion.

Theo takes a moment and then says, 'OK you've been dealing with her up to now. If your advice is to hold back, then I'm willing to follow what you say. DCI Sewell can't report without our input, except in the broadest terms.'

'Perhaps a broadest terms account is the best,' says Donna. 'Enough to show willing, but not enough to give any actual information.'

Theo smiles. 'Just the kind of report DCI Sewell is most adept at giving.'

Chapter 24

Then, thirty-four years ago

It is the middle of the summer holidays. Erika is lying on her bed. It is a hot day. Her schoolfriends have invited her to the park. She will join them later, she has promised her mother she will, but for now, she is indulging in her current favourite pastime – daydreaming. The window is open, a warm breeze is wafting in along with the chirruping of small birds, sparrows, perhaps, or finches. Erika imagines the genial air where those gossiping feathered creatures have come from, in the West. Where he is. Ed.

He has only returned to Erika's church group once since she first met him. They had only spoken briefly, though, Erika feels, intensely. And there have been no letters. Why would he send any? He would know they would only get censored or, worse, 'lost'. Perhaps even cause problems for her. However, she has the napkin, a simple cotton square. But Ed had touched it. When she had collected the plates up after the cake had been eaten, Ed had handed it to her. It even has a smudge of chocolate on it, where he'd perhaps held it to his lips. She holds it close to her heart. *A secret love.* Like in a novel. The words thrill her.

It is common knowledge amongst the church group that Ed has both an American passport (from his father) and a GDR passport along with West Berlin identity papers (from his mother). He uses both to help people escape from East to West. The notion that straight-thinking people might actually want to go to the West, never mind try to do it, had not really occurred to Erika before she met Sofie. There is little in the press. What there is her parents ignore, or they agree with the newspapers' denouncements of 'traitors' crossing the Antifaschistischer Schutzwall. Her new friends at the church tell her that it is getting more difficult for people to breach the wall as it becomes more elaborate and defended. No, Ed gets people out in other ways.

Erika often thinks of Sofie and her family. She has decided Ed helped them. And if he did, then Sofie must be still alive, with her mum and dad, somewhere in the West. However, according to the stories she hears, Ed mainly takes people the direct route, across one of the Berlin checkpoints. 'Right under those bastards' noses,' someone had said with satisfaction. During such whispered conversations, they always get around to who would go and who would stay. There is a good proportion who say they would not even attempt it. It is too dangerous. They have family who depend on them here. Anyway, we must all stay to help transform things, from here, for everyone. Only a very few disagree. They say it is pointless, the regime will never change. The general population are sheep, they don't deserve saving. Only the man who says 'bastard' says this. He also says he has a life to live, he has a right to freedom. There's been some discussion as to whether he should be allowed in the group. He does not share enough of the group's views. He could be a liability. Maybe he is even a Stasi spy, egging them on to be ever more extreme. Erika always has a sleepless night after this is whispered. She vows never to go back. But she does.

She has moved on from merely attending meetings. Now she helps work the cranky printer for the leaflets. They contain carefully worded articles on how best to move the revolution on, on how to promote equality and truly realise the ideals of the GDR. She even takes some leaflets to deliver to various addresses. She does this with her heart beating into her mouth, her throat strangling out her breath. Once she was sure she was being followed and she threw the package of leaflets into a bush and ran. She did not go back to the church for several weeks then. She told them she had been sick when she returned.

She is lying on her bed, imagining Ed lying there with her. They would be naked. No. Erika remembers Ralph pushing himself against her. Ed would be kinder. Ed would be more gentle. Even so, he would have to slip his fingers under her shirt, one of its buttons would be pulled off. He could not help it. His passion would be driving him. His fingers would feel for her bra, expertly unclip it and then tenderly cup her breasts. *Oh.*

Her mother bustles in with a pile of clean laundry.

Erika leaps upright. 'Don't you ever knock?'

'I thought you had gone to the park. You don't want to waste such a lovely day.' She puts the clothes down on the bed and goes out again.

Slowly, Erika stands and starts to put her garments away.

They all seem terribly faded. Most are homemade. They are too childish for her now she has Ed. What if she asked . . . what if he offered . . . would she go? She looks round the box of a room. The wallpaper is a drab cream. The furniture is made of thick compressed wood-effect cardboard – it wobbles precariously every time a door or drawer is opened or closed. She and her father had painted the window frames and skirting board a daffodil yellow. On the chest of drawers, there is a jewellery box with a ballerina balanced on toe-point on top. Her sticky-out net skirt is dusty, the sparkles in it dulled. *Childish, childish.* Erika glares at every book, every object she once cherished and admonishes it for being infantile. She looks at herself in the mirror. She pulls her brown hair up into a tail which falls smoothly to her shoulders. She ties it with a bright green scarf. She had pestered her mother to help her crop her trousers to just below the knees. Her mother, however, had refused to crop a perfectly good shirt, so Erika ties it to reveal a band of flesh which is tanning nicely. She adds a dab of bright red lipstick. Not too much. Who knows whether or when she can replace it. She throws it down. If she were in the West she could have a different lipstick for every bastard day. She could find Sofie. She could be with Ed. Would she go? 'Yes, bloody likely,' she shouts in English, revelling in the new phrase she has just learned.

Chapter 25

Now

The South Bay is a different creature at night. In one direction the white bulbs on the curve of the Spa suncourt form a string of pearls on a dark throat. In the other, the chunky costume jewellery of the amusements. Their gaudy colours melting into reflections on the sands. Donna can hear the sea growling beyond the strand. It is an unimaginably immense rolling flank of pitch. The lights of the town are toys scattered on the rim. The moon and stars are muffled in cloud. Donna stares towards the horizon until it hurts not to see a demarcation, a delineation, some sign that beyond this squabble of buildings clinging to the coast there is something more than an infinite, impenetrable cave.

Donna is on her way to a party at a pub. When was the last time she had gone to one of those alone? Or otherwise? She can't remember. She thinks about going home. She is certain she is wearing the wrong things. She has on a black dress which flounces out from her waist. She bought it years back to show off her curves – now she fears it merely emphasises the weight on her hips. She has a lacy confection in her hair. She has put white powder on her face, bright red lipstick on her mouth and a touch on her neck, plus pink make-up around her eyes. It is Halloween, after all. She thought she should make an effort. However, she is worrying no one else has dressed up. Part of her wants to scuttle home and pretend she forgot to turn up. Another side of her is bubbling with excitement. Harrie had made a point of inviting her and encouraging her to come. As a sop to both her anxiety and her excitement, Donna promises herself, *I don't have to stay long if I hate it.* Then she hurries along the front to the pub. She opens the door. She is almost knocked sideways by the warmth and the noise.

Her comrades have colonised a corner. Some have plunged in with the fancy dress. There is an axe cleaving someone's skull, a knife stabbed through another's neck, and plenty of fake blood, dark mascara and white face powder. Others have come dressed as they would have done for any night out. Donna relaxes a little as she feels she has managed a happy medium. She unwraps herself and asks about drinks. Harrie – who is managing to look like a very stylish Morticia Addams – tells her there is a float behind the bar which she can join if she wants. Donna does so and gets herself a passable red wine. She winds her way through the crowds of drinkers back to the table. She squeezes into the only available space, plonking herself next to Theo. He is doing a passable imitation of a suave Gomez Addams. She returns his grin. 'I've gone for the Bride of Dracula look.'

'It suits you,' he says, chuckling.

'Do you normally come out with the gang?'

He shakes his head. 'I prefer a quiet drink and conversation, not being where I can't hear myself think. Brian asked me to come, to celebrate his exam results.'

She looks around. 'Where is he?'

'Not here yet. Once he arrives and I can shake his hand, I'll slope off. Is this your usual Friday night out?'

'Not for a long while. My husband, Jim, plays golf, so most of our socialising is done around the club.' She mutters it, half hoping he doesn't catch it. He leans in and nods as if he has.

'There's a good local music scene, mostly gigs in pubs which are very welcoming. It's tough moving to a place where you don't know anyone, especially Scarborough, where everyone seems to know everyone else.'

'At least I'm used to small towns. It must have been a bit of a change for you coming from Manchester.'

He takes another swallow of beer. Then he appears to pause before taking a decision to go on. 'There were moments, many, when I wondered if it had been a wise decision. My difference walked in through the door before I did. Well, one is too obvious to ignore and, as for the other, you know the rumour mill in the force never stops grinding. I'd be lying if I said everyone accepted me with open arms. My predecessor . . .' He frowns. 'It was like a tic with him, always finding a way to make some comment or other, but not quite bad enough for me to make a complaint. And he had a following here, still does, so making an enemy of him would not have been sensible.'

'And now you are in charge.'

'And I dare say there are those who say that I don't deserve to be, that it happened because I'm black and gay. There's prejudice, there's ignorance, there's fear and there's downright malevolence, with all shades in between. You get it everywhere.'

'But more in a small town like Scarborough?'

'I'm not so sure. There's also more chance to meet people face to face and build up personal relationships which make it difficult for them to then turn round and bad-mouth you or undermine you. I'm not saying it's easy, but I know who I am and what I am capable of. It makes it harder for ill-thought-out or malicious words and actions to hurt me.'

'You've stuck it out though. I mean, not just here . . .'

Another swallow of beer. 'I give my parents the credit. Especially my mum. She came from Cardiff. Generations back, her family came from the Cape Verde Islands to work in the docks, on the boats. Now there's no question but South Wales is their home. I think it was really her who gave me roots. My dad, on the other hand, I think he always felt he had a foot in each country, because he came here as a teenager, like you.'

'Yes.' She feels the question in his statement. She avoids giving an answer by drinking her wine too fast. When she first came here, she had been desperate to be absorbed into Britain, to disappear into it. Then Jim, utterly, incredibly, incurious about her background, had helped her take on the mantle of Britishness which suited them both. But now? The truth is, since Henrich, thoughts of her past have started to trouble her more than before. She doesn't want to share this. However sympathetic her DI's ear seems, it would take her into a story which would unravel like a scarf with a dropped stitch.

Thankfully she is saved from saying anything else by a

kerfuffle. Brian has arrived. He is already more than a little tiddly. It becomes obvious he is not in a celebratory mood and the reason finally filters through the noise. He has failed his sergeant's exam. Donna can only hear snippets. She sees Harrie approach and offer some consoling words. Then Brian shouts about 'them' only wanting 'women and poofters'. He waves a clenched fist towards her. She doesn't back down, appears about to throw a punch herself. Theo gets up and walks over. Before he reaches the two of them, other colleagues have piled in to pull them apart. Looking strangely apt in what could be a monk's outfit, Trench says something to Theo and he comes back to Donna. He picks up his coat. 'I'd better go before I have to arrest my own officers,' he says grimly.

'I thought Harrie and Brian were friends.'

'Were once. He didn't take kindly to her promotion. Will you be OK?'

'I'll be fine, thank you. I'll stay for another glass of wine, get to know my colleagues a little better.'

He hesitates, then nods. 'Have fun,' he says as he saunters off.

Donna struggles to the bar where she finds Trench with Nicky Fletcher. Whether deliberately or not, Nicky has misconstrued the theme and is dressed as a Princess Leia. If she'd been her mother, Donna thinks, she would have counselled something more flattering. But Nicky appears happy enough. The three of them exchange anecdotes about previous work events where people have fired off at each other. Donna is aware of police officers out on the lash getting into arguments. It's as if the lid has come off a pressure cooker.

Nicky is tossing back the gin. Donna gets herself another glass of wine. She is feeling uncomfortably hot and would rather head off home. However, Nicky pulls her onto the tiny dance floor where they both shuffle around for a bit, Nicky getting increasingly unsteady on her feet. Before she topples over, Donna suggests they go back to the table. She takes Nicky's arm and helps her over to where the others are sitting.

The man with the knife through his neck turns out to be an officer from the drugs team who Donna has only spoken to on the phone or via email. They have a bit of backwards and forwards on how they've ended up in Scarborough and he brings her over a further glass of wine which she drinks too quickly. Nicky has collapsed onto a chair and is giggling at a joke being told by a colleague. She stands. 'You want a drink?' she slurs at Donna.

Donna shakes her head. 'Don't you think you've had enough?'

'Are you kidding? Night's only just got going.' She turns unsteadily and almost collapses onto a grim-faced Brian. 'Hello,' Nicky says, drawing herself straighter. Then, obviously emboldened by alcohol, she adds: 'Well done on your exams, DS Chesters.' Has she not heard? Has she forgotten?

'Fuck off,' responds Brian.

'Wha-at?' Nicky grabs at his arm, partly to steady herself.

His face is right in hers now. 'You taking the piss? You know I didn't pass them.'

'I didna, I didna,' she protests, pulling away. 'I was trying to b'friendly. Show no hard feelings . . .'

He moves towards her, shoves hard at her shoulder and

shouts, 'Are you daft as well as fat, ugly and a slag?' He looks like he might do more violence, until he realises he is being watched and others are about to intervene. He strides away.

'I'm not, I'm not a slag. You – it was you . . .' Nicky blubbers as she begins to crumble to the floor. Donna scoops her up and then realises the young woman is on the point of vomiting so drags her outside where she empties her stomach in the drain. She then slumps onto the pavement edge, hanging her head. Donna sits next to her and puts her arm around her shoulders. It reminds her of when she first became a special and of those young people, drunk and vulnerable, who she had wanted to help. Nicky hiccups and sniffs. Donna finds her a tissue. 'Fuck,' says Nicky.

'It's OK,' says Donna.

'No it isn't.' She's beginning to snivel. 'Everyone heard, didn't they? Everyone knows. And . . .' she looks down. 'I've splashed me dress. I lent it from me cousin, she'll fucking have me.'

'It'll wash,' says Donna, not at all sure it will. It feels like the kind of material which would melt if shown water. 'Let's get you home.'

Nicky shakes her head. 'Me bag's in there. Can't go back in there.'

Donna begins to get to her feet. 'I'll go and get it.'

Nicky holds on to her. 'Don't leave me,' she wails.

Donna sits again. She is beginning to feel cold, damp is seeping through from the pavement. Then a figure comes out of the pub and over to them. It is Trev. He has Nicky's bag and jacket and Donna's coat. He offers to get them a taxi.

'I don't think a taxi is a good idea,' says Donna. 'Do you live far, Nicky?'

The young lass sighs. 'No.'

'I'll walk you then. Come on, love. Let's get you home.'

Chapter 26

Now

'Have you got a hangover, Marmie?'

Donna is annoyed Elizabeth has noticed. And 'Marmie'? Isn't that from *Little Women?* It sounds sinister coming out of Elizabeth's mouth. Donna is also annoyed at herself. Taking Nicky home had made her overtired and yes, she had the extra glass of wine. She'd had to stop several times on the way over to the prison to gulp in fresh air. And boy was it fresh. Wind whipped up in the Arctic raking across the dun-coloured moors with nothing to halt its progress. On the whole, however, Donna would prefer that than the cloying warmth in here, perfumed as it is by body odour. She sips at the plastic cup of water she has been allowed. It is tepid.

Elizabeth lets her glance move round the room and says overloudly: 'I've suggested we have some scented candles in here, but apparently it's a health and safety issue. I think it would improve the atmosphere in here no end, don't you, Ma?' Her gaze comes back to settle on her mother.

How clear the whites of Elizabeth's eyes are now. Donna can remember them when they were virtually yellow and crazy-paved with red. 'How is your treatment going?'

'I'm clean, ain't I?' She shifts her arms so they are laid across the table, the sleeves riding up. The puncture marks are still there. They are old puncture marks, melding into the pale skin almost like birthmarks. 'I don't even smoke any wackie. I tell you, Ma, there's enough spliffs in here to put Amsterdam out of business.'

She has lowered her chin and apparently dropped her voice. It's only a pretence – her words are chiming out across the room and they are getting some glances. Donna wonders whether it is merely for her benefit or whether her daughter is as provoking to her cellmates. She imagines not. She knows what happens to prisoners who don't make and keep friends and it isn't pretty. She was once the liaison for the family of a lass who committed suicide in a remand centre: she had been literally bullied out of her life. *Elizabeth is more likely to do the bullying.* This thought means she has to close her eyes for a moment. She sways as if adrift on a tide warmed by a sewage outfall. She expects a rough comment from Elizabeth, perhaps a pinch on her forearm. Instead her daughter's touch is gentle, her enquiry soft. 'You all right, Mum?'

Donna forces herself back into the room. She nods. 'It's just a bit stifling in here.' She takes hold of Elizabeth's hand.

Her daughter does not withdraw it. She keeps her tone muted. 'You should try living here. At least you get to go at the end of the hour.'

At one time Donna might have jumped in with something placating, maybe about Elizabeth's time on the farm, but it would only have been to make herself feel better. She has come to realise it doesn't help Elizabeth. She gives her daughter's hand a slight squeeze. It is returned.

When Elizabeth resumes talking she does so quietly. Though only their fingers are touching, mother and daughter are holding each other in an invisible ring of intimacy. All the sounds, the smells, the people at the other tables recede. They have become wallpaper. 'I know I deserve this, Mum. Jeeze, I fucking hit that woman over the head with a wooden chopping board. She could have died.' The final word is said as a croaky sob. Elizabeth recovers herself. 'She was a bitch, accusing me of bleeding her father dry to get money for, well, we all know what for . . .' She pauses and takes a breath. 'And she was right. Why would I want to be with an old codger except for his money?'

It is the first time her daughter has spoken so fully about her offence in Donna's hearing. Elizabeth had pled guilty. There had been no trial. As far as Donna could ascertain, her daughter's confession had been minimal. She had still been in the throes of her addictions, so had found constructing sentences, being clear about what had happened, even sitting still, problematic. Donna had assumed she must have explained things more fully to her solicitor. There had been a plea of mitigation. The victim had already threatened to kill Elizabeth if she did not leave her dad alone. The victim had gone looking for Elizabeth to, as she told a friend, sort her out. Elizabeth's solicitor had suggested there were elements of self-defence. But the ferocity of Elizabeth's attack did make that difficult.

Her daughter now grips Donna's hand. 'I am sorry, Mum, for what I did. You do believe me?'

'Yes, Elizabeth, I do.' In that moment she does.

'And, and . . .' Elizabeth moves closer. She is whispering.

'I'm sorry, Mum, for what I put you through. You and Dad and Christopher.'

Donna has waited for this apology so long, she doesn't know what to say immediately. *I forgive you. You don't have to apologise. I'm sorry. I brought you into the world. You are my responsibility.* All these go through her mind. Before she can hook one out to respond, an officer is beside them. They've got too close. The officer wants to know what they've been doing. They're both going to have to be searched, in case anything passed between them.

'Yeah, yeah,' says Elizabeth, sitting back. Previously, she might have followed this with a sharp quip either at the officer's or her mother's expense. However, this time she says, 'Give us a second.' She looks round at the officer and adds, 'Please.' The officer withdraws a couple of steps. Elizabeth turns back to Donna, '"Tarred and feathered you stand,/ your feet mired,/ wound round by tendrils of some creature, raw and poisonous./ You can search amongst the leaf litter for the wormy apple/ – dry flesh, bitter juice –/ or you can reach up and choose a sweeter fruit." Isn't that fab? It's from a poem by Eta Snave, "The Forgiving Harvest". You should read the whole thing.' Then she stands, drops a kiss on the crown of her mother's head and leaves with the officer.

Donna follows another officer out the other way and allows herself to be searched thoroughly. It is only once she is standing by her car that she really hears her daughter's words. 'I am sorry, Mum.' She thinks she might cry. Then she doesn't. She just stares and stares across the brown on brown folds of woven moorland, miles and miles of it in every direction, with hardly a vertical in sight. Only dark smudges cruising the updraughts, their careless caws rattling across the expanse on the wind.

Chapter 27

Then, thirty-three years ago

In the end it doesn't turn out to be the loudmouth. It is the older woman who always brought the cake. Erika cannot even bring her face to mind, merely an impression of some-one short and a bit stout wearing 'old lady' trousers and beige. She never said much. Only listened. So far it is the main organisers who have been taken in for questioning.

Erika is afraid. She tries to recall whether she ever told the woman her full name or where she lived. It wouldn't matter, the Stasi would be able to find out, if they cared to. Erika stays mainly in her room. It is a cold, wet winter anyway, and she tells her parents she has a lot of schoolwork to do. She does, though she finds it difficult to concentrate. Every noise from the street, every car pulling up, every knock on the door, every time the phone rings, she freezes. And when it turns out to be nothing, she has to pace the floor or curl up on the bed, Ed's napkin clasped in her hand, until she can settle once more.

On occasion she does venture out, early in the morning or at dusk, in those grey intervals between night and day. On one of these forays she meets one of the other girls from the group. She is able to tell her the majority of the people who attended have stayed safe. Those who have been detained are not giving up names. 'But,' she adds, just as Erika finds she can breathe again, 'who knows how long they can hold out.' She pauses before whispering, 'Ed is helping those who want to leave.' Erika's heart stumbles. Ed has not forgotten her. He is helping the others, of course he would, but it is her he is searching for. She goes home a little lighter, even her mother notices her smile. Erika allows herself to be hugged. She makes an effort to chat at dinnertime, to be interested. After all, she will soon be off. She glances round the kitchen where they are eating. Out of this drabness, out of this sameness and into . . . into Ed's arms. As she does the washing-up, there's a knock at the door. She loses traction on a glass which falls and breaks in the water. Somehow she nicks her finger. The bright blood is oozing across her hand. It drips, drips onto the draining board. She imagines the splatters of red as someone is hit repeatedly across the mouth. *Tell, tell, tell.* She can hear the visitor is a neighbour wanting to borrow something. She shudders. Next time, though, next time, who knows?

Erika takes to walking the way she did when she met the young compatriot from her church group and finally it pays off. This time the woman appears less keen to talk, looking this way and that. 'I'm busy,' she says.

'I need to speak to Ed,' Erika says, quickly catching hold of the arm of the woman as she turns.

'It's too dangerous,' she hisses.

'Please, please, I can't stay here,' says Erika. For the first time this is totally clear to her. She doesn't want to be here. She doesn't want to be without Ed. One way or another she is going.

'OK, OK. This Thursday go to the Elster Café in Friedrichshain around seven. When a woman comes in to buy matches at the bar, follow her. She will take you to Ed.' She quickly walks away.

Erika hadn't expected this to be the night. She thought she would find Ed and they would set up their escape plan. She hadn't said goodbye to her parents, not properly. She hadn't brought anything with her apart from a small rucksack with a book in it. The book she had forced herself to pretend to read as she sat in the Elster Café for ten, fifteen, thirty minutes, feeling sicker and sicker by the second. But Ed tells her it is now or never. They had set this up for someone else who hasn't shown, who has, perhaps, been arrested. 'They're getting too close,' Ed says. 'I won't be able to come again.' He seems out of sorts, angry. He hadn't smiled at her when she'd arrived, let alone given her the embrace she had been dreaming about. He is chain-smoking.

But you'll come back for me, Erika wants to say, only she doesn't, fearful of the answer.

'Come on, Erika, make up your mind. You're putting us all in danger,' he says aggressively. 'I can't hang about.' He turns abruptly.

'No wait, wait, wait,' the words bump up from her heart and into her mouth. 'Don't leave me here.' She runs up to him, grabs at the damp wool of his donkey jacket.

He stops and faces her. 'Are you sure?'

For a moment she senses his concern for her. She nods.

'Right. You follow me, but at a distance, you understand? Like we don't know each other. And this,' he shoves something metal into her hand. 'This is for emergencies. Got it?'

She nods.

He moves off quickly. She counts to ten and follows. *I mustn't panic*, she tells herself. *I don't want to look a fool.* Not in front of him. She must be grown up in front of him, a lot more than her seventeen years and ten months. Otherwise, otherwise, well the otherwise is unthinkable, so she squashes the attempt of her mind to bring it to her attention. She is feeling younger by the step. She could turn back now. *Run. Run.* Back to her parents. They need never know. She looks up and sees the slick of his dark hair settling on his wide shoulders. He is walking quickly but nonchalantly. *How does he manage that?* She keeps tripping and slithering. They are following a road between sooty industrial units, some brick, some grey metal. It is dusk and getting darker. They avoid the circles of yellow light thrown down by the street lamps. It is cold. It has been raining all day, the droplets like a beaded curtain she is continuously trying to push through. She slips again. She halts. She is panting as if she has just run the last kilometre or so. There is a stitch beginning to ache in her side. As she tries to slow her breathing, she hears a van. It is going fast. The tyres squeal, taking a corner at speed. *Are they coming for us? They must be coming for us.*

She heaves herself forward. He is some metres in front of her now. She wants to shout out to him to slow down. But he had said not to communicate. If they are not seen communicating, they can deny all knowledge of each other. They are out for a stroll. Separately. Why through an industrial estate in the rain would be a question they would have to face. Separately. And come up with an answer. Separately.

Again her mind tells her to flee. Get back to the safety of her parents' flat. That security is still within her reach. She hasn't thrown it all away. Yet. She looks up and sees him receding. He is stouter than she thought he was. She recalls his smell, a mix of cigarettes and aftershave. Then she remembers his smile under his drooping moustache. OK, yes, he smiles a lot, especially at women, but this smile was just for her. She is sure of it. Yes, her parents offer safety, but only if it comes with boredom and restrictions and hypocrisy. He offers adventure and . . . She forms the words with her lips, 'Love.' He loves her, in a way her parents do not. They put everything – jobs, reputation, their own peace of mind – before her. He loves her. He puts her before everything. *Look what he is risking for me.*

She quickens her pace and follows him around the corner. She can see his car hidden in the shadows. There is a young man and a young woman, jeans and denim jackets intertwined as they lean against the side of the vehicle. They are the passengers. They look up as he approaches, but do not unwrap themselves from each other. They nod and swap muffled greetings.

All is quiet in front of her. Inside, her lungs and heart are pumping like parts of a steam engine, overcompensating for her exertion. She stops again to collect herself. She wants to walk up to them as cool as they are. The change in their faces and body language – from relaxed to stricken and rigid – comes before she hears the footsteps and voice behind her.

She turns. He is as startled to see her as she is to see him. *Ralph? What is he doing here? In that uniform?* Her brain cannot compute. Luckily, or perhaps unluckily, surprise appears to have befuddled his brain too. All he can do for a moment is repeat her name. He backs away as well, as if attempting to withdraw from the situation.

She shoves her hands in her pockets. Her right hand hits metal. 'Just in case,' Ed had said before they had set off to this industrial estate. But with a laugh. They had both assumed it would not be needed. Her fingers grip it and pull it out. Merely to frighten him off, make him run away. Leave. Her hand shakes, the other comes to steady it. His mouth falls open. He doesn't move. He is frozen. *Why doesn't he go? Run, Ralph, run.* In that moment, it is as if her hearing has regained its acuity and then some. She hears the flap of a piece of paper as it is caught against the base of the street lamp. She hears a scratching of tiny claws on tarmac. Then she hears the van. The rest of his Volkspolizei squad come to find him. Suddenly there is a detonation of sound in front of her. The retort cracks at her wrist and batters up through her elbow to her shoulder. She drops the gun. It has become a roasting iron.

There is a scream and shouting behind her. Her arm is grabbed and she is flung round. 'Let's get the fuck outta here,' Ed says, his moustache a limp dark worm against the chalk of his face.

Chapter 28

Now

It is possible for someone to just disappear in today's Britain. Donna is surprised. She has been through the usual databases. She has spoken to a distraught sister who hasn't heard from her brother for over a year, though she has provided a decent photo. She has even been through some CCTV footage. However, all she has discovered is that Clive Wallin left the hospital after his discharge, he got on a bus for Leeds and disembarked there nearly five hours later. She is about to ring one of the homeless projects in the city when Theo comes over to her. There are only a couple of officers at their desks this morning. One glances up and then goes back to her screen. The other, Brian Chesters, looks up and stays watching. Donna can see him over Theo's shoulder. Brian doesn't try to hide his interest. She feels mildly uncomfortable. His is not a friendly gawp.

Her DI, on the other hand, does his best to put her at ease. He makes a couple of useful suggestions to help her track Wallin and she notes them down. Then he says, 'It'll have to wait, though. We've got the forensics on Henrich's folder and DS Horne wants a conference call. Have a read of the report and then come to my office at two. OK?' Having received her assent, he goes back the way he came. Donna checks her watch. She'll have to go out and get a sandwich if she's going to eat. She can't miss lunch or her brain won't work. She asks the officer hidden behind her screen and the still watchful Brian whether she can get them anything. The former says no. Brian says he will come with her. She would rather he didn't. Nicky hasn't been back to work since Halloween. Donna hasn't forgotten the exchange between the young woman and Brian. On the other hand it's unwise to make enemies and would be rude to refuse.

Once they are out on the staircase, Brian asks, 'What was that all about?'

'DS Horne from CTU wants to talk about Henrich Grüntor.'

'I can't believe the DI is still thrashing that one. Grüntor died from a ruptured spleen after a mugging and we've got the little bastards who did it.'

He pronounces Henrich's surname as 'grunter'. Donna resists the temptation to correct her colleague. 'I think DI Akande just wants to be thorough.'

They step outside. Traffic is belching at the lights. A fine rain is held in the fuggy air. Someone has discarded a plastic sack of rubbish on the corner. It has been torn open and rifled through by gulls. Donna steps round the resulting outflow of detritus. She will call the council when she gets back.

'There's thorough and there's obsessed,' says Brian as they cross the road. 'He wasn't gay was he, your Grüntor?'

'What? I don't know. He didn't appear to have a partner. What's that got to do with it?'

'Just wondering why the DI is so interested. They stick together you know.'

They? They? 'What are you talking about?' Donna raises her voice. But Brian has already pushed his way into the sandwich shop. She forms all sorts of rejoinders which she doesn't get to use as Brian doesn't wait for her to get her order and clears off somewhere. It rankles. She makes a pact with herself that she will take it up with him later, at a suitable moment. Then she imagines Brian denying it or saying she'd misheard him or, more blatantly, that she'd got it wrong. She is too new. She isn't tough enough. She fears she will let the suitable moment slide.

It makes her more cross with herself than with Brian. In an attempt to collect herself, she dawdles on her way back to work. She pauses by the Cash Converters on the corner, and, with nothing else to do, her eyes scan the window. Donna notices a necklace. *Could it be?* She looks closer. *Surely Jayson Smith would not be this foolish? Right across from the police station?*

She goes in to ask about the diamond and ruby necklace in the window. The man behind the counter is middle-aged with a beard neatly plaited on his chin, no hair on his scalp and a cobweb tatt stretched across his temple. He looks bemused, calls her love and suggests she has mistaken the shop for a jewellers. She insists and points at it. He cranes over and laughs. 'Glass and paste, love. Good, I grant you, but costume.' She digs out her ID card and asks him who brought it in. 'Don't need to check, Jayson Smith from Westfield. Not his usual fare, I'll grant yer. Said it was his grandmother's or summit.' Another customer comes in and he begins to deal with them. Donna takes a photo. *Trixie by name, trixie by nature?*

She doesn't have any time to follow this up. As soon as she has eaten she has to go into the DI's office for the video link with DS Horne. He fills the screen. Donna can't see where he is sitting, though it is likely to be an underground car park if the sound quality is anything to go by. She has had time to devour the forensics report along with her sandwich. She has written a list for herself and 'fingerprints' is at the top. Meanwhile, Gary is explaining that the CTU's interest in Henrich Grüntor has increased. 'You were right about his origins, DC Morris. He grew up in Bautzen . . .' he stumbles over the pronunciation.

'Bowt'n,' says Donna. 'It's down in the south-east corner of Germany which borders Poland and the Czech Republic, slap bang in the former GDR.'

'Yes,' says DS Horne. He's unsmiling, but then the video could be making him feel awkward. 'He went to East Berlin as a young adult. We are still waiting for information about what kind of work he was doing there.'

'And none of this was known to GCHQ?' asks Theo.

'They took his paperwork at face value.'

'It must have been pretty good, then,' says Donna. 'Professional rather than amateur.'

'He never came onto MI5's radar.' Gary sounds defensive, as if it were he who had recruited Henrich.

'But he is now?' asks Theo.

'They are conducting a review. They are also examining whether there has been any chatter about activity in North Yorkshire.' He says it as if he cannot believe he is saying it.

'You have to understand, Russia is still of interest and is certainly not a benign influence in parts of the world, but the risk of violence perpetrated on UK soil comes from other sources.'

'Tell that to Mrs Litvinenko,' says Donna quietly.

The DS replies sharply, 'That was due to a particular set of circumstances, DC Morris. It won't be replicated.'

'Won't it?'

'At least we can be certain,' intercedes Theo, 'it wasn't action on the part of our secret services?'

'Oh no.' The vigour of Gary's dismissal makes his face on the screen go fuzzy.

'One thing ticked off then,' says Theo. He turns to Donna. 'Any thoughts on the forensic report?'

She looks down at her pad. 'Fingerprints. They lifted two sets from the contents. One belonged to Henrich. The other matched a set lifted from cups found at his, er, camp. Which means someone who had handled the documents visited Henrich, perhaps visited him on the weekend of his death, assuming he washed up regularly. We don't know who this person is. Unless Genevieve Lawrence lied about not opening the folder and its origins. Which I don't think she did.'

'And the documents inside the folder?' asks Theo.

'A diary,' says Gary forthrightly. 'There were short entries in German, each dated from 1983.'

'Do you read German?' asks Donna. She finds it difficult to pull in enough oxygen for speech. The same had happened when she first saw attached to the forensics report the photos of the sheets of paper pulled from Henrich's file wallet. Then she really thought she would faint. Now, she forces herself to drag in deep breaths.

DS Horne shakes his head. 'I only have a description from forensics. We will get them translated, we're waiting for the request to be cleared. But I thought you could give us a clearer idea of the content first?'

'What is it, Donna?' says Theo.

She glances at him. His expression is quizzical. He has picked up on the change in her and her uneasiness. 'It is a kind of diary, I suppose. The kind of diary Stasi informers kept.'

'Stasi?' asks Theo.

'East German secret police,' Gary and Donna say almost in unison.

'Is it about Henrich?'

'I don't know,' replies Donna. 'There are no names. It's maybe possible to tell from some of the context. And also there is a reference number on each sheet. Stasi reports are all public now. We could perhaps find a match which would tell us more.'

'We'll need to go through Interpol—' begins Theo.

'I can ease access,' interrupts Horne.

'What are the possibilities here?' asks Theo. 'November 2012, someone from his past contacts Mr Grüntor—'

'Or he makes the contact . . .' interjects Donna.

Then they riff off each other. 'He receives documents . . .'

'Or sends them . . .'

'That's when it all starts to fall apart for him, he is drinking again, taking more drugs than his usual recreational use . . .'

'He loses his job, then his home and begins camping out in Raincliffe.' To Donna it's almost a game, an enjoyable game.

'He must be afraid, why else would he give Ms Lawrence the folder?'

'Is it his insurance?'

'Or his confession?'

'Then there's the meeting in the woods with the other person for whom the documents are significant and . . .' It's no longer a game. 'It's Henrich who ends up dead.'

Chapter 29

Now

It's getting dark earlier. It's night by the time Donna leaves at 6 p.m. and begins her walk home. The streets are quiet, those who are out are rushing to get indoors. She is muffled up. Her mind is moving from work-mode – has she done enough to find Clive Wallin? – to home-mode – what she has in to eat and whether she will give Jim a ring. Their communications have been less tense since her trip to see him. Sometimes she looks forward to speaking to him. Tonight she would rather eat, bathe and go to bed. Yet she knows she 'owes' him a call. From the start, she felt she owed Jim; he wiped away the past or, at least, allowed her to bury it. But hasn't she paid him back by now?

She is turning over the word 'owe' – looking at it from all angles; what a strange little word – when she reaches the path of the old railway. The cinder track starts at the back of a supermarket. The shop was built on the disused goods yard in an area known, Donna has learned from Rose, as Gallows Close. A place of summary execution. A Scarborough Warning was no warning at all; people were hung without the benefit of a fair trial.

The cinder track is sporadically lit. The bushes are unkempt. Branches – skinny and stout, thick with dank foliage and bare – begin to enclose Donna's path. A cycle whizzes past her from behind, its winking red light quickly disappearing into the gloaming. Donna has to stop herself from yelping. She realises her body has tensed in preparation for flight or fight, even as her thoughts preoccupied her. She walks smartly on. It's only a step, as Rose would say, to the intersection with the road with its comforting march of street lights and cars. She passes under a bridge. In the day she has paused to admire the high arch made from hundreds and hundreds of narrow bricks. The Victorians knew a thing or two about engineering, she had thought. Now she is more aware of the shadows, of the moss dripping with water on the sides, of the unidentifiable shapes in the murk created by brick meeting grass – probably discarded rubbish, perhaps not.

'DC Morris.'

She freezes. The arch echoes back her name. It takes a moment to work out the origin is behind her. She snaps round. The person is bundled into shape-concealing coat and trousers. Whoever it is has their hood pulled up, a hat and a scarf obscuring most of their face. Donna's instinct tells her to run. Another thought says she's tired, would she run fast enough?

Gloved hands pulls the scarf down, ''S Derek.'

Relief begins to flood in, only to be damned up when she notices that Derek is swaying. His speech is slurred. *And how did he come to be here?*

As if reading her thoughts, he says: 'Bin following you since the police station. Didn't catch on, did ya? Still got it.'

211

Ex-forces, Donna remembers Lou saying. *Violent*, William Bell had intimated. Donna watches those gloved fingers and wonders what they have done, what they are capable of doing. 'What do you want, Derek?'

'Oh, thas nice. I come to see you and you're all hostile like.' The drink emphasises his Liverpool accent.

Donna makes an effort to moderate her tone. 'I'm tired, Derek, it's been a long day. You could have come to see me at the station.'

'Yeah, oni everyone's watching you there. It'd get back to him.' Derek crosses his arms and slaps at his biceps which are chunkier than Donna had realised. The slapping is rhythmic, at first soft, then firmer.

'What do you want, Derek? I have to get back. I, er, my husband will be wondering where I am.'

'You got someone at home. Thas nice.' Derek sways again, steadies himself with a hand on the masonry beside him. 'No, I mean it, jus cos I'm in this mess, doesna mean I don want others to be happy.' He goes back to slapping at his upper arms.

'I'd be really happy to get home.' The sharpness comes into Donna's voice.

'Yeah, well I'd be happy to have a home,' snarls Derek. He begins to walk around Donna.

I mustn't panic. I mustn't show I am panicking. He's behind her now. It's as if he has dropped ice down her back. She clasps her arms around her. 'Derek, please, I am getting cold.'

'Your home is warm, I bet. It's damn, fucking cold sleeping out here, let me tell you, DC Morris.' He's making another circuit, this time getting closer in.

Donna wonders if she can somehow reach into her bag to get her phone. Her grasp on the straps of her shoulder bag tightens.

'Ah, thas it, think I'm a thief. You're no different from everyone else. They used to hang people out here for nothing more than picking up a handkerchief, you know that? I'd have been hung up there, an example to everyone, and good riddance to me.' He is getting more and more agitated.

'No, Derek, no I don't want . . .' she struggles to find the right words. Then she shrieks: 'Derek, you're fucking terrifying me.'

He halts in front of her. Puts his face into hers. She can smell his sour breath. Cheap cider. Roll-up baccy. It had been Elizabeth's favoured perfume for a while. Donna doesn't move.

Then he steps back, stumbling over a bag of rubbish. Slipping on some mud, he grabs at the bridge wall, scrambling to keep himself upright. He croaks a laugh. 'Almost ended tits up.'

This would be the moment for Donna to take off. All her training tells her so. Instead she moves closer. 'Let me get you a taxi to a shelter, Derek.'

'Nah, love, I've got my place, under the Esplanade, nice and cosy, like.'

'I'll come with you.'

'What about your husband?'

She shakes her head.

'You were that scared of me?' This thought appears to sober him up a smidge.

'What do you want, Derek? Why did you follow me?'

He attempts to straighten himself. Anger is back in his voice. 'Why haven't you arrested him? William Bell.'

'We haven't enough evidence.'

'Evidence? Fuck, he killed Til.'

'She killed herself. Accidentally, I mean.'

'With mushrooms Bell gave her.'

'She also had a blood alcohol level which would have slain an elephant.'

'Aye, well.' Derek looks down at his feet.

'Is there anything you can tell us which could prove Bell's involvement?'

He shakes his head. 'But he wonna stop until every one of us be dead. And nobody gives a fuck.'

'I give a fuck. And I am looking for people who might have been given poisonous mushrooms by Bell and survived. Do you know where I can find any?'

Another shake of the head.

'Clive Wallin?'

'Wasn't he a mate of Til's?'

'Yes. Do you know where I can find him?'

He appears unable or unwilling to look at her. Tears overwhelm his eyes.

'I need evidence, Derek.' Donna searches in her bag and brings out some tissues, gives them to him. 'I am doing my best, but I need some hard evidence.'

Derek blows his nose into a tissue and then uses another to mop at his filthy hands before putting both tissues into a pocket. 'Your best'll have to do.' He lets go of the wall. He sways.

'Derek, let me . . .'

'Na, love, you do your job, thas all I want.' His touch on her hand is cold and rough and slightly slimy. She grabs his fingers so they shake hands properly. She watches him totter away back towards the supermarket. She finally turns for home feeling more weary than ever.

Chapter 30

Now

She wanted to do it. She volunteered. Yet now the time has come, she's not sure she can. Donna has gone to the police station's family room to give herself some peace and quiet to concentrate. It's comfortably furnished and she's sitting with her feet up on the sofa, a cushion supporting her back. The light through the small window is feeble. She has angled the floor lamp so it throws a white beam onto the folder on her lap. She is hesitating. Is she prepared for what she will find within? She feels poised as if about to dive into cold, dark waves from a very high cliff. It is almost like the first time she was given a batch of photographs from a murder scene to look through. *I got through that. I'll get through this,* she tells herself.

In the end, it is her curiosity which won't let her put it all to one side with the excuse of getting one more cuppa. She flips open the manila file. Inside are the contents of the folder handed over by Genevieve Lawrence. There are several sheets of paper. Copies. The originals would have been on GDR paper and she remembers what it felt like. Flimsy. If you pressed too hard your pen went through.

She skims over the document quickly. She can see there were smaller pieces of paper glued onto one sheet of A4 before being copied. The edges of each portion are blurred. They are all different sizes, some are ruled, some are not. The writing is the same on each. Small, precise, with loops on any downward strokes. The writer has been taught to form their letters. Donna recalls being taught in a similar way. There were special exercise books ruled with three lines: one main line, two fainter, above and below. They formed the borders across which her pen strokes must not cross.

She pulls out the sample of Henrich's writing which they had obtained from GCHQ. Though a little bolder, a little messier, there were enough similarities for Donna to say Henrich had written the despatches in the folder. They would have to get an expert to check, but she now believes these reports to the Stasi were by Henrich, not about him.

She focuses on the words, noting down a translation on a pad as she goes. The sentences are uncomplicated; the initial draft doesn't take her very long, though she has to rewrite the phrases a few times to adjust the grammatical construction. When she is satisfied, she reads back through the English versions:

Date: 3rd March 1983
Frau and Herr L. have new curtains. Colour: dark wine. Material: chenille. Ready made.

Date: 23rd November 1983
Frau L. bursts into tears and leaves the room. Herr L. offers me Glenfiddich. He says his wife is not coping with motherhood. The child cries all the time.

And there are more observations from other visits to the L.s' family home. Banal snippets of an ordinary life. Yet Donna can see the accusation in almost every word: 'new'; 'chenille'; 'ready made'; 'Glenfiddich'. The most unpatriotic of all, perhaps, a mother not coping with her new baby. True or not, Frau and Herr L. are being set up for a fall. By Henrich informing to the Stasi.

Then a report which is far more insidious. Once again Henrich is welcomed by Herr L. into the apartment. But almost immediately Herr L. is called away by his wife. Henrich roams the little sitting room (dimensions already given as 4.5 metres by 3 metres). He pulls out a Bible, a leaflet falls out. It is an invitation to a church service. Pastor Eppelmann is to address the congregation. There is to be music. Whether Frau or Herr L. ever meant to attend is immaterial; it is enough that they have the information in their flat and have apparently attempted to conceal it.

There are no more entries. Perhaps Henrich did not make any. Perhaps no one did. Perhaps those that were made were destroyed in the days following 9 November 1989 when the people of East Berlin stormed the Stasi building. Or perhaps these were the only ones which needed to be copied for whatever purpose was intended. Donna desperately wants to know who the 'L.s' are and what happened to them. Puzzling over this stops her mind alighting on the buff folder which may still exist somewhere marked: 'Erika Neuhausen'.

The door opening startles her. It is Harrie. 'Cuppa?' Donna nods. A hot beverage was customary consolation even in the GDR. Idly, Donna wonders whether it is the world over. *Surely not in hot countries. Except India maybe.*

She distracts herself until Harrie returns. Donna plants her feet on the carpet to take her mug of lemon and ginger. Harrie sits on one of the easy chairs. It smells like she has strong coffee. Donna wishes she had asked for some, despite knowing it would probably bring on a headache. Harrie is wearing smartly cut fudge-coloured trousers with a skinny fitting black rollneck. Donna instinctively pulls herself out of her slouch and tightens her stomach muscles under her teal cord skirt.

'What do you think?' asks Harrie. 'Was Henrich the writer?'

Donna nods. Her mouth is too dry for speech.

'Then he was a spy?'

She takes a lubricating sip of the spicy liquid. 'He was a Stasi informer. The official estimate is there was one for every ninety GDR citizens. People were informers for all sorts of reasons. Not just because they believed in what the regime was doing. They were afraid for themselves or for their family. They were greedy. They were trying to survive. Or it made them feel important.'

Shilling's narrow eyebrows tilt. She nods. You don't get to be DS without understanding those motivations. 'What do they say?' Donna passes over her translations. After scanning them, Harrie says, 'They don't look very incendiary.'

'Mostly it's about demonstrating they are getting goods from the West. Though the sin is more in the desiring of them rather than the obtaining of them. People were supposed to be satisfied with living in a socialist idyll.' Donna hears the cynicism flatten her voice.

'Mrs L. doesn't sound happy?'

'I'm guessing postnatal depression. Poorly understood even in this country in the 1980s.' Why does she feel vaguely defensive of the GDR on this point? 'But, in this context, a mark against her for not fulfilling the ideal of the fulfilled mother with the bouncing baby, the next generation of socialists.'

Harrie rereads the last sheet. 'And who is this Pastor Eppelmann? Was it just the anti-church thing? Didn't the USSR ban religion?'

'The GDR didn't proscribe the churches, but they were expected to toe the line. Many didn't and were, in fact, instrumental in the downfall of the regime. Rainer Eppelmann, as well as being a pastor, was a leading figure of the opposition.'

Harrie hands her back the pages and Donna looks at the dates again. 'The early 1980s was a time when the GDR government was getting anxious. I mean it was always paranoid, hence the Stasi, but particularly anxious. The leader who had ordered the building of the Berlin Wall, Ulbricht, had died in the early 1970s. His successor, Honecker, was still committed to a socialist GDR, however he made more overtures to the West. The GDR was desperately short of money and things were getting less reliable to the East. After eighteen years in charge at the Kremlin, Brezhnev was dead. There were two old and sick leaders and then came Gorbachev.'

'Now, I have heard of him,' says Harrie. 'The ending of the Cold War, reform in Russia, the Berlin Wall coming down . . .'

'There's still some discussion about whether the wall coming down was meant to happen. I don't think the GDR leaders were consciously aiming for reunification and hence their inevitable demise.'

'No pig votes for the bacon factory.'

Donna smiles for the first time. A new idiom and it pleases her.

'You left in . . .?'

'1980.' She collects herself and says firmly, 'I left West Berlin in 1980.'

'You are very knowledgeable.'

'I read a lot.'

Harrie nods at the folder. 'Doesn't help us, though, does it? We still don't know who made the copies or why.'

'DS Horne says he can get more information on these reference numbers. It should help.'

'It does look like some kind of blackmail. The question is, was Henrich the perpetrator or the victim?'

'Certainly these pages could be used as blackmail, to let someone trying to hide their past know they have been identified.'

'Maybe to get revenge?'

'Why now? Thirty years later.'

'Best served cold,' says Harrie with relish, whether for the words or for the coffee she has just polished off.

Someone trying to hide their past. Donna isn't sleeping. She avoided the coffee, yet she still has a drill bit turning into her temple slowly, deliberately. She is wondering about the best course of action. Lie still. Try to read. Listen to some music. Get up. Drink tea. Take medication. She used to know how to treat her infrequent ills. Now she is almost permanently under the weather, she can't be certain what will work and what will make things worse.

Donna sighs. She manoeuvres herself out of bed. *Like a beached whale*, she thinks forlornly. Pulling on her trackie bottoms and a fleecy top, she goes downstairs and makes herself a peppermint tea which she takes into the lounge.

Someone trying to hide their past. Her phrase returns to her as she sinks onto the sofa. Memories are like water, they find the slightest flaw in the carefully constructed, reinforced-concrete dam and nag at it. Slowly, slowly the hairline fissure becomes a crack, becomes a fracture, becomes a widening aperture. The memories come tumbling through, racing each other to be heard. They are a torrent. They overwhelm the hard-won fabrications of human ingenuity as if they were formed of mere twigs and autumn leaves.

Her drink slops in the mug. She puts it down. She covers her face with her shaking hands. Her fingers are cold against the furnace of her cheeks. Erika Neuhausen. Donna had closed that particular file a long time ago. But now it won't stay shut.

Chapter 31

Then, thirty-three years ago

She is bent double in a squashed 's' shape under the seat. Her chin is forced against her thighs. The wooden bench flush against her back. Her knees, neck and ankles have gone beyond aching – the pain is searing through the muscles to the bone. The air is fetid. *Maybe the breathing holes they made won't be big enough. Maybe I am going to suffocate. Maybe I am going to die.* She closes her eyes, tells herself not to panic. If she begins to hyperventilate she might well run out of oxygen. She tries to imagine she is in a field, a pasture with poppies. The sun is bright, she is lying on a covering on the ground in the shade of trees, birch trees. She focuses her mind on picturing them. And there is Ed. Ed reaching over to her. The car hits a bump in the road. The impact ricochets through her. She clenches her teeth. Even so a yelp escapes. *It's OK, it's OK, no one can hear you over the engine noise.* She begins to moan softly to herself. It helps. Then the car stops. She can hear voices, harsh voices. The car doors are opened. Something is being pounded on the seat above her. She can hardly hold in the terror, it is a wire of acid ripping through her chest and up to her mouth. The stop seems interminable. From the noises she guesses they are rifling through the boot. Will they pull off the back panelling and find her crouched here? She starts to shake. She starts to pray, *Jesus, Jesus, Jesus*. When she was very small, her grand-mother had taken her to Sunday School. Her parents had not approved and it had stopped as soon as her grandmother had died. But Erika suddenly remembers her grandmother saying Jesus would always be there to save her. If there is any time she needs Him, it is now. *Jesus, Jesus, Jesus*. Is she saying it aloud? She grits her teeth together until her jaws hurt.

Finally, she hears the boot door close, she feels the weight of the woman getting back on the seat above her and more doors being slammed. The car moves off. They must be nearly across by now. Unless the stop was by a patrol, not at the border. *I can't stand it, I can't stand it anymore. Let me out. Please, please, let me out.* She screams it now and thumps her fists against the wood imprisoning her.

Chapter 32

Now

Donna had fallen asleep after all around 4 a.m. She had plummeted into a deep slumber as she lay on the couch. She had, therefore, missed her alarm clock going off upstairs. Somehow something on the radio had brought her to consciousness instead. It was after eight o'clock. Even so, she could not face work without a shower and breakfast.

Which is why she is sauntering into the CID office, attempting nonchalance, as if it isn't thirty minutes after her shift should have started.

'You OK, Don? You look terrible.' Brian swivels round from his desk and does a noticeable time check of the clock on the wall.

It would have to be you who noticed, she thinks resentfully. *And since when did I give you permission to call me Don?*

She turns on a grin which has more than a smidge of the rictus about it. She says she is fine and, keeping her head up, continues to her work station. As she logs in and begins to check through the daily updates before turning to her own emails, she sips from the coffee she bought at the café across the way. Real coffee, 100 per cent caffeine. It smacks into her brain at the same time as the email from DS Horne. He has a response on the reference number on the Stasi reports written by Henrich Grüntor. The reference number has led to a name. A name which stands out from the rest of the message as if typed in Times New Roman 45 and bold. Donna reads it over and over, but it doesn't change. *He should have been dead.* She puts down her cup and stares. Then her mind grasps a straw. *Perhaps it's not him. It's not an unusual name.*

She forces herself to read slowly through all the other information in the email. She hears nothing of the comings and goings around her as she focuses and takes it all in. Herr L. is Ralph Lerner. The date of birth given for him confirms he is the Ralph Lerner Donna had always thought, assumed, had died in 1980. But here he is married to Monika with a baby in 1983, being spied on by Henrich Grüntor. It is unclear whether this changed anything for the Lerners. The other details about them do not come from Stasi reports, but municipal records. Monika Lerner died on 27 January 1985. 'Collided with a tram,' Donna reads. 'Accidental death.' The word 'collided' shrieks non-accidental. Was Monika Lerner pushed? Or did she let herself fall? Suicide was a taboo in the GDR, more than it still is in the UK. *And, oh, so treacherous,* Donna thinks bitterly. For both denying the regime a person and for what the act could say about the system.

Donna would like to walk away, get some fresh air. However, she gives herself another kick of caffeine before reading on. Ralph Lerner also dead, in 2005, heart failure. The child, the one who cried so much as a baby, would have been twenty-two. *Still young to be orphaned.* So now where is she? Donna has gone into full investigation mode. Her brain is clear, her hands and breathing steady. DS Horne's email says no more. However, Donna has a name, a birth date and a place of residence in 2005. Even when resident in another country, people are not so difficult to track down, unless (like Clive Wallin) they are determined to disappear. And Sabine Lerner is no shrinking violet. Her wedding to an Englishman, a banker, made it into the pages of a German woman's magazine. The bride looking strangely old-fashioned in a full-skirted, shin-length dress, with a wide-brimmed straw hat perched on top of an elaborate pile of blonde hair. Donna clicks onto the German embassy website. She zooms in on the smiling woman at the piano. Is it only because she knows that she now sees the resemblance? *Why now?* Her question to Harrie. Sabine Barker, née Lerner, moved to the UK in August 2012. Was it a deliberate act to put herself in the same country as Henrich Grüntor? Or was it a coincidence which she then used to track him down? Was it a coincidence that in the autumn of 2012 Henrich started drinking again?

Donna pulls herself up from her desk and looks around. The office has emptied, with most of her colleagues out following leads or in search of lunch. Donna goes to find her DI. She knocks and goes in without waiting, as appears to be the custom. He is preparing to leave while talking to someone on the phone. She can immediately tell this is a personal call; the timbre of Theo's voice betrays the fondness he has for the person on the other end. He glances up. 'Gotta go. See you soon,' he says softly, before clicking off the connection.

'Sorry.' Too little sleep. Too much screen time. She is not sure she is thinking straight. There's been too much information to take in.

Theo looks at his watch. 'I've a meeting to get to. What is it?'

Maybe I am wrong about all this? She suddenly feels slightly sick. *He went down. He was dead.* She stutters: 'I am sorry, sir, I think I've found . . . a connection . . . Can we ask the German embassy for sample fingerprints of their staff?'

'I doubt it. We don't want to set off a diplomatic incident.' His features are quizzical. The slight tension in his shoulders has eased. He sits and indicates she should do the same. 'What's this about?'

'Sabine Barker. My contact at the German consulate. I think she is the daughter of Ralph Lerner . . .' she has to stop and swallow, force herself to continue with a dry throat. 'Ralph Lerner and his wife Monika were the couple Henrich was informing on in 1983. Ralph and Monika are dead. But Sabine . . .' Then she remembers the interviews she and Trench carried out in Raincliffe: the smartly dressed blonde in the high-end jacket and knee-length boots. 'I think she was seen in Raincliffe the weekend Henrich died.'

'Can you be sure?'

'I can get a photo from the German embassy website and show it to the witness. I can do a trawl of CCTV. She must have travelled here somehow, by train or car? I can talk to traffic.'

'Do it. Once we're certain, we'll think about fingerprints.' He smiles.

The adrenalin which has been keeping her upright

deserts her. Donna could just lay her head on her arms on the desk in front of her and weep. The freight of memories is too heavy.

'Donna, this'll wait. Go home and get some rest,' Theo says kindly.

She nods, but cannot find the energy to move.

'You got your car?'

'I walked.'

'I'll drive you. I can go that way to my meeting. Come on. Do you need a hand?'

She shakes her head. She stands. She puts one foot in front of the other. She is glad Theo is at her shoulder. He doesn't touch her, but it's as if his presence is a plaid blanket being wrapped around her for comfort. It reminds her of another time: when she was a young girl, swathed in a coverlet, she was carried and gently placed in the back of a car.

Chapter 33

Then, thirty-three years ago

Perhaps she blacks out for a while. In any case, she drifts into a woozy, grey haze for a short time. She is only vaguely aware of the car halting and fresh air tumbling in on her. Hands take hold of her shoulders. *This is it, I am going to die,* her mind manages to think before she realises these are friendly hands. They guide her into a building, up a wide staircase and into an apartment. A woman, the woman who had bought the matches, assists her in using the bathroom – *Oh, the shame of it* – and gives her a long cotton nightgown to put on. Only then does Erika realise the smell of urine was wafting off her. *Ed must have smelt it. If only the floor could swallow me whole.* The woman takes Erika into a small room where she tucks her into a narrow, low truckle bed. *I will never sleep again,* Erika thinks. Then she does.

It is late when she wakes. She stumbles to the bathroom. On her way back, she notices the door to the kitchen is open. She can see the woman who bought the matches. Ed is sitting at the table. She is saying to him, 'Give her time, she's just a kid. Why you brought her I don't know. It broke all your rules.'

'I know,' Ed says. 'Carried away, I guess.'

'Foolish,' says the woman.

Ed gets up from the table. 'I thought you liked it when I got carried away,' he says. He puts his arms around her, kissing her passionately on the mouth. It's the way he was supposed to be with Erika. Only more realistic. She whimpers as she shuffles back to the bed and hides herself under the covers. *What have I done?*

The woman is kind. She brings Erika drinks and snacks. Erika hardly acknowledges her. She goes over and over her 'relationship' with Ed and realises what an idiot she has been. A naïve idiot. She decides she will go back. Then she thinks about Ralph. The gun shaking in her hand. The gun going off. Ralph falling. She can't go back. She would be arrested. Her parents too, probably, despite their credentials. Or they would have to disown her. *It would be better for them if I were dead,* she thinks. She feels dead anyway. Dead from shame. She burrows down again, even as the idea of how she might live comes to her.

The next morning, or perhaps the next, she gets up and has a shower. The woman gives her some clean clothes which don't quite fit. The woman is taller, more willowy. She makes coffee and waffles for Erika in the kitchen. The radio is playing, the music is lively, sassy. Erika can't quite catch the lyrics, but the song eases the stiffness and the aching in her muscles. 'You like it?' asks her host. 'It's "State of Independence" by Donna Summer. I went to see her when she played here. She was fabulous.' Any woman the woman Ed loves thinks is fabulous, must be beyond compare.

The following day, Ed appears. He tersely tells Erika she must go to the embassy to get her papers regulated. His girl-friend says Erika can wait a little longer if she wants. She has a warm, kind smile. On the other hand, she has let Ed put his arm around her narrow waist and has kissed him on the cheek. Erika looks down at her mug of coffee and says, not to worry, she was planning on leaving anyhow.

The woman says she will take her to the embassy, which she does. The drive takes them along streets which are full of colour and people. Even more exuberant than in Sofie's wildest descriptions. Erika shrinks down in her seat. 'It's a bit over-whelming at first,' says the woman. 'You get used to it. Here' – she pulls into a parking space – 'let's get some chocolate.'

'I've no money,' Erika mutters.

'I'll treat you.'

The shop feels immense. The long lines of shelves are full to bursting with every kind of packaging, bright and glit-tery. Despite herself, Erika moves closer to the woman, who takes her hand. 'Here,' she says when they arrive at the con-fectionary aisle. 'You choose.' Erika is stunned. She begins to count and stops when she reaches ten different types of chocolate bar. *How could anyone choose?* Ridiculously, panic begins to rise in her chest. Her hands twitch. The woman notices. *Oh the shame, the shame.* Erika glances down at the clean shiny tiles. 'Here, this is my favourite. You want this?' asks the woman. *Will it make Ed love me?* Erika nods. She dumbly follows the woman to the checkout (there are eight!) and then into the car. *Idiot, stupid Erika*, she berates herself.

'You needn't worry,' says the woman kindly as she pulls away from the kerb and joins the continuous line of traffic.

'Everyone is the same. It is overpowering. It's good you remind me that we really don't need so many choices.' She smiles at Erika.

Erika stares at the rucksack on her knee, small and shabby, with the gleaming chocolate bar inside. *Don't try to get me to like you.*

The woman hums along to the tape playing. Donna Summer singing about being hot stuff. 'Once you've got your papers, you can come back and stay with me,' she says. 'Until you sort yourself out.'

'No, thank you,' says Erika stiffly. 'I'll be OK.'

'Well, take a card.' She picks up one from a pile in an indent by the gear stick and hands it over. On one side is her name, the word 'artist' and a phone number. On the other is a reproduction of a sketch of a naked woman. 'One of mine,' says the woman. 'You like it?'

'Yes,' says Erika politely. She stuffs it into her bag, attempting to crumple it up at the same time.

'Here we are.' The woman pulls up at the kerb in front of a large building, its door flanked by square cut pillars.

'Thank you,' Erika forces herself to say. She finds she cannot force herself to move.

'We can leave it for another day, if you want,' says the woman. She reaches out to pat Erika's arm. 'It's OK.'

'No,' says Erika, overloudly. She flinches out of the way but the woman's fingers touch her. Grabbing at the door handle, she practically falls out of the car. *Very elegant, Erika*, she tells herself crossly.

'Take care of yourself,' the woman says as Erika slams the car door.

She takes a deep breath and pulls herself up to her full height, not inconsiderable for a girl of seventeen years and ten months. She could pass for older. She takes one step towards the stone portico, then another and another. It becomes easier. Everything which has been flitting through her mind over the last few days abruptly solidifies. She has to leave the young, the silly, the adolescent Erika Neuhausen behind. She doesn't belong here in the city of traffic, of shops, of hustle and bustle. She enters the building and crosses to the wooden desk, her footsteps echoing up to the mosaic on the ceiling. She stands in front of the receptionist who is finishing with a telephone call. When the receptionist turns to her and asks for her name, Erika says, 'Donna, Donna Newhouse.' She says it firmly and clearly. It too resounds up to the rafters.

Chapter 34

Now

She wakes. The hours before dawn are the worst. Memories come to her more vividly than they have in a long time. The moment in front of the receptionist when Erika Neuhausen became Donna Newhouse reruns in technicolour.

After only a short wait, Donna had been ushered up some broad stairs to a cluttered room. The official who greeted her had not believed a word she said. She was not Donna Newhouse. She had not come across the border alone by swimming the River Spree. She had not lost her GDR ID card in the water. She was not eighteen years and ten months old. However, nor was the official a Stasi. It turned out he had little interest in forcing information from her. She was not on any list of 'undesirables' gleaned by special agents operating in the East. She was, therefore, a desirable. If she wanted to be eighteen-year-old Donna Newhouse, then he saw no reason why she should not be.

'Right, you're set,' he said once he had handed over her new ID card with which she could apply for a passport, along with the slim wad of West German marks given to all 'returnees'. She had tried to get up. Donna recalls her legs felt like scaffolding poles screwed to the chair. 'Is there anything else?' the official had asked. She had shaken her head. 'You have somewhere to stay?' She had shaken her head again. He had sighed. Nevertheless, he found her a place in a hostel and had paid for a month.

He was a kind man. I was met with such kindness, Donna thinks. *Even, especially, Ed's girlfriend. I wish I had been more grateful.*

She had spent the month discovering the city, her eyes trying to take in everything around her, her heart trying to process everything she had done, counting neurotically her dwindling supplies of money. She spoke to few people. Those she did talk to immediately recognised her accent and knew where she had come from. They wanted to know all about her, what it was like, how she got out. She gave the vaguest answers and moved on. Those details belonged to Erika Neuhausen not Donna Newhouse. She began to speak more and more English so no one could place her. She was assisted by an English girl she met in the hostel who was working there to help pay for her studies. 'You're good,' the girl said once. 'You should go to England, be an au pair.'

The month was coming to an end, as was her small stock of money. She had to do something. She went back to the official. He obligingly found her a place through someone who knew someone who was leaving the British embassy to go back home. She stepped out onto the street again. She was now Donna Newhouse, going to be an au pair in Ludlow, England. For the first time since February she felt a sense of excitement, a sense of freedom.

***

Donna nods off uncomfortably on the sofa. When she wakes, her neck and shoulders ache, she is cold. The heating has only just clicked on. She makes herself some scrambled eggs and bacon for breakfast and sits at the kitchen table to eat it. *I never thought to go back? Not once during that month?* she interrogates herself. She cannot remember. *I didn't think of my parents, how frantic they might be?* Probably not, she realises. Understanding what it is to be a parent and to lose a child only comes with becoming a parent. *I thought it was for the best if I was dead to them,* she defends her younger self. But she also knows that she became caught up in the adventure, the adventure of being Donna Newhouse, of discovering a new country, a new language, of making friends who had never known Erika Neuhausen. She never wrote to her parents. What would her father have done if he had been forced to censor his own daughter's letter? Oh yes, she had long worked out what her father actually did. And this had been her argument which had worked for a long time. It was the heartlessness of youth, and is why she understands Elizabeth, can forgive her, over and over. Jim has never been anything but the dutiful, loving son. He is not able to get his head around throwing off your family.

She puts her plate and cutlery in the sink and goes upstairs. Why did she never try to find them after 1989? *I was too busy, too caught up with Elizabeth and Christopher, too caught up with my own family. The one I had constructed.* It rings discordant. She pulls out the bag she had taken to Kenilworth. From an inside pocket she takes the battered envelope and, without pausing to give herself the chance

237

to change her mind, extracts the photo. Erika Neuhausen flanked by her parents on her fifteenth birthday. They are both beaming. Her mother is wearing her smart dress. Donna remembers the silky material and the swirl of blue. She thought it was the height of sophistication. In the photo it looks handmade and dowdy. Her father is in his suit, his one and only suit. The camera does not show it, but it was shiny at the elbows and bagged at the knees. Erika has already grown to the height of her mother and is well on the way to catching up with her father. She is decked out in a white lacy dress which is too tight across the chest and too short. She looks incredibly uncomfortable. It was the day, Donna realises, that specific day, when Erika realised her parents were not perfect, were not able to protect her. That was the day when she began to separate herself from them. *My fifteenth birthday*, Donna breathes out. *Mine*. It's a concept she finds hard to fully grasp, so fully has she slipped this particular skin.

There is something else in the envelope. She pulls it out. A faintly blemished napkin. The white cotton slightly yellowed. She goes to deposit it in the bin. Then she pauses. *He gave me my second life.* She returns it with the photo to the envelope.

She has been walking briskly, as if the memories might not keep up with her. They do, of course – they are inside her, beside her, dancing in front of her. Images, glimpses of a past she still cannot quite accept is hers. It is more as if she is reviewing stories she has been told. Whenever she thinks of another scene, she has to tell herself, *This was me*. She has to receive her recollections back in.

238

She is panting slightly, both from the vigorous movement and from anticipation. She heads down the steep hill, round the corner and there it is. Vastness. Openness. A horizon which luxuriantly sculpts itself to the curvature of the globe. The sun has only recently detached itself from the water, leaving a glittering trail across the waves. It is nudging into white low cloud. But above the sky has been scoured blue by the stiff breeze which now scuffs at Donna's face. She wraps her scarf more securely around her and pulls on her woollen hat. Unexpectedly this immensity of shades of blue has become her tonic to be sipped and gulped whenever she can.

She reaches the beach. It is gleaming from a recent tide. She steps onto the sand. Gusts of wind brush swirling patterns into its compact tawny surface. She heads towards the harbour. The stalls selling crabs and whelks and ocean tails (whatever they might be) are just opening up. The amusements and the pubs on the other side of the road are still shuttered. Only Zoltar in his glass box mechanically offers to read her fortune as she passes.

For a long time she has left one part of the story unremembered. Not at first. Not during the early years, when she was recreating herself as Donna Newhouse and then Donna Morris. She couldn't escape it then. It would catch her blindsides, felling her. She would cry without reason, or no reason she could admit to anyone else. She would feel scared, frightened of what she was capable of. She would play it over and over in her mind. The part where she turned to see Ralph Lerner in the VoPos uniform. The part where she pulls out the gun. The part where she squeezes her fingers towards her thumb. The part when there is a terrible explosion of noise. The part when there is a moment of silence into which Ralph falls. She had asked herself over and over, how deliberate was her act? Was it the shaking? Was it intentional? She had never come to a definite answer. Truth be told, she had tried to unremember, only never quite succeeded. When she had heard what Elizabeth had done, she'd relived it all over again and wondered if the propensity to violence is handed down in the genes. It was why she had taken Elizabeth's side more than Jim. *Desperation. Desperation does terrible things.*

Donna strides out onto the quay towards the lighthouse. There is a strong smell of diesel. The rigging on the yachts in the harbour clink musically. She reaches the end of the jetty. Before her is only water once again. A sculpture of a woman stands there in the act of diving off. *But he wasn't dead.* At last she is able to think it clearly. *All these years I thought he was dead in 1980 and he wasn't. He married. He had a daughter.*

The chill is sharper, the sun is more muffled by a pale bank of cloud. Donna looks across the waves hissing and twisting in eddies. A herring gull divebombs a smaller, lighter-coloured gull, making it drop a hard-won sprat, which the bigger gull then swoops and retrieves for itself. *All these years I thought it was me. But it wasn't. I didn't. I didn't kill him.*

Chapter 35

Now

Of course, the witness from Raincliffe has gone away for a couple of days. When she comes back, she identifies Sabine as the woman she saw the weekend Henrich died. However, as Harrie points out, witnesses are notoriously unreliable, especially after a passage of time. Theo agrees. He says he will seek advice. Donna continues with her quest to find out if/how Sabine Barker got to Scarborough. She searches relevant CCTV, as well as putting in requests to Traffic and to the BTP officers at the railway station.

It's the middle of another afternoon when Donna gets a call from the desk sergeant. A rough sleeper, Derek Wyatt, is asking to speak to her. She goes down. Derek greets her like an old friend. There's something different about him. Maybe he is a tad less dishevelled? Certainly Donna cannot smell alcohol on him. 'I've found him,' he says triumphant. 'Clive Wallin. I can take you to him. He's in Hull. Come on, there's a train at four.'

'Derek, I can't . . .'

'Can't or won't?' His voice is elevated. 'There's more of us going to die and no one gives a fuck because of who we are.'

The desk sergeant looks up from a conversation he is having with a young woman. 'You OK, Donna?'

'Yes, yes, everything's fine.' She waves Derek out into the street and wishes she had thought to put her coat on; the chill slices through her layers as if she were naked. 'OK, OK, I will come with you but not this minute.'

'There's a train every hour.'

Not only is the temperature falling, but so is the night. Hull, a town she does not know – to go there when it's dark would be foolhardy.

Derek's face becomes pleading. 'He could move on any time.'

'I'll get my bag.'

The train from Scarborough to Hull rattles through the dog hours of the day. It meanders from one halt to the next, the land mostly flat fields to either side except when the towns bustle in with their red brick. Donna is unnerved by how long it takes. She had thought maybe thirty minutes. Half an hour in and they are hardly twenty miles down the coast. She now understands Harrie's raised eyebrow and 'Are you sure?' when she had said what she was intending on doing. *Ah well, nothing to be done.*

She breathes in the stale warm air of a carriage which has made this journey several times already this day, carrying bodies and dogs and damp coats and walking boots and burgers. Derek had forced her to buy provisions and now she is glad. They've both had a bacon buttie and cup of coffee (she didn't bother with decaffeinated, she needs the boost). Derek is now polishing off a cereal bar. He is telling her how he managed to find Clive: through social media; through trips to Leeds and talking to people he met on the street; through questioning bus drivers. Derek's story unfurls like the track under their wheels, curving inevitably though unhurriedly towards its destination. 'You should join the force,' Donna says at one point. Derek laughs and continues with his tale. She glances at her reflection as the dark now makes a mirror of the window. She sees a face which has lost some of its definition. She sees striations around the throat. She sees skin which is too red over the cheeks and nose and looks bruised around the eyes. *Perhaps the eyes are the same?* The colour of bluebells, her mother had once said. She closes the lids. They have already seen too much in her lifetime.

She must have dozed, lulled by the rhinoceros-like sway of the train, because Derek is nudging her. The lights of roads and shops and housing smear the gloom. As they get off into the bright station, there are people and traffic. *Maybe it's going to be all right.*

Derek leads her down a series of pedestrianised streets. Shops and cafés are closing for the day, restaurants opening. Derek wants her to notice the grand Victorian edifices in honey-coloured sandstone of the maritime museum and art gallery. Then they are following a harbour edge past more pubs and eateries.

'Where are we meeting Clive?' asks Donna. *Maybe I should have ascertained this before.*

'Over there.'

She has to scurry slightly to keep up. He is walking taller and straighter than she has ever seen him. Over the harbour lock gates. They pass a statue depicting a family emigrating to what to them would have been the New World. Then they go past some new office buildings in glass and steel, part of the regeneration of present-day Hull. The path is getting lonelier, more industrial. Donna grasps at Derek's arm. 'Where are we going?' There's a hint of panic in her voice.

'I told you, over there,' he says firmly.

She stops. 'Where is over there?'

He grabs her elbow. She can feel his fingers pinching into her skin. He puts his face close to hers. She can smell bacon. 'Don't bail out on me now,' he says angrily.

'Don't, don't you threaten me,' hisses Donna, pulling backwards.

He lets go of her and puts his hands up.

She pivots back towards the lights, the people, the traffic. Even that damn train was better than this.

'Please,' says Derek softly. 'It's not far now. I'll look after you.'

She turns towards him. 'Will you?'

'Yes.'

She looks him up and down. He's wearing layers of clothing which are none too clean, topped with an anorak with greasy cuffs and a pocket hanging off. He is wearing his bobble hat over his scraggy mousy hair. His face shows the ravages of his lifestyle. His nose is too large for its narrow confines. His skin is scored with purple veins and scabs. *Can I trust you?* She holds herself back.

'DC Morris, Donna, please,' his voice cracks. 'For Til's sake.'

She thinks about Nat and Lou, Til's sister and niece. After a moment she relents and goes with him. They cross a car park and then a metal bridge over water the colour of sump oil. A few lights glow on the brick buildings to either side, but as they move onto a path following the Humber, these fade. Derek produces a torch. 'Where the bloody hell is this?' Donna whispers. *Why am I whispering? So as not to wake the river spirits?*

'Albert Dock.'

Donna crunches on glass at every step. The windows it came from are now boarded and graffitied.

'Became used by the fishing fleet in the 1970s,' Derek continues. Perhaps he thinks it will soothe her to have a history lesson. 'The famous Hessle Row is a step over there.' He waves his arm inland. ''Course, there's nothing like the fishing done from here that there used to be.'

And the Humber continues to wash by, a broad, dusky-skinned serpent, much as it had always been, Donna imagines.

'Clive, Clive!' Derek's sudden shout breaks through the torpid air.

Donna realises how wound up she is as her heart springs up against her ribcage. 'Derek . . .' She begins to remonstrate with him.

'Shush.'

They stand close to each other, their body warmth melding in the frost-bitten air. They listen. At first, all Donna can hear is the thump of her own heart and the gasp of her breathing. Then she hears the slip-slap of water against the wall at the edge of the walkway they are on. Then something grey rises from the river. A spectre in tattered robes. Donna recognises the wide wingspan and long legs of a heron launching. And finally she hears something human, a grunt or a call of sorts.

'There he is.' Derek grabs her arm and pulls her towards a large ornate doorway. Once a shipping company had built it to flaunt its wealth. Now it is Clive's bedroom. On the top of the three steps, he is wrapped up in several sleeping bags. Around him are plastic bags of what could be clothes. There is an unlit Primus, a half drunk bottle of cheap cider and a box of cigarettes. The entryway is littered with detritus, some discarded by Clive, some not. A dim illumination is thrown by a security light on a boatyard behind the building.

'Hey, Clive, wake up.' Derek goes up to the prone man and hauls him to sitting. 'God, you fucking stink, man.'

'Derek?' Clive slurs. 'Whadyawan?'

'I want you to tell this nice policewoman what you told me about William Bell.'

'Police?' Clive blearily scans around him, perhaps checking to see if anything illegal is on show.

'She doesn't care what you've been up to, man . . .' says Derek.

Don't I?

'Just tell her what you told me about William Bell.'

Clive pulls his legs round, so he is sitting with his back against the large door with its large brass handle. He props his head on his hands which are shakily leaning on his knees. He groans. Donna is reminded of an illustration of the caterpillar in *Alice in Wonderland* in a book of Elizabeth's or Christopher's. She recalls that the character is not very helpful. She wonders whether Clive will be equally difficult.

However, with some more gruff encouragement from Derek, he does begin to speak and is relatively coherent. He had been in Scarborough for a couple of years from the spring of 2011 to earlier this year. He had met Til. 'God, I loved that woman, you know?' He looks at Derek for understanding. Derek nods. 'I can't believe she's gone.' Clive scrunches over further. It appears as if he might fall silent.

But Derek won't let him. He says, 'Come on, Clive, Clive, man . . .' and on, his voice rising to a shout. Then he punches the other man on the shoulder.

'Ow, that fucking hurt,' says Clive.

'Well, tell the lady about William Bell.'

Clive obliges, slowly, with frequent sips from his bottle of cider. The romance with Til had been idyllic according to Clive; they shared so much.

'Yeah, like bottles and gear,' mutters Derek derisively.

'Wha?' Clive glances up.

'Nothing, get on with it.'

Til had taken Clive to St Jude's and William Bell had seemed a good sort. 'He said about foraging,' Clive uses the word as if it were a foreign language. 'Blackberries and stuff. Then he said about the mushrooms. Til said, weren't it dangerous and he gave us the leaflet. But when I tried it, man, I was sick. I had to go to the hospital. And when I came out Til had gone home or summit, didna want nothing more to do with me. I was heartbroken, you know, man?' He takes another swig.

'Yeah, I know.'

Donna allows a short space, then rallies herself. She is getting cold. She would rather be off home. 'And do you have a copy of this leaflet?' Clive would be a disastrous witness, but the leaflet, that could lead them somewhere.

'Wha?' Clive looks at Derek.

Derek punches him again, this time harder, rather too hard for Donna's liking. 'The leaflet William Bell gave you about the mushrooms.'

Clive seems untroubled about being hit. He begins to sort through his plastic bags and eventually, surprisingly, he retrieves a piece of paper from one of them. 'I wan it back, mind.'

Donna takes out an evidence sleeve from her bag and puts the leaflet in it. She immediately sees why Clive is so attached to it. In one corner is the message: 'Love you babe, Til xxxx.' 'I'll have to take it,' she says. The paper is splotched and torn. It has been produced on a computer with images. She doesn't hold out much hope for it, but it may yield something.

'No.' Clive tries to lunge forward.

Derek easily deters him with a forceful push. 'For Til,' he says gently.

Clive subsides, cradling his cider bottle. 'Yeah, for her.' Then he says angrily, 'The bitch, she left me with nothing, just walked out when I was sick, the bitch.' He looks like he might be about to struggle to his feet.

Derek steps between him and Donna. Clive doesn't manage to stand upright, either because of the sleeping bags or because of the alcohol. He slumps back onto the top step, his chin on his chest.

'Should we get him to a hostel?' says Donna.

Derek shakes his head. 'He'd be in one already if he wanted to go.'

Clive emits a snore.

Derek gently arranges him back into a prone position, on his side. 'So he doesn't choke if he vomits,' he explains.

Donna has done similar for Elizabeth many times. Even so she's reluctant to leave Clive there. It's going to be a cold, raw night. 'What about hypothermia?'

Derek makes sure Clive is well tucked into his sleeping bags and hauls some cardboard over the top. 'Come on.' He walks away, then stops when he realises Donna isn't behind him. 'Come on,' he says roughly. 'You can't save everyone, DC Morris. Especially when they don't want to be saved.'

'I think deep down we all want to be saved,' Donna says softly.

'I'm going. Are you coming?' He begins to stride away, taking his torch with him.

Donna takes another look at Clive's snoring figure and then dashes to catch up with the point of light which is beginning to recede into the night.

Chapter 36

Now

Donna had insisted she was not leaving Hull until she had contacted an appropriate service for Clive. 'He might freeze,' she had said with some passion. 'I'm not having it on my conscience.' Derek had raised his eyes to the heavens as if a conscience was an irksome encumbrance. 'He'll be fine,' he started to say. 'He's used to it.' But Donna stood her ground and they spent the next hour or so trying to raise someone to assist. Plenty cared, but no one felt moved or able to do anything concrete except suggest another number to call. Eventually, Donna stood frustrated and disoriented in the elegant square named after Queen Victoria. Derek has slumped beside her on one of the deep steps leading up to a statue of the lady herself. Then they were approached by two people wearing high viz jackets inscribed 'Street Angels' with the name of a church underneath. 'Are you all right, love?' the portly man asked. Both were bundled up against the cold. Above their scarves both sported those smiles Donna always associated with true believers. She grabbed the man's arm as if he were a lifebuoy thrown from the ark and gabbled rather incomprehensibly about Clive. 'Down by Albert

Dock?' asked the woman, her voice sounded young, though it was difficult to tell under her layers of clothing. 'Yeah, we know him, Clive, we'll pass by and see him tonight. We've got him a place in a shelter, but he hasn't taken it up. Likes his drink too much.'

'Told you,' Derek muttered, using his arms on his thighs to push himself upright. 'Now can we go?'

After garnering several more assurances, Donna followed Derek to the station. They both dozed in the fuggy warmth of the carriage, only to find themselves turfed out at Bridlington. Derek looked at the departures board and swore eloquently – there were no further trains to Scarborough that night. So Donna paid for a taxi ride for the last twenty miles. Derek insisted he had somewhere to be. Donna went back to the almost deserted CID office to send the leaflet to forensics and an image of it to a fungi expert. When she finally reached home at midnight, her limbs were weighted as if they had anchors on them and it felt like a rudder had been rammed through her head.

It's mid-morning, thirty-four hours later, that Donna gets to her desk. There's a response from her email to the fungi expert. He has sent a photo. Donna stares at it. A white stem. A white bulbous top. It doesn't look so unlike the button mushrooms she bought at the supermarket the other day. On the leaflet the photo had been entitled 'field mushroom'. Incorrectly, the email tells her. It goes on, 'This is most definitely a photo of *Amanita virosa*. Highly toxic, damages liver and kidneys, usually fatal.' It is the common name Donna rereads: 'destroying angel.'

Harrie comes over to her desk. 'It's our lucky day, Donna. We get to speak to our Mr Bell again.' She is looking sharp and fresh in her dark trousers and tweedy jacket.

Donna is feeling frumpy in her cords and cardi. 'What have we got?'

'There were several sets of fingerprints on the leaflet you extracted from Clive. One set match one of the unidentified sets of fingerprints found on a mug at Henrich's campsite. We've been able to cross-check with Derek's, Til's and Clive's as they are all in our system already. Til's and Clive's are on the leaflet, as we would expect them to be, but not matched to the fingerprints on the mug. Derek's are on neither.'

'Where's the connection with Bell?' Donna is struggling to work up the enthusiasm to move.

Harrie regards her a tad impatiently. 'Clive says William Bell gave him the leaflet, so we need to at least ask him about that. You've seen what the mushroom expert has said?'

Donna nods slowly.

'What's up?' Harrie perches on the edge of the desk. Her thigh is compact, muscular. 'This was your line of enquiry, you chased all the way down to Hull for it, and took the next day off' – this is said with a slight tinge of disapproval either for the trip or the sick day – 'now you've got results.'

'Yes.' One of the Street Angels had told her Clive had moved on, no one knew where. She has the sudden thought that one day his body might be pulled from the Humber. She had lived in fear for years of Elizabeth turning up dead. *At least I know where she is now.*

'Donna? Are we on our way?' Harrie stands.

She reaches down for her bag. 'Yes, I've just got to go . . .'

'To the toilet, I know. I'll meet you by the garage entrance.' Harrie walks off.

For a moment Donna allows her head to sink on the bag she has hauled onto the table. Heat floods through her to her cheeks. If she could scrunch herself up and throw herself into the waste bin she would. Then she thinks, *Just you wait, Harrie Shilling, just you wait. Twenty years down the line . . .* The vehemence of this helps heave her to her feet.

William Bell lives on South Cliff in an early-Edwardian villa. Generous bays flank a generous front door and the upper sash windows show off heavy swags of plush curtaining. Harrie and Donna walk up the path through a neat combination of lawn and shrubs. Harrie uses the stout door knocker to rap against the solid wood. It takes a few moments for a woman to pull the door open. She is maybe in her late thirties or early forties. She is small, slim, with a mass of dark hair tied up on her head with a bright scarf. Her skin is pale and faintly freckled. She is wearing jeans and a cream shirt. Her long fingers sparkle with fancy engagement and wedding rings. She identifies herself when asked as Moira Bell, William's wife.

As Harrie explains that they would like to speak to William, a child of about eleven appears, attaching herself to Moira's arm. She waves shyly at Donna and Donna waves back, smiling. The child also grins. Donna wonders why she is not in school, then thinks maybe the Bells homeschool. This turns out to be the case, as Moira obviously feels the need to give an unrequested explanation to the two police officers standing on her doorstep. She does not invite them in. 'We're busy with lessons, aren't we, my lovely?' She touches her daughter's silky hair. Donna recalls doing similar to both Elizabeth and Christopher when they needed reassurance, or Donna did. The feel of their hair was like fine strands of embroidery silk. Harrie is asking where they can find William. Moira explains he is in Newcastle on a course. He is training to be a pastor. She is vague about when he might return home. Donna pulls out from her bag the photograph of the leaflet in readiness for showing it to Moira. The woman turns to look and appears on the brink of denial when her daughter pipes up, 'That's one of Daddy's.'

Mrs Bell says quickly, stiffly, 'Holly, off you go now. Haven't you your maths problems to finish?'

'I've done them, Mummy.' She smiles proudly.

'Nevertheless, you go in, Mummy has—'

Donna interrupts, 'You're a clever girl, Holly, I can tell. Are you sure this is one of your daddy's?'

'I don't think you should be . . .' Moira tries to say firmly to Donna, a little notch appearing in her smooth forehead.

I know I shouldn't be questioning your daughter without your permission, thinks Donna. She smiles encouragingly at Holly and holds her breath.

Holly responds with an assurance which goes beyond her years, 'Oh yes, I am certain. He showed me. He was using Publisher to make it look nice.' She looks up at her mother and says crossly, 'What, Mummy? You always said we should be truthful to everyone and not just God. Though it doesn't really matter with God. He knows whenever we lie.'

Donna notices Moira's fingers are now gripping her daughter's shoulder and turning her back towards the interior of the house. 'Go inside,' her voice is now commanding. Holly sighs theatrically and then complies, waving at Donna and Harrie as she does so.

'Well then,' says Harrie, her voice light. 'I think it would be best if we talk to Mr Bell at the station. We'll send a car to pick him up.'

'He won't be back until very late,' says Moira, flustered.

'You said you didn't know when he would be back,' says Donna with some satisfaction.

'I don't, I mean I don't exactly, but I am sure it will be late.'

'Look, Mrs Bell,' says Harrie congenially. 'Tell your husband we'll expect him at the station tomorrow at ten. And here is my card if he wants to rearrange.'

Moira snatches the card. 'Yes, fine.' The door would have slammed if there weren't draught excluders impeding its progress.

Harrie grins at Donna. 'We've got him.'

As they walk back down the path, the satisfaction Donna is feeling dissipates. 'Perhaps we should have insisted she say where he is, get him arrested?'

'Possibly,' Harrie slides easily into the car, 'though it might be a push to arrest him now. It's not illegal to produce a leaflet which has the wrong photo on.'

Donna thumps herself down into the passenger side. 'She'll be on the phone to him now. Maybe he won't even come back.'

Harrie clicks her seatbelt in place, pausing before turning

on the engine. 'Trust me, Donna, William Bell thinks he's done nothing wrong, and he will want to tell us exactly how much on the side of right he is.'

Chapter 37

Now

Harrie was correct. William Bell does come in the following morning. He even agrees to having his fingerprints taken without a fuss. 'Like a lamb to slaughter,' Harrie mutters as Trench leads him away.

If he's a lamb scenting the abattoir, William Bell is unconcerned. He ambles into the interview room and sits back relaxed. He is wearing a tan pullover with a white open-necked shirt and dark brown slacks. He smiles. 'What can I do for you two ladies?'

Once Donna would have accepted this, maybe even found it flattering; over recent years it has really begun to grate. She wants to grab him by the lapels and punch him on the nose. *Patronising git.* She senses Harrie tensing beside her.

However, Harrie's tone is smooth as she very pointedly says, 'For the tape, Detective Sergeant Harrie Shilling and Detective Constable Donna Morris are in attendance. Mr Bell, would you say your full name, please?'

'This is all very formal.'

Harrie's gaze does not waver.

He shrugs and complies.

Harrie resumes, 'Mr Bell has kindly agreed to be interviewed about some leaflets connected to the deaths of Mr Henrich Grüntor and Ms Til Shearer.'

'I've said I don't know anything . . .'

Harrie lifts up her hand. He stops, sighs and crosses his arms. Harrie indicates to Donna that she should continue. She takes the photo of the flyer from the folder in front of her and slides it across the table. 'Do you recognise this, Mr Bell?'

'William, please. I've said already I don't know anything about this.'

'You haven't looked at it.'

'I don't need to, to know I haven't seen it before. I haven't seen any leaflets ever about mushrooms or foraging.' He is very convincing.

'Your daughter said she had seen you preparing it on your computer.'

'Oh, she's a poppet, but she's only eleven. She probably thought it a good story to tell two lady detectives.'

Has he really overemphasised the word 'lady'? Donna's shoulders tighten. She wishes she had some sunglasses for the dazzle from his many white teeth. 'Clive Wallin told me you had given him the leaflet and also showed him how to forage mushrooms which then made him sick. He was in Scarborough hospital after eating *Amanita virosa*.' Donna points at the photo. 'They look very like edible varieties, but are extremely poisonous.'

'Indeed, DC Morris? I'll bear that in mind the next time my wife forgets to buy mushrooms at the supermarket.'

'This isn't funny,' snaps Harrie. Her hand slaps the table top. 'Two people have died and several others have been made very sick from eating these mushrooms.'

Creases appear on Bell's forehead. He rubs at them with brawny hands. 'And if I could help you with this, I would. Did you talk to Clive?' He turns to Donna. She nods. 'How is he? I used to enjoy his company when he came to St Jude's. Has he found somewhere permanent to live?' Donna doesn't answer, but William Bell catches hold of the merest flicker in her face. 'I thought not. He settled for a while when he was with Til. But when that all ended badly, he wasn't going to stick around. He used to joke, "no moss grows on Clive Wallin".'

In other words, he knows we won't necessarily be able to find Clive when we need him. Donna sees this certainty take hold in Bell's face as he sits back again, his hefty paws in his lap.

'You were kind enough to allow us to take your finger-prints, Mr Bell,' says Harrie. 'Will we find they match those lifted off this flyer?'

'I have no idea,' says Bell. 'It won't prove I made it or gave it to Clive. I understand there are more and more questions around the validity of fingerprint evidence.'

Donna thinks about the South Cliff villa. William Bell is likely to have the money for a lawyer to plant the seeds of doubt. 'What if we go into your house or your computer, Mr Bell?' she says. 'Will we find copies of the leaflet there?'

'No. But unless you are going to arrest me, you're not going to get the chance to look. I wouldn't give permission. It would be too upsetting for my wife.'

This Donna can believe. Perhaps because Moira knows what her husband has been up to. Donna thinks Holly would probably love it. 'And will your fingerprints match those taken off a mug at Henrich Grüntor's campsite?' asks Donna, keeping her tone conversational.

Does she detect a slight tautening within those hefty fingers? If so, it is gone in a moment. Bell smiles genially. 'If they do then it's only evidence of how untrustworthy fingerprint evidence is. I didn't go to see Henrich. I didn't know where he was sleeping.'

Donna latches on to Bell's tone. 'But you knew him?'

'I, er' – he falters, probably remembering he had claimed not to – 'a lot of people come through St Jude's. If Henrich came in, then no doubt I spoke to him. I try to be welcoming to everyone.'

'Derek said he saw you speaking to him at length.'

It is in the relaxation that Donna recognises Bell has tensed. He smiles broadly. 'Ah Derek, I like the guy, I really do.' He sighs. 'Shame about his drinking and, well, you know . . .' He is immediately sad.

His theatrics could rival his daughter's, Donna thinks tersely.

'What, Mr Bell?' asks Harrie, after a pause.

William shakes his head. 'There's just not enough support for ex-servicemen, to help them manage their anger, their violence. Derek, now he made it his business to get to know anyone who came to St Jude's. He knew Clive and you say Clive got sick. Derek was very close to Til and she died. Now I come to think of it, Derek did mention a Henrich he was getting to know.' He doesn't add the fact of Henrich's demise. He doesn't have to.

Donna remembers meeting with Derek under the bridge. Her palms turn sweaty. Has she been believing the wrong person?

Chapter 38

Now

It's now a month and a half since Henrich Grüntor's body was found in Raincliffe Woods and there are still so many unanswered questions, It is, therefore, satisfying to close another case log. That of the so-called diamond necklace reported missing by one Trixie Benson from her holiday cottage at the fancy hotel in Ravenscar. Donna had seized the necklace she had seen in the pawnbrokers. The manager had not appeared surprised, only keen to show he had followed the legal requirements. The investigator at the Insurance Fraud Bureau had also been keen, eager to give Donna the lowdown on Trixie Benson, which was only the latest in a long line of her aliases. The bureau's investigation had stretched over almost two years, but still they didn't have a watertight case. If Donna could come up with something, they would be eternally grateful.

Donna took Trev with her to see Jayson Smith. He didn't need much persuading, once he realised he might get caught up in a fraud prosecution. He claimed the door of the Bensons' lodge at the hotel had been left open for him and it was Lex who had done the damage. Jayson said he thought he was merely acting as a go-between, taking the necklace, left on the kitchen counter for him, to the Cash Converters, because Trixie didn't know the system. He kept his cut and gave her the rest. 'It wasn't much,' he offered with a wily smile, 'for glass and paste.' His statement gives the Insurance Fraud Bureau what it needs to move in on Trixie.

Donna does not believe in Jayson Smith's innocence as the jemmying of the door looks more like his known handi-work than anyone else's. However, the bureau is happy to overlook this. And if they are, the DCI tells Theo who tells Donna, the Scarborough police are too. 'A nice tick in the clear-up-rate box,' says Theo. 'Well done.'

This buoys her into the weekend, which she is determined will not be overshadowed by thoughts of the past. Trev has told her Nicky has not returned to work since the Halloween party, and he has almost suggested that a visit from Donna might be useful to find out what is happening to her. 'She says it's flu, but I don't believe her,' he'd said.

So Saturday afternoon Donna finds her way to Nicky's home, a neat, square, modern detached house, cheek by jowl with the higgledy-piggledy terraces which run down to the harbour. 'Within a sea-spit of the foghorn,' Trev had described it as. Nicky's mum answers the door. She says of course Nicky will be pleased to see a friend from the force and leads her into the front living room.

The amount of time Nicky is taking to appear suggests she is not as enthusiastic as her mother suggests. Donna sits on the comfortable sofa. Every flat surface in the room sprouts photos in every kind of frame. Some are formal,

262

family groups, especially weddings, others are snapshots, children playing on the beach or lovingly embracing grandparents. Donna and Jim have never managed to grow such a collection, mainly because her side is lacking. She wonders whether she will ever frame the photo from her fifteenth birthday. Whether, indeed, she will ever show it to Jim.

Nicky's mother bustles in with a tray. The tea would put hairs on your chest and there are homemade Yorkshire curd tarts. Donna compliments her on a fine family. She smiles broadly. 'There's a lot of us, that's for sure,' she says, laughing. Then she becomes serious. 'You brought her home after the Halloween night out, didn't you?'

Donna nods.

'It was kind of you. Nicky was in an awful state. She hasn't been . . . hasn't been herself for a while now. She won't tell me what's happened. I hope she will talk to you.'

Then Nicky walks in. Her mother gives her a quick hug. 'Here she is, my princess.'

'Oh, Mum,' says Nicky, though she's smiling.

Elizabeth would be snarling.

Nicky settles herself in the armchair. She's wearing joggers and a baggy sweater. She looks as if she has just got out of bed after a broken night. She certainly doesn't have flu. Her mum gives her a mug of tea and leaves them, as she says, 'to it'.

The conversation does not get off to the best of starts. Donna asks Nicky how she is and she shrugs. She has the same response to Donna saying she is missed, that her friends are worried about her and, finally, when she asks what she has been up to.

There's a pause while Donna searches for another way in.

Nicky is looking down into her mug. She says, 'I'm not coming back. I haven't told Mum yet, but I can't go back.'

'Don't say that, Nicky.' Donna's mood plummets, though she had been half expecting it.

'Why not? It's true.'

'It isn't. You can come back. DI Akande, DS Shilling, PC Trench, me, we'll all help you.'

She doesn't respond.

'Don't let him win.' Anger flares and then dies again as she notices the young woman's resignation.

'He already has.'

Donna sits forward. 'No, Nicky, if we speak to the DI, he'll help, he's already said—'

'You haven't told him anything?' Nicky is aghast.

Donna shakes her head.

'He can't do nothing,' Nicky says grimly. 'It's the way it is.'

'No.'

'Yes.' She glances up with some fierceness. 'It's like my uncle says, I should never have gone for it. Lassies aren't up to the job, that's what he says.'

'Well he's wrong, Nicky.' Donna sits up straighter, her tone becomes more strident. 'You did a great job that day in Raincliffe. No one else could have got those witnesses talking like you did and kept such meticulous notes.'

Nicky repeats, 'I'm not coming back. I can't face it. Everyone is laughing at me—'

'No, it's not true. DI Akande says he won't tolerate—'

'What can he do? My uncle says he doesn't know what

the force is coming to with a black poofter in charge.' The words spill out of her pretty mouth, then she claps her hand over her lips. She seems surprised at what she has said, embarrassed. A flush creeps up from her neck.

'You don't really believe that, do you, Nicky?' says Donna crossly.

She draws her knees up to her chest to shield herself. 'Well, he's family,' says Nicky defiantly. 'And he was a police officer for all his working life. He knows a thing or two.'

'He's still wrong.'

The two regard each other, Donna grinding her teeth, Nicky peeping over her kneecaps. Then her mother sweeps in again. She's about to say something, probably something about it being so nice to see Nicky talking to a friend, however the atmosphere brings her to a halt. 'Oh.'

'I'm off to bed,' says Nicky, seizing the opportunity to escape. She pushes past her mother and can be heard thudding up the stairs.

'Nicky,' her mother calls after her. 'You can't spend all your time hiding away up there.' Her voice loses its energy as it gets to the end of the sentence. Nicky's mother plonks herself on the end of the sofa. She looks strained. 'What's wrong with her, Donna? Why won't she tell me?'

Donna gets up. 'I'm sorry, Mrs Fletcher, if Nicky won't tell you, I can't. But' – she touches the other woman on the shoulder – 'I am sure she will tell you in time.' She is certain. Nicky and her mother are no Elizabeth and Donna.

Mrs Fletcher grabs hold of her hand for a moment. 'I hope you are right, love.'

'Tell her – tell her to call me any time.'

'I will, love. Thank you.' Nicky's mother's tone is full of tears.

Maybe if I can't save my own daughter, I can save another mother's, Donna thinks, not a little bitterly, as she takes her leave.

Chapter 39

Now

'I don't get why we are still talking about it,' says Brian.

'Because there are still things which haven't been sorted,' responds Harrie.

They are bringing chairs into DI Akande's office for a review meeting this Monday morning. As they jostle for space in front of Theo's desk, Brian continues: 'Jordan Smith and his mates mugged Henrich which resulted in a ruptured spleen. End of.'

'Only it isn't end of, is it?' says Harrie, plonking herself down. 'What if William Bell is going round encouraging rough sleepers to eat poisonous mushrooms?'

'Doing us all a favour.' Brian is good at muttering, Donna has noticed, a careful mix of audible and muffled. She thinks about Nicky and Fleur.

'It's murder,' snaps Harrie.

'DC Chesters and DS Shilling,' Theo intervenes in the same tone Donna remembers using to a bickering Elizabeth and Christopher when they were around eleven and nine. Elizabeth had begun to be irritated rather than charmed by her baby brother and Christopher was trying to assert his autonomy from the older sister he had once revered. 'I believe,' Theo continues mildly, 'it is up to the senior officer to decide when a case is closed, and that would be me.'

For a moment both Brian and Harrie hang their heads. Then Brian sits back and exaggeratedly shrugs while stifling a yawn. Harrie straightens in her chair. She opens her notebook.

Donna brings coffee over for the others and a fruit tea for herself before sitting at the corner of the desk.

'OK,' says Theo, 'updates. Jordan Smith is currently on remand, charged with GBH. Calvin Davidson and one other are on bail, charged with GBH under joint enterprise.'

Donna secretly hopes the joint enterprise won't stick for Calvin and the shock will have been enough for him. Then she recalls the number of times Elizabeth was given second chances. *But prison would teach Calvin nothing,* she continues to argue with herself, *except how to be scared and how to be violent. Luckily,* she tells herself, *it won't be my call.*

'Some good news,' says Harrie. 'Donna was right. Traffic has placed Sabine Barker arriving in Scarborough on Saturday September 28th, just before one o'clock. She is last picked up on a camera by the hospital. Then a couple of hours later by the camera on the A171 going north. It would have given her ample time to turn off to Raincliffe.'

'We can get her into interview then,' says Donna in a rush.

'Unfortunately, no,' says Theo.

Donna and Harrie turn their attention to him. 'Why not?' they both say, almost in unison.

'When I told him about our interest in Ms Barker, the DCI decided to have an informal word through diplomatic channels.' Theo's explanation appears littered with invisible quote marks. 'What's come back is that Sabine Barker had good reason to be here; she was returning to Edinburgh from the Hull ferry. She'd had a meeting in the Hague. Unusual to take her car instead of flying, but not unheard of. Plus, the DCI informs me, she has left the consulate. Recalled.'

'What!' Donna's exclamation drowns out Harrie's less strident response. 'No. I have to speak to her.' She had not even comprehended this until she had spoken it. *I have to speak to Ralph's daughter. I knew your father,* she tries out. She realises the others are staring at her. Harrie has one tweezered eyebrow raised. Even Brain has overcome his carefully curated nonchalance.

'Frustrating, I know,' says Theo gently, his tone also querying the virulence of her outburst. He doesn't have to add that frustration is an almost constant ingredient of their work.

Donna drags in a breath. It's stuffy. She can smell Brian's aftershave. She shakes her head, as if it will shake her free of the memory. More than a memory in her mind, it is in her body. *Folded over. Her nose to her knees. Under the back car seat. She had been told it had taken only an hour to reach the other side. It had felt like months.* She pulls herself back to the present and her colleagues' features, two concerned, one curious, perhaps calculating. 'I was merely keen . . .' She pauses to collect herself further. 'Keen to speak to Sabine about, about Henrich Grüntor. I suppose there's no chance of catching up with her?'

'I can pass the request along,' says Theo, not sounding convinced. He turns to Harrie. 'What about William Bell?'

'We haven't got anything that will stick. He tried to implicate Derek who also knew all the victims.'

'So-called victims,' says Brian. 'Til's death was ruled accidental. Clive isn't dead and is hardly what you would call a reliable witness. Henrich died from a ruptured spleen.'

'William Bell's fingerprints were matched to one of the unidentified sets found on a mug at Henrich's campsite,' says Harrie. 'To be clear, not the set also found on the folder of Stasi reports, they remain outstanding. However, this latest match does suggest Bell visited Henrich during the last few days of his life.'

'Or during the several weeks previous,' says Brian. 'I don't suppose Henrich was meticulous in his washing-up.'

'Or,' says Donna, 'Henrich stole the mug from St Jude's.' Harrie and Brian turn their gazes on her. Harrie looks displeased. Brian grins. 'Just thinking aloud,' she says defensively.

Theo nods. 'With this in mind, what about Derek? Donna, you know him better than the rest of us.'

'I suppose . . .' she starts slowly. The disappointment over Sabine is nagging at her mind. Perhaps she's not up to judging Derek's character? She rallies herself. 'I suppose if you are looking for opportunity, he has it as much as Bell. But then why bring it to our attention? If it was him, he was getting away with it.'

'Classic psychopathic behaviour,' Harrie says with confidence. 'Wants to challenge himself, show he can beat us.'

'I don't think Derek is psychopathic,' counters Donna. 'He seems to have too much empathy for that.'

'Maybe "seems" is the operative word,' says Harrie.

'OK,' says Theo, 'you two invite him in and take a formal statement.'

Donna wants to protest as she can't imagine any interviewing of Derek ending well. However, focusing on him will take her away from scratching after the one who got away, Sabine. 'OK, I'll set about searching for him.'

'You sure you're up to it?' says Brian, his tone a mix of negligible concern with a spit of derision. 'You looked like you might pass out earlier on.'

'I am perfectly fine, thanks Brian,' says Donna, her poise regained. 'Shall we get on?' She stands.

'I thought that was my line,' says Theo.

For a moment, Donna fears she has overstepped an indiscernible boundary she should have been aware of. When both Harrie and Theo begin to chuckle, relief floods in.

Chapter 40

Now

The sky is grey. The air is cool and damp. Donna is searching for Derek. He had said his usual pitch was somewhere under the Esplanade within the South Cliff Gardens. This had been confirmed by people who know him at St Jude's. Consequently, she takes this twisting path. As it dips down, the underside of the road and pavement rise to one side. They balance on concrete buttresses where the cliff has been nibbled away. Donna wonders whether those blithely walking or driving along above realise what lies beneath, or rather what doesn't lie beneath. The props, with the road as a roof, create alcoves. Donna gingerly makes her way up the steep bank to investigate. There's a discarded sleeping bag and some squashed beer cans, nothing more.

She looks down towards the slate-coloured waves. Bushes and trees gramp tenuously to the slopes. The branches of the beech, charred by rain, bend around each other, as if ashamed of their nakedness. There's still enough foliage from evergreens to create screens and hidden places. Little birds – a robin, a bluetit, a tiny wren – are flitting in and out.

Donna tentatively calls out for Derek. Nothing comes back except the rustle and clap of a disturbed pigeon.

She makes her way back to the main track. The trees thrust up to road level. Their roots reach out to claw at the tarmac path. Dusk is shouldering its way in from the sea. Donna wonders whether she should leave further searching until the next day, Derek being such a mercurial, an unknown, quantity. Still her feet take her onwards, down a further level, around another turn, away from the peopled street above.

These had once been pleasure gardens. In daylight, corseted and bustled ladies would have walked here to take the air. And, no doubt, every now and again, they would have had to sit down. Hence the periodic appearance of a wooden shelter. Once fancifully carved and painted, they now look rather weather-worn and some have been sprayed with graffiti tags. An unexpected needle-point shower sends Donna quickly into one of these shelters. She sees the supermarket trolley first and then the pile of blankets which could have been the leftovers from an abandoned camping trip. 'Derek,' she says, softly at first, then more loudly.

Until finally: 'Wh-what?' He wakes up fighting off invisible foes.

Donna leans in closer. 'It's me, DC Morris.' She immediately steps back, the pungent odour of alcohol and lack of dental care hitting her.

'Who? Who?' Derek struggles to sit up and unglue his eyelids. Then he recognises her. 'Oh, it's you.' He slumps backwards and closes his eyes.

'We need you to come in and make a formal statement. And we need you to be sober.'

'Yeah.' He's almost asleep again.

She sits on the bench by the side of the dirty foot end of his sleeping back. Looking outwards there is a narrow strip of scraggy lawn, the shoulder of the land falling away and then the sea. It is flat, almost motionless, as if it has been capped by a layer of beaten nickel. To one side is the castle mound with the red crumbling crenulations. Below it is the sweep of the harbour arm, the white lighthouse a protruding thumb. But they all seem dwarfed by the extent of the water, each of its molecules silently swaying in unison. 'I can see why you like it here,' Donna says.

'Mmm?' He opens one eye and then the other.

'The view.'

'Ah yeah, the view. You'd pay a premium for it up there,' he jerks his head towards the Esplanade. 'But then you'd have things like heating, security, a bathroom. What ya want, DC Morris? Can't you see I'm busy?'

'We need you to come in to make a formal statement and we need you to be sober. So either you come in with me now and spend a night in the cells – which are heated – or you lay off the booze for twelve hours and come in tomorrow afternoon.' She keeps her gaze on the sea, its movement hypnotic.

'I'm going nowhere. I've said all I'm going to say. You didn't arrest Bell. Why should I help you anymore?'

'We haven't got enough.'

'Not my problem.'

'Someone else could die.'

'Your fault, not mine.' He rests his chin on his chest, apparently readying to sleep again.

She'd like to sleep. She can imagine herself slipping into the water, being cradled by it, rocked backwards and forwards. 'You said you saw Henrich the Friday before he died at St Jude's.'

'I did.'

'Did you go with him to his campsite in Raincliffe?'

'No, I would have said if I had.'

It's the soothing sway of the sea which keeps her going with the questions; she feels cocooned, safe. 'And were you with Til when she died?'

'No, I wouldn't have let her die if I had been.' Something is changing in Derek's voice. Belligerence is being replaced by distress.

'Are you sure, Derek? You'll feel better if you say.' There's a sub-aqua movement, as if the nickel is being melted at some tremendous heat and is buckling. The tremor skids through the water until there is a lifting and a pushing which is becoming visible, and a wave suddenly launches itself at the sea wall below with an incredible *vaaar-umph!* At the same time Derek throws himself forwards, all sour breath and yellowing fingernails, shouting into Donna's face: 'I never, I never hurt her, I never would. Get out, get out you bitch.'

He isn't sober enough and is hampered by the sleeping bag still clutching at his waist, so Donna is able to jump out of the way. 'Derek, Derek, what are you doing?'

'Get out,' he shrieks. 'This is my gaff. You can't stay here unless I invite you to. I know my rights.' He's picked up a piece of wood which he had secreted under the blankets and is waving it at her.

Shaking and stumbling, Donna moves out of his reach. She clutches at the edge of the shelter for support. She realises how far away she is from others she might call for assistance. 'Derek, calm down, I'm just trying to find out what happened. Did you see Til the evening she died?'

He hesitates. 'No,' he says, while nodding his head. 'I tried to tell her not to trust William Bell, but she wouldn't listen to me, so I left.'

'And if you'd stayed,' Donna says softly, 'you might have been able to get an ambulance to her.' She has to duck as the piece of wood comes sailing towards her.

'Get the fuck out!'

'I'm going, Derek, only because I don't appreciate being attacked. But you've got to come in and make a statement.' She turns on her heel, a tidal wave of invective coming after her. But Derek doesn't follow. Donna begins to control her instinctive panic. On the whole, she doesn't believe Derek played a part in Til's death. Though he does. And many would.

Chapter 41

Now

Donna leans in close to observe the grainy figure moving against the shadowy background. Often there is some measure of uncertainty with CCTV images, especially with those from cheap equipment like this one. However, not this time. The tall frame, the stooped gait, the bobble hat, the supermarket trolley. It's Derek. She searches the screen. The time and date put him just around the corner from Til's place well within the ToD timeframe provided by Professor Hari Jayasundera. As Brian points out, rather too gleefully in Donna's opinion.

'Are you working for Bell's defence now?' she asks.

'It is your boy, isn't it?'

'He's not my boy.'

'Well, right now he's in our cells.'

'What's Derek in for?'

'Criminal damage and offences contrary to sections 5, 4A, 4, of the Public Order Act 1986 and section 91 Criminal Justice Act 1967.'

Despite her budding dislike of the lad, Donna has to admit, when he can be bothered Brian does know his stuff. 'What did he do?'

'Threw a brick through Bell's window and stood in Bell's front garden shouting obscenities and that Bell is a murderer. Oh, and Derek was completely plastered, of course.'

Donna allows herself a cup of real coffee before going down to the cells. They are subterranean, in a wide corridor which links the police station to the magistrate's court next door. The only natural light comes in through skylights. The overwhelming smell is of bleach which presumably masks a multitude of the night's sins. Though of this particular night the custody sergeant is able to report a fairly quiet time. 'It's the full moon and when the wind blows from the north-east that brings them in,' he says with a grin. Donna has heard from other custody sergeants about the mythical powers of the full moon to fill police cells, but the north-east wind? 'Straight from Siberia,' comes the explanation. 'You want to see Derek?' Derek is obviously no stranger to the custody sergeant either. 'He's quietened down a lot. Feeling pretty rough, I would imagine. I think' – he checks his screen – 'yes, he's had a cup of tea and is decent enough for a visitor.'

Derek is sat sideways on the plank-bed, a blanket around his hunched shoulders. He's dressed in a sweatshirt and some trackies which Donna guesses have been provided for him. They are clean and the trouser legs a smidge too short. Donna can see Derek's ankles, bony, the skin discoloured. His feet are encased in some very fluffy pink socks. He grunts a greeting to her.

She stands, folding her arms and resting a shoulder lightly against the wall. There is nowhere to sit apart from the bed. 'What did you do it for?'

'Is this a formal interview?' growls Derek. "Cos I want me lawyer here and all I'll say is no comment.'

Donna sighs. She can't help it. The rush of exasperation escapes before she even acknowledges it. *My mother is sighing again*, Elizabeth would have said. *Must be bad.* Or if she was in a worse mood: *Fuck off out of here if all you can do is sigh.* Derek doesn't respond any better. He pulls the blanket closer around him and ducks his head. Donna can see the sparseness of his hair, the rawness of his scalp, normally hidden by his bobble hat. 'You know you've played right into Bell's hands.'

'You'd never have arrested him anyway,' Derek mutters.

'We needed more evidence.'

'Yeah, like another fucking body!'

Donna catches her sigh in time. She knows he has a point. 'Did you feed Henrich Grüntor *Amanita virosa?*'

'No comment.' His voice is indistinct as his chin sinks further into his mantle.

'Did you feed Patricia Shearer *Amanita virosa?*'

'Get out.' He lifts his gaze for a moment and shouts at her.

Another chute of frustration is threatening. Frustration, not just with Derek, but also at her own impotence, and at a process which, on the whole, will give more credence to the likes of William Bell than the likes of Derek. Or her daughter. Donna leaves.

Upstairs she puts in a phone call to the hospital to ask to be told of any future cases of *Amanita virosa* poisoning, and leaves her phone number with a harried receptionist.

Chapter 42

Now

It is the fear of suffocation. It is the burning in the muscles of her shoulders and her legs. It is the sting in her bladder, the roiling in her stomach. No, most of all it is the fear that she will suffocate. Donna starts to try and push herself upwards. She is now on her back, her fingernails scratching against the wooden lid. *This isn't right,* she tries to tell herself. Still she scratches and pushes until her hands run red with blood. It comes to her, she is in her coffin. *But I am still alive,* she yells, and wakes herself up. It takes a moment for her to orientate herself back into the little bedroom in the little brick house on the corner of the little cul-de-sac in this little town flung onto the east coast. The skin under her armpits and the fold of her breasts is squeaky with sweat. It takes another moment to realise the rising melody is not from a chorus of angels attending her demise. She grabs her phone. 'Yes?'

'DC Donna Morris?' a young woman's voice asks.

'Yes.' Her mouth is so dry even getting that much out is a major operation.

'Er, there's a note on the system to call you if we have any poisonings from *Amanita virosa?*'

'Yes?'

'Well, a patient was brought in about an hour ago.'

Donna glances at her radio-alarm; the luminescent figures tell her it is 2 a.m. 'Who?'

'A little girl, Holly Bell. Was I right to call you?'

'Yes, yes, absolutely. Thank you.' The connection is broken. However, Donna still holds the phone to her ear. She is unable to move. *Holly? He can't have.* But then, who is 'he'? William Bell feeding poison to his own daughter or Derek exacting some kind of twisted revenge? *No.* She shakes her head. *Neither can be possible. Can they?*

A shower is imperative. A coffee and some toast a necessity. She puts in a call to Harrie. It goes to voicemail. As does her call to her DI. But Theo calls her back almost immediately and says he will meet her at the hospital.

She walks there. It's not far and she does not trust herself to drive. The cool darkness will slough her of her dream. *Nightmare.* It had been years since she had had this nightmare. It had been very frequent in the early years after she left the GDR, even well into her marriage. The first time she had had it Jim had woken her, telling her she had been thrashing about, the worry in his features fighting with a kind of horror. She had almost seen the words passing through his brain, 'What have I married?' He had become more blasé as things went along, presumably coming to believe she was not a dangerous axe murderer. Her life with him had eventually quietened her nights. She had slipped her skin one more time. Now she knows she is not a different person, only grown older and maybe wiser. Erika Neuhausen is still breathing within Donna's ribcage.

It hardly feels like the early hours of the morning at the hospital. Light spills out onto the forecourt banishing night, and inside there is a full complement of staff in different-coloured tunics, along with people in varying states of distress. Inpatients are wandering around in nightwear and dressing gowns, nipping out for a sneaky ciggy just beyond the 'No Smoking' signs or just for a gasp of fresh air. Accident and Emergency patients and their consorts are seated on plastic chairs, some reading, some stoically staring at the creamy-coloured walls, some sniffing into tissues, some holding various limbs which have been tied up with makeshift dressings. Those already being seen or needing to lie down are in curtained-off areas. There's one ambulance crew attending to a new arrival, an elderly man loudly claiming he wants to go home, even though his arms are sticks and his face bloated and yellow. It is all industrious bustle and managed messiness.

Donna isn't immediately sure how to break into the flow. She is young Erika balancing on the bank, watching the water swirl past, not at all sure she wants to venture forward. Luckily, just as she is thinking of walking out again, Theo arrives. *How does he manage to look dapper at this time of the morning?* Donna becomes more aware of her thrown together ensemble of polo neck, sagging pullover, elastic-waisted jeans under the anorak she last wore at Rose's allotment, to its detriment.

'What do we know?' asks Theo.

'I've just arrived,' she says, conscious that she's not really clear how long she's been standing there watching everyone swill around her. 'I was waiting for you.'

'OK, let's go. Who rang you?'

'I – er – I'm not sure, a junior doctor I think. I didn't get her name.' She could kick herself.

Theo, however, is addressing a nurse on reception and she looks something up on the computer. She agrees to call the doctor overseeing Holly's care, but says it may take some time. She looks wearily at the waiting area.

Theo gets them both a barely drinkable tea from a machine and they sit by the big windows which overlook the car park. The elderly man has been wheeled off. Two other trolleys have appeared. *Like buses*, Donna thinks. The paramedics chat easily with their grey-skinned charges, presumably anxious to be off on the road again but not showing it.

After a moment, Theo says casually, 'I've been thinking about what you said after you interviewed Genevieve Lawrence . . .'

'Mmm?' She is half distracted by the constant stir of people, even so she tenses for whatever is to come next.

'Ms Lawrence said Mr Grüntor had the same accent as you and then you said you had an East German accent. But you always said your birthplace is West Berlin.'

'Mmm.' Could she spin another tale? That she had inherited her accent from her parents perhaps? Or that West Berliners have an East German accent? She probably could. She probably could manage to be convincing, at least convincing enough. However, does she want to? She deflates slightly. Is it time to tell someone the truth? Is DI Akande that person? Her story is coming apart at the seams and there's something in Theo's gaze which suggests he knows it. 'I was born in Dresden, East Germany. I moved with my

283

parents to East Berlin when I was fourteen. I left East Berlin in 1980 when I was eighteen.'

'Left?'

She doesn't want to say any more. This has already been too much, the first time she has articulated the truth out loud to another person in her adopted country, in her adopted language. 'Left,' she repeats.

'DI Akande, DC Morris.' A young woman in a uniform of blue tunic and trousers stands before them. She has an afro of coppery hair tucked up into slides and grips, skin the colour of hazelnuts and dark eyes. 'I am Dr Fran McDonald. You want to talk to me about Holly Bell?'

The seats are screwed to the floor, so Theo moves over in order for the doctor to sit between him and Donna. Fran explains that Holly was brought in by her mother around quarter to midnight and immediately taken to ICU. 'We've stabilised her, but she's very poorly.'

'And you are certain it is *Amanita virosa?*' asks Donna.

'We haven't got confirmed toxicology, that'll come in the next couple of hours, but one of the nurses recognised it from a case she'd seen earlier this year and the consultant confirmed it.'

'Can we talk to her mother?' asks Theo.

'I can't stop you. There's a café on the fifth floor by ICU. She's in there having a coffee and a bit of a break.'

'Has she said anything about what happened?' asks Donna.

Fran shakes her head. 'She's very upset. We haven't got a very coherent story as yet. She just says she looked in on her daughter before going to bed and found her splayed across

284

her bed, struggling to breathe. It would help us to know whether it is definitely the mushrooms and when they were ingested, if she could possibly tell us.' Fran's pager buzzes and she gets up. 'The nurses on reception will always be able to find me.' She strides away.

Compared to the noise and agitation of downstairs, the fifth floor is quiet. *As the grave*, Donna's mind supplies. Their shoes on the tiles make the most noise there is as they walk along the corridor. There is a wall decorated with mosaics representing the seaside on one side and a succession of closed doors on the other. At the far end windows replace the wall. The dark is uplit with the orange glow from the street lamps in the car park below. There is a square of floor which has been carpeted and furnished with sofas, comfy chairs and low tables. In one corner is a coffee machine and a kettle with various beverage supplies. Moira Bell is seated on a sofa, leaning forward, seemingly intent on watching the milky liquid in the mug she is holding. She looks up when they approach her and Theo says gently, 'Mrs Bell, I am DI Akande and this is DC Morris. I believe you two have already met.'

Moira gazes at them as if they are a conundrum she can't possibly fathom.

Theo pulls over a chair to sit in and Donna sits beside Mrs Bell.

'You must be very worried about Holly, Mrs Bell,' Theo starts. 'We'd just like to understand what happened so we can help her.'

Moira Bell is beside herself. Donna has always liked this

285

English phrase, imagining people popping out of their skins and standing next to their hollow facsimile, but she has never really understood it properly until now. The rational Mrs Bell, the polite one, is a pile of crumbled self at Moira's feet. All that remains is anger, fear and guilt, but mostly the anger. 'It was him, of course it was bloody him. He has a vendetta against us, throwing a brick through our window, shouting obscenities.'

'Derek Wyatt fed Holly mushrooms?' asks Donna. 'How?'

'He must have broken in, put them in our fridge. Holly made herself a mushroom omelette yesterday lunchtime. She loves to cook.'

'When did he break in?'

'Yesterday morning, while we were at the shops.'

'Derek was in our cells until 3 p.m. yesterday afternoon. Then he was remanded into custody for a hearing this morning.'

Moira does not hesitate. 'Well then, the day before.'

'Did you see any signs of a break-in, Mrs Bell?' asks Theo.

'I must have left the back door on the latch, yes that was it, while we were doing our lessons. He'd have come over the back from the lane.'

'Didn't you notice anything strange in your fridge?' asks Donna.

'I don't keep an inventory.' Her tone is taut, each word snaps out. Her hands are gripping each other in her lap.

'So you'll give us permission to enter your house to check for Derek's fingerprints?' asks Theo.

She shakes her head, or at least it shakes as her whole

body trembles. 'He would have worn gloves. It was him. Arrest him.'

'Mrs Bell,' Theo says soothingly, 'where is your husband?'

Another quake racks through her. 'He's got another of his training days, in Newcastle. He's going to make a fine pastor.' This appears to cheer her for a millisecond. Then she goes on in a dull voice, 'He's on his way home. I called him and he's coming back. When are you going to arrest that man?' For the first time she looks up and directly at Donna. Her eyes are dreadfully red.

'Let me get you a fresh cuppa, Mrs Bell,' says Donna, standing and going over to the kettle.

'I want you to arrest that man. He poisoned my daughter. The devil has his soul.' Her voice has gone up an octave.

'He is under arrest, Mrs Bell,' says Theo.

Donna finds an array of tea bags. She makes a strong brew for herself and Moira, adding sugar to Moira's. Theo says he doesn't want anything. Donna sits again. The activity has eased some of the tightness that had been creeping into her shoulders. Mrs Bell, too, seems to have loosened. She takes a sip from her mug and says softly, 'She's such a sweet little girl, my little girl, always smiling, always willing to help.'

Donna nods. She doubts it. It is rare for any child to be always smiling, always willing to help. *Indeed, would that be a good thing?* And, anyway, Holly had not reached her teenage years. Something catches at the breath in Donna's throat; she fervently hopes Holly will get to be a rebellious teenager.

Theo's phone rings, he looks at it, stands and turns away. He does not move away. Donna realises this is deliberate.

He wants Moira to hear. 'Yes, Trev?' 'Is he now?' 'Yes.' 'No, thank goodness, Holly is still in ICU. Charge him with child neglect.' He closes his phone, turns back and sits down. He leans towards Moira. 'My officers have been at your house. Your husband arrived back and started throwing plastic food bags from a fridge in the shed into the bin. My officers have arrested him. Forensics have taken the bags. What do you think they will find?'

Moira begins to hum, then words form: 'Our Father, Who is in heaven, may we praise You . . .'

Theo continues to speak. 'Mrs Bell, they will take his computer and his phone. What will they find?'

Liquid slops from the mug Moira is holding. Donna takes it before it slips to the ground. Moira continues to half hum, half recite, 'May we have Your Kingdom on earth. Give us what we need, not what we desire. Forgive us our many sins. Look after' – here she chokes, tears drip down her nose onto her clasped fingers – 'keep my baby safe . . .'

'Mrs Bell,' Theo says firmly. However, he is interrupted by Fran coming over and asking Moira to come with her.

Moira jerks her head back. 'Is she, is Holly . . .?'

Fran smiles. 'She's still very woozy, but she's gaining consciousness.'

'His will is done,' says Mrs Bell, before leaping up and rushing away.

'Will we be able to speak to Holly, Dr McDonald?' asks Theo.

'Later, maybe later.'

Theo stands and hands her his card. 'If she says anything about where she got the mushrooms, please let us know.'

She nods, and then is off back to her patients.

'We let him stew for a bit,' says Theo. 'We've got to wait for forensics on those bags. And a time in our cells could unnerve him if he's not used to it.'

'Only he's not unaccustomed to police cells,' says Harrie. She had been the lead for the officers waiting for William Bell at his home. All organised by Theo while Donna was munching on her toast.

It's why he's in charge.

The three of them are gathered in the DS's enclave in the corner of the incident room, Harrie at the desk. She now reads off from the computer screen a list of offences from drug possession to dealing, from burglary to assault. 'All over ten years old, committed in Liverpool.'

'He mentioned having "issues" when we first talked to him,' Donna recalls. 'The way he spoke it sounded to me like he'd been through the twelve-step addiction programme.'

'So he comes to Scarborough to rebuild his life,' says Theo. 'Remembering what it was like to be in custody just might rattle him.'

'He's one of those who thinks he has immunity,' says Harrie.

'God given,' says Donna.

'What do you mean?' asks Theo. His voice a tad sharp, perhaps because of the early start.

Donna hesitates. *What do I mean?* 'Um, well, I don't know. Maybe – maybe if he's doing what his God wants him to do, then He'll keep him safe. His God, I mean.'

'Interesting,' says Theo.

Donna glows.

'Poisoning rough sleepers was somehow God's will?' asks Harrie.

'They'd be more comfortable in heaven,' says Donna. 'At least, that's what William Bell might believe, or say he does.'

'I want to know where he was coming back from,' says Theo. 'Donna, get on to that. Once I have anything back from forensics we'll reconvene.'

Harrie's comments about William Bell's sense of impunity come back to Donna as she works. He has hardly bothered to cover his tracks. When arrested, he had handed in the contents of his pockets which included a mobile phone and a wallet. The phone will have to wait until the young (overly young, in Donna's opinion, *When did work colleagues begin to look like sixth-form students?*) tech analyst comes in. A wallet, however, Donna can deal with. In it she finds a credit card receipt for a stay over the previous two nights at a B&B. Not in Newcastle, but in Liverpool. A phone call later and she finds out Mr and Mrs Bell are frequent visitors. The description of Mrs Bell – buxom, blonde, late twenties – makes it clear this is not Moira. A helpful DC in Liverpool gets her some relevant CCTV which clearly shows William Bell on a street in the city, arms around a young woman at a time when his wife thinks he is in Newcastle training to be a pastor and when his daughter is bedding down after having ingested poisonous mushrooms.

Donna finds herself unwilling to go to Theo with this news. She understands her reluctance when he tells her what he wants her to do.

'It will break her,' she says.

'If she doesn't already know. Maybe she's been turning a blind eye.'

Donna knows everything about turning a blind eye. Who really wants to face up to what a loved one is capable of?

Theo leans forwards on his desk, his face set, his tone implacable. 'There is a slim possibility Mrs Bell really did not know what her husband was up to with his bags of mushrooms. But her readiness to point fingers at Derek makes me wonder. If she knew, was she actively assisting him? We could be looking at murder, conspiracy to murder, perverting the course of justice. All these are serious charges. I need you to talk to Mrs Bell and then get back here. I want you to interview Mr Bell with Harrie. Dr McDonald rang to say Holly said she had taken the mushrooms from her daddy's fridge in the shed. The one William Bell emptied when he rushed back from his assignation. He didn't, we might note, rush to his daughter's bedside as fast as he could, but covered his own back. Final confirmation on what was in those freezer bags should be with us in the next couple of hours. I want us to be armed with the maximum amount of information possible before we confront our suspect.'

Moira Bell is turning into the weird twin of the neat little woman Donna had first met. Her face appears to have grown thinner and sharper, her skin is the colour of one-day-old putty. Her hair is a bedraggled heap on the top of her head. 'What do you want?' she asks crossly when she enters the small café area next to ICU. She had refused to come out to meet Donna, but has been gently ejected while a couple of health assistants wash and change Holly.

'I hear Holly is doing better,' says Donna.

'What do you care?' She pours herself neat strong coffee.

'I care a lot.'

'Which is why you are keeping my husband from his daughter's bedside.'

'He's keeping himself from his daughter's bedside, Mrs Bell. You heard Holly say she had got the mushrooms from the fridge he has in the shed.'

'She shouldn't have gone in there, she knows that.' There's less stridency in her voice. She swigs her coffee and half turns away to look out the window. Dawn has been and gone. Neither woman saw whether it was spectacular or not. The sky is a flat grey. An ambulance can be heard arriving at A&E downstairs.

'Did you know what he kept in there, Mrs Bell?'

She shakes her head slowly.

Donna is not convinced by her denial. 'Did you know what he was doing with them?'

Another shake of the head, with even less conviction.

'How about the flyers? We've found them on his computer, you know.'

No response.

'Mrs Bell—'

'I have to get back.' She takes another gulp from her mug and puts it down.

'Mrs Bell, where did you say your husband was these last two days?'

She turns and lifts her chin, her gaze is steady. 'In Newcastle, he's going to be a pastor. God guides him.'

This Moira believes, Donna can see. She steels herself with the thought that she is following her DI's (if not God's) guidance. 'Mrs Bell, your husband was not in Newcastle. He was in Liverpool, booked into a B&B with a young woman who called herself Mrs Bell.'

Everything is so near the surface for Moira, Donna can see the shock twitching through her.

'You're lying.'

Even so, Donna gets the sense that this was not a complete revelation. At turning a blind eye Mrs Bell appears to be practised. 'I'm not. I checked with the B&B and I have also seen CCTV footage.'

Moira walks away. 'I have to be with my daughter . . .'

'Mrs Bell, you need to think about this. Holly could end up with both her parents in prison. Is that what you want?'

She finishes her question to empty air and the flapping of the door Moira Bell has rushed through.

Chapter 43

Now

William Bell has opted for 'no comment'. No doubt on the advice of the smartly dressed woman sitting next to him. 'The solicitor's from York,' Harrie hissed to Donna as they walked towards the interview room. 'Don't know her.' There was censure in her voice. Perhaps because it suggested Bell didn't rate locals, an anathema to Scarborians. Or maybe simply because on the whole officers like to know something about whoever is in the interview room with them. But although he has chosen 'no comment', Donna can see how much he wants to say more. He wants to explain his actions, Donna supposes, because of his certainty that he could bring these two 'ladies' to his point of view.

Harrie is taking Bell through the evidence. First the computer and the flyer. 'Mr Bell, we took this laptop from your house.' She has a photo of it which she puts on the desk. 'Is it yours?'

William Bell appears to scrutinise the image before saying, 'No comment.' If he can't grandstand, he can at least play games.

Donna feels the irritation ripple through her. *It was your daughter*, she wants to say, *you nearly killed your daughter.*

However, Harrie continues at the same measured rate. Her litany of questions punctuated by his rote response. 'Does anyone else use this computer?' 'We found this flyer on the computer. Did you create it?' 'We have a printed copy of this flyer –' she produces a facsimile of it '– it has a fingerprint on it which belongs to you. How did it get there?' 'It was in the possession of a Clive Wallen who said you had given it to him and had encouraged him and Patricia, Til, Shearer to forage for these mushrooms pictured here. Did you do that?' 'Do you know what these mushrooms are?' She taps the picture on the flyer with a fingernail painted incongruously with a sparkly baby pink varnish. 'Do you know they are *Amanita virosa*, which are extremely poisonous?'

Donna is struck again at how benign they look. A more domed version of the field mushrooms found in most supermarkets. The 'no comment's have been coming robotically after each question. Now Bell hesitates. Donna wonders if he is going to claim he didn't know, he had been mistaken, he had been trying to help. She can almost see the thought flicker through his mind. Then comes the 'no comment'. He has sat back, legs wide. He is dressed in a sweatshirt and jogging bottoms. They are not the regulation ones which would have been provided for him when he was taken into the cells and his clothes taken off him. They look new. Perhaps his solicitor brought them in, so William Bell could appear less like an accused and more like a witness who has helpfully dropped by on his way from the gym.

'Clive Wallen said these mushrooms made him sick. He

was treated in hospital. The records show he had been poisoned by *Amanita virosa.*' Harrie leaves a pause and then says, 'Are you sure you have nothing to say to us, Mr Bell? It always looks better in court if you have helped us in interview.'

'There is no saying this will end in court, DS Shilling,' says the solicitor, her accent clipped from years at a top-flight university. 'My client has chosen a no comment response as is his right.'

William Bell grins at her.

Harrie straightens her shoulders. Her trouser suit is almost as smart, though not quite, as the solicitor's. 'Very well,' she says stiffly. 'Mr Bell, do you recognise these packages?' She has images of freezer bags of mushrooms. 'When you were apprehended you were putting these in the bin. Why?' 'Do you know they contain *Amanita virosa?*' 'Do you know similar bags were found at the home of Patricia Shearer and the campsite of Henrich Grüntor?'

'I daresay the bags are pretty standard, available from any shop,' William Bell says. He cannot help himself. His solicitor's pen lifts off the paper. Maybe she is considering whether to repeat her advice to him. She decides not to. William Bell grins again.

Your daughter nearly died, thinks Donna. She holds herself back. Harrie has a bit more to go through.

She carries on: 'Your fingerprints were found on the bags found at the home of Patricia Shearer, as well as on a mug at the campsite of Henrich Grüntor. Can you explain how they got there?'

Donna can see how tempted he is to give them his

treatise on the unreliability of fingerprints. His solicitor glances round at him. William Bell shakes his head.

'Mr Bell?' says Harrie firmly.

'No comment.' He sounds weary.

'Did you know Patricia Shearer?' 'Ms Shearer's sister and niece say you did. They say you paid for her to go to see her sister on her birthday. Did you do that, Mr Bell?' 'Did you know Henrich Grüntor?' 'Previously you denied knowing Mr Grüntor, yet you were at his campsite, can you explain this?' 'We think you supplied *Amanita virosa* to both Patricia Shearer and Henrich Grüntor knowing the mushrooms were poisonous and with the express intention of poisoning them. That is murder, Mr Bell. Have you anything to say?' 'Why did you do it?'

For this last question William Bell is finding it extremely hard to say his 'no comment'.

Harrie puts her head on one side and waits.

It's possible that all three of the women in the room are holding their breath. Finally William Bell says something. 'No comment.'

Harrie gives a quick nod, Donna is to take over.

It was less than an hour ago that Moira Bell had phoned her and haltingly explained her husband's crusade. Bizarrely, in Donna's opinion, Mrs Bell had finished her tale with the words, 'He is a good man, DC Morris.' *Define good,* she had thought. Now Donna sucks in air. It is laden with perfume: hers, Harrie's, the solicitor's and Bell's aftershave. It makes a heady mix.

'Mr Bell, your daughter Holly is in hospital. She too has been poisoned by *Amanita virosa*. How did this happen?'

Bell's chin drops to his chest. He takes a couple of heavy breaths. His shoulders hunch.

At least you feel something. I hope it's for Holly, not for your own arse.

'No comment.' His tone is quieter.

Donna doesn't immediately speak. She is rewarded.

'I . . .'

'Yes, Mr Bell?'

'She shouldn't have—'

'Mr Bell,' says the solicitor quickly, 'my advice remains the same.'

'No comment.' He says it so quietly it is barely audible.

'Mr Bell, where have you been since yesterday morning, that would be Tuesday 19 November?'

'Newcastle. I am training to be a pastor.' He's talking to a spot on the floor just in front of him. His solicitor sighs loudly.

'You were staying at the Cliffs B&B in Liverpool with a woman calling herself Mrs Bell. Who was she? Are we looking at a charge of bigamy in addition to murder?'

'I . . .' He looks sidelong at his solicitor, then shakes his head. 'No comment.'

'When Moira, your wife,' she emphasises the word, 'calls you about your daughter, you drive back from Liverpool. But you don't go to the hospital. You go home and start emptying the contents of a fridge you keep in your shed in the garden. Why is that?'

'No comment.'

'Weren't you worried about Holly?'

'No comment.'

Distress is creeping into his voice. He doesn't meet her gaze. Donna feels like she has him on a pin and is sticking him to a board, as if he's a specimen. An insect. A shabby one. 'Don't you care about your daughter, Mr Bell?'

'Of course I fucking care.' He throws himself forward so he ends up with elbows on the table, chin on his forearms. 'I love my daughter.' He sounds choked up. His eyes glitter. He rubs at them with his thumbs.

'But she ended up eating those mushrooms you were storing in your fridge. The ones you were keeping to give to people you met through St Jude's. People without homes. People addicted to alcohol. Vulnerable people. Why did they deserve to be poisoned, Mr Bell?'

'Destroying angel,' he mutters.

Harrie says sharply, 'What?'

He does not reply.

'Destroying angel,' says Donna. 'The common name for *Amanita virosa*. Is that why you did it, Mr Bell? You see yourself as some kind of angel?' Her voice is rapping out the words. She wishes she could feel more surprised. It was as Moira had said.

'They're in a better place, with God,' he mumbles.

'Mr Grüntor is dead, Mr Bell, not in a better place.'

'That depends on your opinion.' He is ignoring his solicitor's increasingly frantic headshaking.

'Dead is dead, Mr Bell. That's not my opinion. Are you saying Mr Grüntor wanted to be dead?'

He moves his head so he is staring at her. His skin is a strange blotchy pink. Tears slide out of the sides of his eyes. He sniffs. 'He didn't want to be alive. He told me.'

This Donna can believe. Elizabeth had said several times she didn't want to see the following day. *But it was the drugs, the drink. She wanted to get away from her life, not life in general.* 'And Holly?' she says softly.

He drops his forehead to his arms and sobs.

'I think my client has had enough,' says the solicitor stiffly. 'I suggest we take a break.'

Harrie calls a PC to take William Bell back to his cell. Once he has shuffled out, followed by the clipping heels of his solicitor, Harrie turns to Donna. 'Well done, DC Morris.' She gives a faint smile. However, neither of them feels like celebrating.

Chapter 44

Now

Though it is not her mess, Donna decides to clear it up. She searches out Harrie who agrees with her. 'Not your job,' she says, 'but best to know it is done and done properly.' It gives Donna a boost to think Harrie trusts her to do a proper job, even if it is in comparison with Brian.

She drives out to the isolated house, perched between moor and sea. There's a 'For Sale' board optimistically by the gate. It has already begun to lean precariously. Fleur Greene is out in the field with Lily and Freddy. The uncompromising wind yanks at the bushes and flattens the grass. Fleur is dressed in several layers, a faux-fur-lined hat pulled down over her ears and a scarf over her mouth and nose. Only her pregnant belly, wrapped in a stripy jumper, is exposed where the duffel coat she is wearing doesn't meet. Donna is glad of the thickness of her clothing and that she had put on the wellies she now carries everywhere in her car. She approaches Fleur across the muddy ground. The donkey (Lily or Freddy?) sees her first and bobs its head. Fleur turns from the bucket of feed she's been shaking into a trough. 'You again?' she says.

'Could we go inside, Ms Greene?'

'Have you got something useful to say?' She scratches at the donkey's neck as it reaches its nose into the bucket and crunches on whatever is contained there.

'I have some information.'

Fleur finishes what she is doing and the donkey transfers its attention to the trough. Fleur gives it a final stroke and walks off to the house.

Inside is hardly warmer than outside. 'I won't take your coat,' says Fleur, 'but please take your boots off. There's spare woolly socks if you need them. I'll make us some tea.' She indicates Donna should go into the sitting room. There's evidence of a fire in the grate and the room is a smidge less icy. There's bedding on the settee. Donna sits on the upright chair, leaving the armchair for Fleur. It takes a while, but she eventually reappears with a tray bearing mugs, teapot and milk jug and an opened packet of bourbon biscuits.

Putting it down, she says, 'Take what you want.' Then she sees the sofa. 'Oh.' She rolls the duvet, sheet and pillow up to one end. 'Not used to having visitors,' she mutters. 'You can sit there if you like.'

'I'm fine here.'

Fleur takes the mug Donna has filled for her with a biscuit and retreats to the armchair. She waits, expectant.

'Ms Greene,' Donna starts.

'Fleur, call me Fleur, I prefer it. I've been thinking of using my maiden name again, anyway.'

'Fleur, I read what happened to your husband. I am so sorry.'

'You mean what he did? Hanged himself? It didn't just

302

happen. An accident I could cope with. But he took his own way out, DC Morris.'

'Donna. I imagine he must have been going through a really tough time. He must have thought you would have been better off without him.'

Fleur slurped her tea. 'He wasn't thinking of me. And he certainly wasn't thinking of this little one.' She puts her hand tenderly on her protruding abdomen. 'Selfish. A coward. He couldn't face the future. Well, he left me to do it, didn't he? Alone.' Her angry tone wavers. She bangs her mug down onto the coffee table and searches out a tissue to blow her nose. 'Is this why you've come, to offer tea and sympathy? Oh no wait, I brought the tea. I don't need sympathy, Donna.'

Donna allows Fleur's fury to lap around her, feeling secure on her hard chair of composure. She is confident she can navigate the tides of emotion rolling towards her. 'I have reviewed the file concerning the fly-tipping and I have spoken to the investigating officer . . .'

'DC Chesters.'

Donna nods. 'I am sorry to have to inform you, he found your husband—'

'It was him, wasn't it? Sid.' Fleur breaks in. 'I knew it. Not at the time, no. But when I looked back, he'd been so much happier just before it happened. He even said he had found a solution. How much did he get paid?' She tries to sit forward, though her bump gets in the way.

'Seven hundred and fifty pounds.'

She flops back. 'A measly seven-fifty. He killed our lambs for a measly seven-fifty?'

'I don't suppose he meant to—'

'No, Sid never meant to. He was salt of the earth according to everyone, such a nice man. But he never used this.' She hits her temple with her finger with a force Donna fears may do some damage. Then Fleur drops her hands to her lap.

'He never thought, never considered the consequences. Never thought about us,' she finishes sharply, arms cradling her unborn.

'I am sorry,' says Donna into the quiet between them.

Fleur shakes her head. 'Not your fault,' she says softly. 'At least you had the balls to come and tell me, not like that other one, DC Chesters, another fucking coward.'

Donna is not inclined to defend her colleague.

Then something else occurs to Fleur. Points of red appear on her cheeks. 'Seven hundred and fifty pounds? And where did that go? I never saw any of it. He didn't settle any of our debts. He blew it, the fucker. When I thought he was up all night trying to sort our finances. When I was throwing up every sodding ten minutes with this little mite. He was blowing it all at an online casino. The fucker.' She shouts the last word and repeats it several times loudly to the ceiling. Then she seems to run out of steam and deflates. More quietly she says, 'Well, we're selling his precious farm now. That's what he couldn't face. He always said his dad would turn in his grave if we let this place go. They can both whizz round like fucking tops in their respective coffins now.'

Donna pulls from her bag the letter she has prepared. She has already done some initial enquiries, Fleur can get practical and psychological support from specialist midwifery services and from several charities. They will help her with communicating with the bank and utilities. Donna explains it all as she passes it over, finishing with, 'You should never have been cut off. You should have been categorised as vulnerable.'

A small smile appears on Fleur's lips when she hears this. 'Tough as old boots, that's me,' she says quietly. She peruses the paper. Then she glances up. 'Thank you Donna, you've been very kind. I am sure some of this will come in useful.' She takes a deep breath and stands. 'To be honest, I could have done with you months back. I feel like I've pulled myself out of a very deep hole. Well, I guess I haven't done it all myself. Lily and Freddy have helped and this little one' – she caresses her abdomen – 'and my sister. They all stuck around, even as I fought to give up. Now we're out of here. Not Lily and Freddy unfortunately, but they'll be happy in their new home with the neighbours over the way.'

'Where will you go?'

'Darlington. My sister is there with her family. She'll help me get back on my feet. I trained to be a teacher back when – I can find work in a school or maybe private tutoring.'

The amount of relief which floods through her tells Donna the level of anxiety she had been feeling for this woman and her unborn child. She too stands and takes her leave. 'I hope everything turns out for the best,' she says as they reach the front door.

'So do I,' says Fleur, a brief laugh in her voice. 'Sometimes it's a leap of faith, isn't it, life?'

Donna sits in her car for a moment watching the clouds form grey Alps on the horizon. Two ink blots float in on the bluster. As they land, the crows settle their feathers. They do a little jig before zealously tearing into a lump of carrion. She will now go back to the office and complete the case file for the Greenes. She is not like Brian. She can't leave loose ends when they can be tidied up. Fleur won't go unencumbered into her new life. A poor credit score from the debts will no doubt follow her and, perhaps, trip her up in the future. The past, Donna surmises, can rarely be totally swept away.

It is that time of the evening when the CID office is particularly quiet. The day staff have gone home. The night shift (fewer in number) have gone out to get some tea, as they term it, in Scarborough. Donna could have left an hour ago. She toys with the postcard. She has written a date and time on the blank side and addressed the envelope to the Federal Foreign Office in Berlin. Even so, she is not certain she should send it. The image on the card is of a version of a 1930s train company advert with 'See You in Scarborough' emblazoned across the top. The colours are bright and primary. There's a woman in a red dress walking along golden sands. She is hanging onto a wide-brimmed straw hat. *Hats don't perch*, Donna thinks. *They need to be secured.*

She is aware of someone coming into the room and she quickly tucks the card into its envelope. She looks up to see Theo. He is on his way out, but diverts to her desk. 'Working late, Donna?'

'Just finishing up a few things.'

'So Harrie told me.' He sounds slightly displeased. 'The Greenes' case.'

'I thought it best—'

'What you have done is fine,' he says quickly. 'And this afternoon I approved your contribution to Derek Wyatt's pre-sentencing report. I thought it fair. Hopefully it will get him a non-custodial sentence and a referral to the addiction service. Good news about his mate offering him the maintenance job on the holiday park.'

'Even better, it comes with accommodation.'

'Was that your doing too?'

She shakes her head. 'It's a friend from his old regiment and he had always said the opportunity was there. If Derek gets clean.'

'Let's hope he does then.' He pauses. His expression becomes weary. 'PC Nicky Fletcher isn't returning.'

'Oh.'

'I understand there was an altercation between her and DC Chesters on the Halloween night.'

'I think everybody was a bit drunk.' *Why am I defending him? Or am I defending Nicky? Or me?*

'Still, things were said which have led me to certain conclusions. But I can't act on hearsay, I need Nicky to make a complaint.'

'I tried to persuade her.' She's grateful she hasn't had to snitch. She assumes Harrie is less bound-up by outmoded customs.

'Yes.' His tone is one of sadness. Then he seems to gather himself. 'In that case there is nothing more to be done for now. I will just have to be more vigilant.' He walks away, telling her to get off home. He moves as if his coat has a brass collar.

Chapter 45

Now

'A penny for them?'

'Mmm?' Donna rouses herself. She had not realised the silence between them had gone on so long. As usual the tide of chatter around them continues; sometimes it will rise to a crescendo of anger or distress, but right now the conversation is at murmur level. Perhaps everyone, like Donna, is feeling soporific, due to the stuffiness of the visiting room. Outside a cold front from the west is clattering over the moors with hail and wind bending double anything above grass level. As she'd driven to see her daughter, Donna had felt it whipping at the car, almost shoving it to the wrong side of the road. The sheep were hunkering down against fences, shabby quilts of damp bundles of fleece. Maybe this is why one of the prison staff has thought it proper to ramp up the thermostat.

'You seem distracted, Mum,' says Elizabeth. She appears in good shape today, healthy and relaxed. She has had a decent hair cut. Her light brown tresses feather around her face, which has regained its bonniness. The sallow, gaunt features in a lank frame, with hair which had been badly chopped-about and dyed, has all but gone.

'Am I? Sorry.' What she was thinking had come up to her tongue and then stalled. She had tried out various openers on the way over: *You know what I said about coming from West Berlin* . . . Or, *You know what I've always said about my parents being dead* . . . None of them sounded quite right. She couldn't get started. *I can tell my DI what I can't tell my own daughter.*

Elizabeth leans in and says gently, 'You know you can tell me anything.' She says it with all earnestness. Then she laughs and sits back.

Donna smiles too. How many times has she said this to her daughter, only to be rebuffed, usually offensively or violently?

Elizabeth nods. 'Yeah, I never went for it either. But you know what? Somewhere inside me I always knew it was true and that helped.'

Oh, Lizzie. Donna feels the tear slip its tether and skid down her nose. Followed by another one. Previously, she might have tried to hide it. This time she finds herself a tissue and dabs at the little rivulet until it slowly ceases. She looks up and discovers her daughter also has glassy eyes. *I ran away, I escaped, I* . . . The words present themselves. They do not blurt out, not yet.

Instead Elizabeth says, 'OK, you don't have to say anything. But I want to be the first person to hear you are leaving Dad.' She's found her own tissue and, after wiping away her tears, she holds it crunched up in her hand lying on the table.

Donna is tempted to take her daughter's fingers in her own, despite knowing it will lead to another body search for both of them. 'I'm not leaving Dad.'

Elizabeth is looking at her slant-wise. 'Chris rang me . . .'

'Oh, I'm glad—'

'Only to recruit me into persuading you to stay.'

'But it was good to talk to him, I bet,' says Donna. Her mind is tidily crating up her own concerns. *For now,* she tells herself.

Elizabeth shrugs, her half-smile seems more sorrowful than anything. 'It's not like it used to be. It's really difficult to know what to say and he doesn't ask me anything. He doesn't want to know about, about here.'

'It'll take time,' says Donna, more to fill in the space. She's not at all sure her son will ever forgive his sister. It is possible Elizabeth has completely missed the boat on that one. *Maybe when Christopher has his own children, he'll understand,* she tells herself, unconvinced.

'Patience, you've always had patience in shedloads. Luckily for me.' Elizabeth grins at her mother. 'I'd like to learn that from you.'

'I learned it from you.'

Elizabeth drops her chin to her chest and the grin tumbles. 'I guess I deserve that.'

'I didn't mean it as a criticism,' Donna says quickly. Only it's too late, she can see her words have grazed her daughter. Donna expects Elizabeth to storm off or hit out with something.

She doesn't. 'I do feel a bit sorry for him. Dad, I mean. He'd be lost without you. He's built his life around you. You're his brick. His foundation stone. Everything'd crash down about him if you went.'

'I don't think that is true. He's managing fine without me at the moment. But,' Donna finishes firmly, 'I am not leaving him. Once this probationary year is over, well, we'll assess everything then.'

'You mean you'll assess the situation I'm in. I doubt I'll be out of here any time soon.'

'You'll have had your first parole board by then. We shouldn't second guess the result.'

Elizabeth smiles wanly. 'Always the optimist, Mum. I guess I taught you that too.'

The lines Donna wants come easily to her: '"Let me take your hand,/ tell me your story and I will tell you mine./ Together we will blend a gentler truth/ of plums, crushed mint, rue and honey mixed".'

Elizabeth's features light up. 'You read it. The poem. Eta Snave's poem.'

'Of course.' Again and again until she had it by heart. The first thing for years her daughter had suggested she share with her. Why wouldn't she?

'And you love it?'

Donna nods. Before she can respond more fully, the buzzer goes for the end of the session. The room erupts into clatter and commotion. Her daughter leans in, close enough for Donna to feel her breath.

'You're my brick too, Mum.' She puckers her lips and blows a kiss. Then she's gone.

Professor Hari Jayasundera is slighter and younger than Donna had expected. He is also more welcoming. The 'prof' is not only a practising pathologist, he is also a renowned academic with an international reputation. Despite the other calls on his time he'd said without hesitation, 'Sure, come on over. Saturday afternoon is fine. I'm on duty.' The morgue is in the basement of the hospital, however Jayasundera has his office on the second floor, with a window onto a courtyard garden. It's not a big room, and every available space is taken up by shelves of books and folders or by the two filing cabinets. The prof shakes Donna's hand. His fingers are long and delicate. His skin is the colour of aged cherry wood. 'So you are doing your probationary year here, DC Morris?' he asks as he indicates she should sit.

She nods. She can tell he wants more explanation. 'I'm a late developer.'

He returns her smile. 'I think it's useful to have a bit of life experience to do your type of work. What can I do for you? You said it was about Henrich Grüntor. Not exactly a straightforward case, nevertheless I understand from DI Akande you've got some results.'

'Yes.' She hesitates. She had explained to Jayasundera that this was part of her training. But, can she really justify it beyond her own curiosity? She sees his eyes lift to the clock on the wall behind her head. For all his geniality, this is a busy man. 'Yes, it was about the puncture mark on the back of Herr Grüntor's neck. I wondered whether you had any further thoughts on it?'

'I reread my report before you came over, I don't have anything to add. A puncture wound, maybe a very fine knife blade or perhaps a hypodermic needle. Though there was no evidence of an injection, at least not from the tox tests we were asked to perform.'

'Could it have been a hat pin?'

This startles him. 'How very quaint. Do people have hat pins anymore?'

Yes, if they want to keep a straw hat balanced on top of their head on their wedding day.

He does that thing of leaning back in his chair and letting it swing a bit while he steeples his fingers. 'If it were sharp enough, I guess it could be.'

'Could it kill?'

'A hat pin? I doubt it. You'd have to be pretty accurate or lucky, and the force required . . .' He turns back to her. Shakes his head. 'Not impossible, but unlikely I would say.'

'Thank you, Professor Jayasundera.'

'Is that it? Would you like to see the morgue, as part of your training?' He appears keen. She doesn't refuse. She is interested. She doesn't admit to having visited several morgues in her career so far. She is unsurprised to find this one the most shipshape she has seen.

Chapter 46

Now

After days of grey, the sky is a tenderised blue. The sun is revealed. It is in a weakened state. Donna has bundled herself up for her walk. And possible wait. She has no idea whether her card was forwarded from the German Federal Foreign Office. Nor, if it was, how it was received or whether it was received at all. Perhaps the envelope remains unopened, either unseen or deliberately ignored. She walks past the Spa. There are a few hardy types sitting in the suncourt with their tea and scones. A big truck is parked in the roadway, disgorging the trappings for a travelling show playing at the theatre for 'One Night Only'.

Following the path, Donna passes the brightly coloured beach huts and skirts the former lido. A few people go by, dogs at their heels or straining at a stretched leash. This is the time of year when the town belongs mainly to the locals, except for a clutch of serious walkers on the coastal path. Donna suddenly realises she counts herself amongst the natives.

She pauses for a moment to scan the eggshell-blue sea. It's as if it is being held in a porcelain cup formed by the curve of the bay between the Castle Cliffs and White Nab. Unseen fingers tip the delicate vessel this way and that. The water ripples and sparkles. It slops over the brim at Donna's feet. Tomorrow she will head back to Kenilworth for a couple of days with Jim. She has decided face to face is the best way to tackle telling him about how she really came to be in Ludlow. She tries to envision his response. Will he be angry because of the lies she has told him over the years? Will he be curious and sympathetic? He has shown himself more capable of empathy over recent months. However, her worst fear is that he will be uninterested and dismissive. It won't matter to him, and, by extension, he won't understand how much it matters to her.

She quickly turns and walks away from the edge. She is moving with more vitality than of late. She reminds herself to notice when she is feeling well, especially as the days when she is poorly are becoming more frequent. *I don't want to think of myself as a sick old woman.* She takes the steep steps by the side of the Holbeck. Here the hotel slid into the sea twenty years ago, dragging with it, some say, tables set with linen and silver for breakfast. Round another corner and she finds the secluded bench. Hedged in on the path-side by privet and hawthorn, it nevertheless has a commanding view to the horizon. It is the first one along from the easy-to-spot clock tower, yet tucked away enough for a clandestine meeting.

Sabine Barker is on time. Donna knew she would be. Sabine is taller and with a bigger build than the photos Donna has seen suggest. She is dressed in jeans, knee-high boots and a raspberry-coloured woollen jacket. Her beret is of the same colour and her blonde hair is tucked up into it. She takes off leather gloves to shake Donna's hand with warm fingers. Then they both sit on the bench and take a moment to size each other up. Maybe Donna sees something of Ralph in his daughter's face, but then perhaps Donna is superimposing it on there. Sabine has a long face, a narrow nose. Donna recalls Ralph's as being more heavy set.

'You wanted to see me, DC Morris,' says Sabine, her clipped accent adding to her air of composure.

Donna feels anything but composed. She wonders why she organised this. She has rehearsed an opening speech. It has deserted her. Eventually it comes out rather more garbled. 'Your dad, Ralph, Ralph Lerner. I knew him – we were at school together.'

'Oh?' Her eyes widen a little.

'You thought we were here to talk about Henrich Grüntor? I want to talk about him too.'

Sabine does not respond. Donna can see she is going to have to do the hard work of reeling her in. *In any case, I want to know.* 'Did Ralph, your dad, ever mention an Erika Neuhausen?'

Something eases in Sabine's face. 'We used to visit her parents. Dad said it was a kindness as Erika had died, when she was in her teens, I think. I didn't mind. They are a nice couple.'

Donna feels a restriction on her lungs. 'They are still alive?'

'I haven't seen them in a while, but they sent a card last Christmas. Are you OK? You look peculiar.'

Donna puts her chilly hands to her chest as if to force air in and out, as if to force her heart to beat. 'I'm fine,' she says, knowing her voice sounds strangled. 'Did Ralph, your dad, say how? I mean, how Erika died?'

Sabine looks to one side, narrows her eyes. 'Car accident, I think.'

There's a pause. Donna finds she cannot force any further words out. She lets her gaze rest on the undulating blue below their perch.

Then Sabine says, 'Look, you say you were at school with Dad, so you know what life was like in the GDR. I don't, not really, I was only six in 1989. I mean, you read about it, but it's not the same as knowing, is it? And Dad didn't say anything. I might have asked more, but he passed, you know, when I was only twenty-two. I'm not sure I can tell you much.'

'You knew enough to go after Henrich.' The statement blurts out. 'What did you do? Access the Stasi reports?' For a moment the two of them lock glares.

'I don't have to stay here,' says Sabine, standing.

'I am Erika Neuhausen,' shouts Donna.

Sabine crumples back down onto the bench, shock washing over her face.

Donna goes on, each phrase being awkwardly torn from her throat. 'I killed your dad, at least I thought I had. He was in the VoPos. You knew that? Of course you did. He wasn't, wasn't, kind to me. He caught me trying to escape and I shot him. I really, genuinely thought I had . . . All this time I thought I had killed him . . .' She shudders to a halt.

Sabine leans her forehead on her hands, rubs at her skin with her nails.

'All I'm trying to say is' – Donna bends forwards, speaks more quietly – 'I know. I know how it is to do something in

318

fear, or anger, and then regret it, spend your life regretting it. I know . . .'

'You missed. You didn't even graze him,' says Sabine, rearing upwards and back against the arm of the bench. 'You didn't kill him.'

'Nor did you kill Henrich Grüntor.'

'He's dead.'

'He already had a ruptured spleen and had ingested poisonous mushrooms. A hat pin to the back of the neck was the least of his worries.' Donna is feeling calmer now. *I missed!*

'He, he fell forward.' Sabine's hands are visibly shaking in her lap, as is her voice. 'I left him there. I should have called for help. I was scared.'

Donna nods. 'He was likely beyond help. The ruptured spleen was twenty-four hours previous. But you could have made his last minutes or hours easier.'

'He didn't make my mother's last months and years any easier,' Sabine spits out. She sits taller. 'His reports meant they were never left alone. My dad was even taken into custody twice. Ralph Lerner, the darling of the Volkspolizei. He didn't go back to it after Erika, after you, shot at him. It ceased being a game for him, I suppose. He, he became a good man, a kind man.'

Donna feels a revulsion against this; she doesn't say anything, but maybe it shows on her face.

'Yes, a kind man,' says Sabine. 'He told your parents the truth about what happened to you. He was the only person who did. The authorities told them it was a car accident, said you were too smashed up to be seen.'

'My parents knew? What did they—?'

Sabine continues as if not hearing Donna. '*Mein lieber Papa.*' Her voice cracks. She puts her fingers to her lips. 'He was a good father to me.'

'I'm glad,' says Donna half truthfully. Erika still wants her vengeance. *He hurt me.*

'We're none of us perfect,' says Sabine, curling over on herself once more.

'Your mum?' says Donna quietly.

'I understand it now – postnatal depression they'd call it now. Made worse by that, that man's reports.' The shiver runs through to her fingertips. 'But all I remember was there were no hugs or kisses. I, I didn't feel like she loved me . . .'

'I'm sure she did.'

'. . . And then she was gone. For ever.'

Donna touches Sabine's hands which are now freezing. 'She loved you.'

Sabine cocks her head upwards. 'Then why kill herself? Why abandon me and Dad?'

An image of Fleur's anger flits through Donna's mind.

Sabine hurries on: 'Henrich Grüntor, that's why. He killed her just as surely as if he pushed her under the tram. Without him, I'd still have my mum. Then Dad died from grief. Grüntor killed them both.' Some of the power goes out of her voice. 'I wanted him to understand. I just wanted him to understand. Say he was sorry for what he had done. But he turned away. He was walking away from me. I didn't even know I had the blasted pin in my bag . . .'

I didn't know the gun was in my hand.

'. . . I only wanted to hurt him, like he'd hurt me. I didn't think it would do any damage, it wasn't sharp enough . . .'

Was it the shaking or did I squeeze the trigger?

'Then he fell and I thought . . . Well, I don't know what I thought, I just ran.'

I wanted to kill him. I wanted to make him pay. He had assaulted me. He would have raped me. The thoughts leave Donna momentarily paralysed. She can't say these words to Ralph's daughter, nor can she summon up any others to replace them.

Sabine withdraws her fingers from Donna's hands. She searches in her bag for a tissue, finds one and wipes her eyes, blows her nose. 'I'm done here,' she says, her voice once more under control. She stands: 'You can arrest me if you like, DC Morris, but I wouldn't advise it.'

'What about my parents?' Donna says. But she says it too quietly to a retreating back.

In reality, Sabine does not come.

In reality, Donna sits for the hour on the bench waiting for Sabine Barker to arrive. In reality, Donna replays in her mind what the encounter might have been like, each time with some slight alterations, until she comes up with this final scenario. It is the best she can do. Yet she still doesn't get to hear (even in her imagination) more about her parents, especially how they feel about what she has done. There are some things which stretch invention to its limits.

Nor does Donna get the absolution from Ralph Lerner's daughter she feels she needs. She sits for another thirty minutes and then another, before she lets herself admit that Sabine Barker is not coming. A desolate smog settles at the centre of Donna's being. It won't be as she had envisaged. It won't be simple, this clawing back of her story.

A tar-soaked rag flaps onto a nearby branch. Then another, then another. Crows. Morrighan and her companions. They had overseen the striking down of Henrich Grüntor. First came Calvin and Jordan and their mates, self-absorbed, boastful and cruel. Then came self-righteous William Bell with his destroying angels. Finally, Sabine with her desire for revenge. Or maybe just comprehension. Yes, Donna will give her the benefit of the doubt. Now the birds regard Donna, their heads on one side. Is she beaten? 'Not yet,' she tells them. 'Not yet.'

With a deep breath of salty air, she pushes herself to her feet. The porcelain cup is tipping in the other direction, the sea is drifting away from the land, leaving the tea-leaf-coloured sand to encrust its edge as if waiting for the divining of a new future. Donna's celebrated optimism is reasserting itself. It's difficult to remain wretched while feasting on this rippling expanse of silver-gilded water. She sees at the bottom of the cliff a group of people in wetsuits crossing the beach. Among them is probably Rose. She issued her sea swimming invitation again last night. Again Donna refused. She watches the group below plunge in amongst the waves. Some strike away strongly, others float and body-surf. They have turned from rather ungainly land-creatures into overgrown seals. Donna smiles. She has signed up for intermediate swimming lessons at the pool. Only to boost her confidence, to bring her to fitness, she tells herself. Yet, she recalls, Erika was a fine swimmer once.

Author's note

This is a work of fiction. However, Scarborough, North Yorkshire, exists and the vast majority of settings I have used are real. On the other hand, HMP North Yorkshire does not exist. There is no prison slap bang in the middle of the Yorkshire Moors, though it sometimes feels as if there might be.

Following a chance meeting over a mallet in a Krakow campsite in 1978 which created a firm friendship, I have been fascinated by the history of East and West Germany and the famous wall. I have always made efforts to follow what was going on in the once divided, then reunified, country. I have visited Berlin and Dresden both pre- and post-1989, although unfortunately, since this novel was written during 2020, a planned return to Berlin to re-check my memories could not happen. For this book, I also dived into *The Berlin Wall, 13 August 1961 – 9 November 1989* by Frederick Taylor (Bloomsbury, 2006) and *Border: A Journey to the Edge of Europe* by Kapka Kassabova (Granta Books, 2017). Also essential viewing was *Deutschland 83* and *Deutschland 86* (created by Anna Winger and Jörg Winger, 2015 and 2018) and *The Lives of Others* (directed by Florian Henckel von Donnersmarck, 2006).

All errors in the text which remain are my own.

Acknowledgements

Thank you to my dear friend Charlotte Cole and to Krystyna Green, Hannah Wann, Amanda Keats and all the crew at Constable/Little, Brown for making this happen. It has quite literally been a life-long dream.

Thank you to my German friends, Claudia Hempel and Angelika Scheffler, for giving me the East–West perspective. Thanks go to my sister, Ros, and all my lovely friends – readers and writers alike – who supported me with my writing. It's been a long road travelled, but generally a good one.

And finally, to my wonderful husband, Mark Vesey, who, when we first got together over thirty years ago, instead of laughing when I said, 'I am going to be a writer,' bought me an Amstrad.